ROAD TO BLISS

ALSO BY JOAN CLARK

Girl of the Rockies

The Hand of Robin Squires

Wild Man of the Woods

The Moons of Madeleine

The Dream Carvers

The Word for Home

Thomasina and the Trout Tree (picture book)

The Leopard and the Lily (picture book)

Snow (with Katie MacDonald Denton)

ROAD TO BLISS

JOAN CLARK

Doubleday Canada

Library and Archives of Canada Cataloguing in Publication has been applied for.

ISBN: 978-0-385-66687-9

Printed and bound in the USA.

Published in Canada by Doubleday Canada, a division of Random House of Canada Limited.

Visit Random House of Canada Limited's website: www.randomhouse.ca

10 9 8 7 6 5 4 3 2 1

For Jack

1

Without his guitar, Jim Hobbs felt like the loneliest guy on the planet. Here he was on a sweltering August afternoon, parked on the running board of a transport truck waiting for the driver inside to wake up. Above him ABC HOUSEHOLD MOVERS was printed on a shiny white door. Not a lick of shade anywhere, not a tree in sight, nothing to shield him from the sun smashing down. Though he'd taken off the woollen tuque he wore winter and summer, sweat dripped from his forehead onto the pavement, where it sizzled like drops of water in a frying pan before being sucked up by the sun. Water. What he wouldn't give for a drink of water. He saw a farmhouse way off in the distance, but if he hiked over there to ask for water he might miss a ride, and if he missed a ride he might change his mind, might turn around and go home. No way was he going home, at least not yet. It wasn't the first time Jim had felt like leaving home, but it was the first time he'd made it this far, and he didn't want to quit. He had something to prove, even though he wasn't sure what it was. To pass the time, he drummed the empty water bottle against his knee before squeezing it until the plastic buckled and he tossed it away.

He glanced at his watch. Three o'clock. Six hours since he left the café forty miles back. It had taken six hours to travel forty miles, not what you'd call progress. The café was where he'd grabbed breakfast and used a pay phone to leave a message on the condo voice mail saying he was okay but wouldn't be home again tonight. He didn't expect anyone to answer the phone. His mother, Paula, was out of town for three days, and his sister seldom picked up the phone. He'd lost track of the number of times he'd watched Carla stand beside a ringing phone to read the incoming number before deciding if the caller was someone she was willing to talk to. Truth was, Jim didn't want anyone to pick up the phone. He wasn't ready for a conversation about why he'd decided not to go home but to clear out of the city instead. The situation at home was complicated in a way he couldn't put into words. It was a normal family—parents split like Solly's and Web's. After six years he should be used to it, but he still missed his father. If Zack were around more often, maybe Jim wouldn't get fed up living with two women. Maybe he wouldn't feel so lonely. How could he explain all this stuff to his mother? If he said, *I'm lonely, Mom*. Paula would say, *Why are you lonely?* And he would have to tell her about missing Zack big time, and that would make her unhappy. The strange thing was he was lonelier at home than he was now, parked on the running board of a transit truck in the middle of nowhere. It didn't make sense except for the fact that he had *chosen* to be alone, and there was no one around to make him feel like he shouldn't be here. At home his sister often made him feel he shouldn't be around. The night before the subway accident, after Paula had left with Ron and Jim had gone out for pizza, Carla had locked him out for *two whole hours* so she and her snorky boyfriend could make out without having a younger brother around. After hammering on the door until their neighbour told him to pipe down, Jim sat on the hallway floor when he could have been in his bedroom trying out a new piece on his guitar. When Carla finally condescended to let him in, she said, "C'mon in, bro," as if locking him out was normal. No apology—his sister didn't go in for apologies. No point telling her she was a bitch. Whenever he used the B-word to her face, he got a lecture about being sexist. According to his sister, the entire English language was sexist, and the words *priest* and *God* assumed to be male. Jim couldn't be bothered arguing. Carla never gave up an argument until she'd won.

Another complication in Jim's life was Ron, Paula's on-again, off-again boyfriend who was sixty at least—way too old for his mother—and tried to seem younger by spiking his dyed-black hair. Pathetic. Whenever Ron turned up at the condo, he'd pat Jim on the back. *How're you doing there, buddy,* he'd whisper. *Scoring any chicks?* Jim didn't see what Paula saw in the creep. Luckily, she didn't go away with him often, and whenever she did, she came home happier, so Jim kept his mouth shut.

If he'd still had his cellphone, Jim would have tried using it to call home. Unfortunately, his cellphone was inside his backpack, which for all he knew was still under the seat inside the subway car where he'd shoved it before the accident, when the subway had screeched to a stop, plunging everyone aboard into total darkness. Sometime during the accident, he'd lost his Walkman, too. He figured it must have fallen off when he and the other passengers were pitched sideways. Lucky for him he hadn't taken his guitar with him on the subway; it was still safe at home in his bedroom. If it had been strapped to his back, it would have been smashed when he lost his grip on the slippery subway platform and fell backwards, hitting his head on the iron track. If he hadn't knocked himself out cold, he might have remembered to go back to the subway car and look for his Walkman and backpack, but his head was so messed up, he wasn't thinking straight. Concussion, the nurse in the subway told him. It's important you not fall asleep. Stay on your feet as long as you can. If your head still hurts in the morning, see a doctor.

No problem, Jim told her; he was used to walking and used the subway only to get to his summer job. What's your summer job? she asked. Gardening, Jim said. Mowing lawns and stuff.

Apart from his job, Jim walked just about every place his life took him—to school, to the city malls, to the Cineplex and video stores—so it was no big deal to keep on walking. He told himself he could walk all night if he had to. But most of his walking had been in the city centre, near the condo where he lived with his mother and sister. Yesterday, when he'd finally emerged from the subway after being in the dark so long, he was blasted by sunlight, and like some pale, weak-eyed creature, he blinked at what he saw. What he saw were streets jammed with buses and trams, cars and trucks, campers and trailers, vehicles of all kinds, none of them moving. But people were moving. Wandering back and forth through the glut of stalled traffic were people who seemed at a loss about what to do with themselves. There were thousands of people out there, some sitting on café chairs or the curb or standing alone. Most stood in huddles of three or four, chatting, gesturing, talking on cellphones.

Standing near the subway entrance was a bearded man in a pale blue business suit. He must have seen the lost expression on Jim's face, because right away he began to explain. We're in the middle of a massive power failure, he said. The entire electrical system in the city has crashed. There's no electricity for miles around. No one knows why. Some fault in the system. Computers are down and elevators aren't working. The traffic lights and gas pumps aren't working either, so all these people on the street are stranded downtown waiting for some kind of transportation to take them home. They'll be waiting a long time. Jim heard the defiance in the man's voice when he told him *he* wouldn't be waiting around—*he* was getting out of downtown. Jim watched in admiration as the bearded man, holding his briefcase over his head, plunged like a swimmer into the crowd.

The electricity wasn't working, but the sun sure was. The blinding light hurt Jim's eyes and he tugged his tuque lower to shield them. "It's a frigging party out here," he grumbled. "A big noisy street party I don't want to join." His head and eyes hurt, and like the bearded man, he couldn't clear out of downtown fast enough. Head down, eyelids shuttered, he shouldered his way through the crowd and kept on shouldering until the crowd gradually thinned out and the sidewalks were clear enough for him to hit his long-legged stride. He'd gone more than twenty blocks before he noticed that the office and apartment buildings were gradually becoming shorter and less important-looking, and that there were vacant lots and playgrounds with kiddy swings and slides. Every few blocks the streets were bordered by rows of shops and boutiques, each one with a Closed sign hanging in the door. All this Jim passed with barely a glance.

It wasn't until the sun had slumped out of sight behind a stand of trees, colouring the sidewalks a chalky grey, that Jim awoke as if from a trance, and stopping to look around, realized he was in the suburbs, where low-roofed houses had tidy fenced gardens and there were small strip malls and gas stations on street corners. By now the business centre of the city, with its banks and skyscrapers, its crowded streets and grubby alleyways, was far behind, so far behind that when he turned around, he couldn't even see the tallest skyscraper of them all, a needle thrust into the sky. The landscape had entirely changed.

He knew then that he was a long way from home. It was the first time in his life that he'd been this far from home on his own. The aloneness excited him, gave him a sudden thirst for independence. He felt the faint stir of rebellion. Maybe he wouldn't go home tonight. Maybe he wouldn't go home tomorrow night either. With Paula away with Ron and Carla getting it off with her boyfriend, Jim didn't see a reason for going home, except for his guitar. Why should he? Why not give himself a break and head out on his own? His mother and sister were doing what they wanted, and now that the pain in his head had eased and he was ordering his thoughts more clearly, he couldn't think of a single reason why he shouldn't do what he wanted. What he wanted was to head somewhere different. He'd never been west of the city, and going by the pink blush of the setting sun lighting the sky behind the houses, he knew he was heading in that direction. Why not keep going west? He began walking again, more purposively now, driven not by the nurse's instructions to stay on his feet, but by the adrenalin rush of adventure.

As the miles behind him lengthened, so too did the shadows, and gradually the unlit streets deepened to charcoal grey and then to black. Without the spawn of city lights, the stars stood out sharply in the night sky, but their flickering light was so distant it barely touched the sidewalk, and Jim began to stumble over unseen cracks and concrete shards. Still he kept on, walking slowly, groping his way through a canyon of darkness. Exhausted, he stumbled on, passing no one, though occasionally a vehicle drove past, its headlights casting houses and lawns in ghostly light. It was close to midnight when a car pulled into a driveway directly ahead of him, and in the wash of headlights Jim saw a low rambling house off to one side, with candles lighting two windows and a chaise longue on the lawn. As soon as the driver shut the front door behind him, Jim felt himself being pulled toward the chaise longue. Soon he was stretched out on it sideways, hands pillowing his head, feet hanging over the end. He was asleep within seconds.

It wasn't until the stars were disappearing into the dawn sky that he shifted onto his back and the tender bruise at the base of his skull woke him. By then the pain in his head was completely gone and the bruise was the only reminder of yesterday's subway accident. He got up at once and moved on before the owners of the chaise longue even knew he'd been there. Hungry and bleary-eyed, he made his way through the city's fringes, walking in the direction of the freeway. Now that it was daylight, cars and trucks were on the road, and he had hopes of thumbing an early ride. The café where he stopped for breakfast and used the pay phone was a couple of miles from the freeway, but close enough for Jim to hear the distant thrum of traffic.

Leaving the café, he headed for an overpass he saw in the distance. In less than an hour, he was standing on the highway with his thumb stuck out. He tried to look harmless, which wasn't easy, given his size—like his father, he was six feet tall and broad shouldered. Zillions of drivers zoomed past without a sideways glance. The glass face of Jim's watch had cracked in the accident, but it still worked, and at first he checked it at fifteen-minute intervals. But with the prospect of a ride fast fading, checking the time only discouraged him more, and he soon gave it up.

Four hours dragged past. It was noon, the sun beating down hard. Jim was beginning to think that maybe heading west wasn't a good idea, and he felt his sense of adventure leaking away. Still he walked on. Finally, when defeat seemed inevitable and he thought he'd have to turn around, a battered station wagon pulled over and the driver, a housepainter wearing splattered overalls, offered him a ride. Going far? the man asked. The nearest truck stop, Jim told him—a truck stop was almost as familiar to Jim as home. It's thirty miles on, the housepainter said. I'm only going twenty-five, so you'll have to walk the rest of the way. Sure, Jim said. He'd never been to the truck stop ahead, but he already knew what it looked like, just a big flat lay-by alongside the road. Though the truck stops where he'd stopped with his father had all been to the east, Zack said they were all more or less alike.

It had been years since Jim had been on a trip with his father, and except for a fishing weekend last summer, they hadn't spent much time alone. Jim missed going on short hauls with his father. So why was he heading west and not east? Because if he headed east, there was an off chance

Zack would pick him up on the road, and then Jim would have to tell him he was leaving home and Zack would want to know why. Jim wasn't about to tell his father that Paula was away with Ron—he'd rat on Carla, but he wouldn't rat on his mother. He wouldn't do anything to spoil the chance of his parents getting back together. So he was heading west. But to reach the West he'd need to hitch a ride with a long-distance driver, which was why, thirsty and hot, he'd parked himself on the running board of the ABC HOUSEHOLD MOVERS truck, waiting for the driver to wake up.

2

Another hour passed and still Jim waited, knowing that soon the driver inside would have to get up. There were regulations a long-distance driver had to follow—only a four-hour driving stretch, Zack said, before a driver was required to take a short break, three hours max. Problem was, Jim had no idea how long the driver had been sleeping before he showed up. A second hour dragged by. Just when Jim was convinced he'd croak if he didn't get water and shade, he heard movement inside the truck, and lurching to his feet, he tapped on the glass. A wiry, balding guy squeezed between the front seats and opened the window partway.

"Howdy," he said. "What can I do for you, sonny?"

Jim's mouth was so dry the words stuck to the back of his throat.

"Take your time."

On the second try Jim worked up enough spit to say he was looking for a ride west.

The guy scratched his cheek above a patch of unshaven bristle.

"'West' covers a lot of territory," he said. "Where in the west?" There was a twang like a guitar string in his voice.

"Somewhere on the Prairies," Jim said, by which he meant far away from the city.

His answer seemed to require a closer look, and opening the door, the guy manoeuvred himself until he was sitting sideways on the driver's seat, his sock feet dangling above the running board. He looked at Jim, who looked right back, taking in the dome-shaped head, the grey hair straggling shoulder-length below a bald spot. The guy had sad hound-dog eyes and wore a gold cross on a chain around his neck; both his arms were tattooed with flags. Reaching behind the seat for a pair of cowboy boots, the driver took his time pulling them on, as if he was stalling about whether or not he'd give Jim a lift. Once the boots were on, he asked if Jim was running away.

"No," Jim said. He didn't think he was running away—he was *getting* away. Big difference.

"So where's home?" the guy asked, suspicious.

Jim tilted his head back, to indicate the city.

"Then why are you going in the opposite direction?"

Jim shrugged. "Because I want to head for someplace I've never been."

The driver looked dubious. "You on anything?"

He meant drugs. Jim had toked up a few times, tried OxyContin once and been wasted on booze twice, which made him more or less clean. Even so, he didn't appreciate being grilled, especially by a stranger. But he swallowed the urge to tell this guy that the cops were after him and he was addicted to crack. That kind of smartass talk could cost him a ride. It had taken last night and most of the day to get this far, and he didn't want to mess up now. "I don't do drugs," Jim said, then added, "My dad's a trucker," which he thought might help. Who knew? There was the off chance this guy might know his father.

"That so," the guy drawled. "He got a name?"

"Zack Hobbs," Jim said.

"Haven't had the pleasure. What's your name?"

"Jim."

"Silas Stamps." The guy stuck out his hand. "Hop in."

What a relief not to be left standing in the blazing sun a second longer! Jim climbed onto the passenger seat and watched as Silas switched on the ignition and pushed the air-conditioning button. A river of cool air flowed across Jim, who nodded toward the cubicle behind the seat and asked, "Didn't you find it too hot in here to sleep?"

"Nope." Easing the truck forward, Silas said, "I got me a battery fan back there that keeps me cool enough to nap. I didn't want to sleep too long anyways and woke up when I began to feel warm." Without taking his eyes off the pavement, he added, "There's a cooler behind you. Help yourself to water."

Jim leaned over the seat and his long arm snaked down and groped for the cooler. He opened the lid, lifted out a bottle of water, unscrewed the plastic top, took a long swallow and buckled himself in.

Silas manoeuvred the truck out of the truck stop and into the traffic stream. Soon they were bouncing along at a brisk clip, reminding Jim that when he was on a short haul with Zack, the truck seat would bounce like this, making him feel like he was sitting on a springform bed. Another reminder were the two electric blue Smurfs dangling from the mirror, where Zack hung a rabbit's paw. Once they were up to speed, Silas punched in a CD and what Zack called "hurtin' music" came on. Like Silas, his father went for these pathetic cryers who crooned about lost loves and all that crap. Not Jim's kind of music at all. The kind of music he picked out on his guitar was a combination of rap and jazz—he carried the tune while Solly played drums and Web played piano. The crooner was making Jim sleepy, and slouching lower in the seat, he tipped his head back and closed his eyes.

Silas gave him a sideways glance. "Looks like you didn't get much shut-eye last night."

"Yeah, I spent the night on somebody's lawn furniture."

"No wonder you're whacked," Silas said. "Go ahead and sleep. It'll be a few days before we reach the Prairies."

"Days!" It had been a long time since Jim had looked at a map.

"It's a big country."

=

Jim slept until late afternoon, waking just as they were passing an enormous lake glittering like mica in the last rays of sun. Silas announced that he intended to stop just ahead and asked if Jim wanted a coffee. Jim told him no thanks, he'd buy himself a Coke. He didn't say he had his own money, over a hundred bucks—the old lady had paid cash for a month's gardening, counting the bills into his hand one by one. He'd been on the way to a banking machine when the power crashed and the subway shut down.

Inside the service-station store, Silas headed for the washroom while Jim bought a Coke and three Mars bars, finishing them off in five minutes flat.

Riding a sugar high, Jim sat up for the next few hours as they passed more rocks, woods and lakes. Although there was a sameness to the land, there was a difference too, because no lake or clump of trees or rocks was exactly alike. When he grew bored with looking around, Jim asked Silas about the flag tattoos on his arms.

"Before I became a trucker, I travelled all over the world, hitching rides wherever I could. I was a drifter, a kind of Don Quixote," Silas said. He glanced at Jim. "Do you know who Don Quixote is?"

"No."

"He's a storybook character, a dreamer who wandered all over Spain with his sidekick, Sancho Panza, looking for his true love, Dulcinea."

"Did he find her?"

"Naw. She wasn't real. She was a dream."

Weird. Jim couldn't help snickering. "You were looking for a dream?"

A sheepish look washed over Silas's face. "I guess I was," he admitted, "but I didn't find my Dulcinea until I came back home. Now we've got eight-year-old twins, a girl and a boy." He reached out and batted the Smurfs. "The twins always give me toys when I go on the road so I won't forget them. As if I would.

"My wife, Ellie, has never been to Spain," he went on, "but I'm aiming to take her and the kids there next year." Silas glanced at Jim again and said, "Do you have an itchy foot? Is that why you're heading west?"

Jim didn't feel like talking about himself, but because Silas was doing him a favour, he owed him an answer. "I wanted to get out of the city," he said. "I was underground in the subway when the power went out."

A massive power failure. Silas knew all about it. "Biggest

one ever. Wiped out the power in this part of the country. Even wiped out parts of the USA."

"I was stuck in a frigging dark tunnel for over half an hour with a bunch of passengers," Jim said. "After a while the generator lights came on and a couple of subway workers showed up with flashlights to help us get out of the car. I figured I didn't need help, and I was in such a hurry to get off that I jumped onto the tracks and ran ahead of everyone else. I was holding onto the edge of the platform to boost myself up when my hands slipped and back I went, hit my head on the subway track and knocked myself out cold."

"How long were you out?"

"Ten, maybe fifteen minutes," Jim said. "By the time I came to, all the passengers had left and a subway worker took me to a nurse upstairs. She said I had a mild concussion and to not fall asleep. She told me the best thing I could do for myself was to walk, and if I wanted, I could walk to the hospital. It wasn't far away. When I told her there was no way I was going to the hospital, she warned me to stay awake. So I started walking, first to keep myself from falling asleep and later because I wanted to clear out of the city. It's hard to explain . . ." Jim's voice trailed away. He didn't want Silas to know he'd been scared shitless when the subway car had jolted to a stop and the lights went out and people started screaming. Jim didn't plan on telling anyone that just before the power failed, he'd been listening to a Walkman tape of DJ Buddy's. DJ's joke of the day was that Mars had broken out of its orbit and was heading straight toward Earth. Look out, Earth! Buddy screamed before the power went out, and for one terrifying minute Jim was convinced Planet Mars *had* collided with Planet Earth. He was embarrassed to admit to anyone, even to himself, that he'd been taken in by the dumb joke.

"You don't have to explain," Silas said. "You're talking to someone who can't stay long in a city before taking to the open road."

"My dad says he's addicted to the open road."

"Yup. It's an addiction, all right."

"When I went on short hauls with my dad, I liked sitting up high, looking down on all the cars and smaller trucks."

"Like you were king of the castle."

They chatted on and off like this while Silas slipped in another weepy CD. Later they pulled into a roadside diner for supper. Jim put away a chicken dinner, two slices of banana cream pie and two more Cokes. When he finished eating, he left Silas at the counter and, going to the pay phone, dialled zero and placed a collect call to Paula. She might not be back from her shack-up with Ron, but if she was, Jim figured that by now he was far enough away that talking to her wouldn't persuade him to change his mind and go home.

Carla picked up the phone.

"Finally, *finally* you call," the Drama Queen shrieked. "I told Paula that you'd call again, but she was convinced something *awful* had happened to her precious little man. She called Zack and he told her to give it another day and if you didn't phone she should call the police."

The police. Jim hadn't given a thought to the police.

He reminded his pain-in-the-ass sister that he'd phoned that morning and left a message. It was as if she didn't hear.

"Zack said that maybe you just needed some breathing space," Carla went on. "Personally, I think you're *totally* irresponsible. That's because you're a sooky baby, a mama's boy."

That hurt, big time. Jim asked to speak to Paula.

"She's lying down. She has a *terrible* headache. That's how *upset* she is. She *never* lies down. *WAIT.*" Jim heard the receiver clatter against the hall table. Moments later there was a faint cry and the brush of feet against the carpeted stairs. Paula picked up the phone.

"Jim! Is it really you?"

"Sure, it's me." He heard her sobbing, which she never did.

"Are you okay? Are you hurt or anything?"

"I'm okay, Mom."

"Thank God for that. When Carla phoned Ron's cabin and told me you didn't come home last night, I thought something awful must have happened to you. You've always been so reliable."

Jim explained about the blackout and having to evacuate the subway car, leaving out the part about the concussion. He asked if she'd got the message he left on her voice mail that morning.

"About not to expect you home tonight? Yes, I got it," Paula said crossly. Now that she knew he was okay, she was angry. "What I want to know is *why* aren't you coming home."

"I'm taking a break."

"A break."

"Yeah."

"From *what*, may I ask?" The sarcastic Paula was back.

"From everything. Mostly I want to clear out of the city for a while."

"What's got into you, Jim?"

Jim knew his mother was furious at him, which she seldom was—he seldom gave her reason. How often had she said that he'd never given her a lick of trouble? His sister was the shit disturber in the family; he was the goody-goody, or as Carla put it, the sooky baby. He hadn't anticipated that his mother would be so upset. Why the big deal? After all, Paula had gone away herself and he'd phoned home earlier today. Had she forgotten that three years ago, when his sister was his age now, Carla had taken off for a week, and it was two days before she phoned? Once again he told Paula that after being cooped up in the subway, he'd felt like clearing out of the city.

"So where are you?"

"On my way to the Prairies."

"Say that again?"

So Jim did.

"Okay, but why the Prairies?" She was calmer now.

"I want to see the West."

"And after you've seen it you'll come home."

"I don't know. I'll see how it goes."

"You don't *know* if you'll come home!" Paula shrieked. "I can't believe what I'm hearing."

"Calm down, Mom. Calm down."

"Calm down! Do you have any idea how worried I've been? I'm a basket case, and you tell me to calm down!"

"Sorry."

"I want you to come home. Promise me you'll come home."

"I can't."

"Can't! What is this *can't?*" She was shouting.

Jim had forgotten how fast Paula's moods could change, how quickly anxiety could turn to anger. But he stood his ground. "I won't promise."

Silence while his mother shifted gears.

"What about school?" He could tell she was making the effort to calm herself down. "It begins in two weeks."

"I know." How could he forget?

"You *have* to come home in time for school. Until you're sixteen, quitting school is against the law."

"I'm not quitting school. It will still be there when I get back."

"Which is when?"

"I haven't decided."

"You should have told me you were leaving," Paula said, her voice petulant and accusing.

"I didn't know myself. Why are you on my case, Mom?"

Paula ignored the question and asked if he was travelling by bus.

"I hitched a ride with a trucker."

"Your father's son."

Jim let it pass.

He saw Silas heading for the door and said, "Gotta go, Mom. My ride's leaving. I'll call you in a few days." He hung up just as Paula was reminding him once again about school. He felt badly cutting the conversation short, knowing his mother wanted to keep him talking. But he felt good, too, knowing that he'd stuck to his guns and hadn't caved in to the one person in the world who could persuade him to turn around and go home, back to the city where he'd spent his entire life.

3

While Silas was busy merging the truck with the traffic stream, Jim closed his eyes, feigning sleep so he wouldn't have to talk. He wanted space to think about the phone conversation he'd had with his mother. He was thinking that it was a good thing he'd called home from the roadside diner, because if he hadn't, the police might be out looking for him soon. Paula's reaction had caught him off guard. Because she'd been away herself, it hadn't occurred to Jim that she'd be so upset about him not phoning home last night. What was the big deal? Maybe he *was* a mama's boy, like Carla said. It was okay for his mother and sister to do what *they* wanted, but just let him try to do what *he* wanted and they were all over him. Talk about a double standard. And to think it had taken a concussion to knock some sense into his head, to wake him up to the fact that like the others in his family, he had choices—he could head out to someplace on his own if he wanted.

Although he'd never done anything about it until now, sometimes Jim had felt like leaving home. He often got tired of the way his mother and sister carried on, talking and laughing, totally ignoring him. Did they think he was hard of hearing? Or did they think he wasn't worth talking to? They didn't even notice when he left the living room or kitchen to play guitar in his bedroom. True, he found it easier to play guitar than to make conversation with the women in his family, but that didn't mean he wanted to be ignored. The fact was, even his mother didn't know him—she thought she did, but she didn't.

She often told him he was laid back like his father. But if his father was laid back, why had he moved out? Something must have been bothering him. When Jim was nine he got up the nerve to ask his dad why he left. Zack told him that it was complicated, that the separation might be only temporary. When you're older, he said, I'll explain. Well, Jim was older. Six years had gone by since he asked the question, and he was still waiting for an explanation. When he asked Paula, all she said was that both she and Zack needed breathing space. Well, Jim knew about needing breathing space. He needed breathing space from his mother and sister. And he needed breathing space from school.

He hated school. It was boring and useless and a total waste of time. He didn't think that what he was expected to learn in school had anything to do with him, which was why he dozed through most of the classes, slouched low, hoping the teachers would forget he was there. Every once in a while a scrap of information would wake him up, usually in science class, and he'd listen closely, but most of his time was spent waiting for the bell to ring. He couldn't get away with faking the flu or whatever and skipping school. He and Solly had tried that the year before and had got away with it twice before the principal called them in and read the riot act.

Besides total boredom, Jim made a mental list of what else he hated about school:

Teachers. Bugging him about wearing his wool tuque in class. Bugging him about applying himself, paying attention and working harder. None of the teachers came out and called him lazy, but that was what they meant.

Tunny. Because of Jim's size, drug pushers who hung out near the school left him alone unless a mastiff named Tunny was with them. Whenever Tunny caught Jim by himself—his timing was perfect—he set his gang of terrier junkies on him, ordering them to rough him up. Once they blackened his eye, even cracked a rib, until he gave Tunny thirty bucks and was handed a plastic bag of white powder. Though he and Solly had done OxyContin, there was no way he was doing crack, and he flushed the bag down the school crapper.

Girls, a.k.a chicks. They were a humungous problem. When he was near a girl he thought he liked, Jim could hardly keep his eyes off her, even if her breasts were covered up. Later he couldn't stop himself from imagining they were having sex. The problem was, the chicks came on way too strong and gave him no room to manoeuvre, no time to think. Their boldness made him feel awkward and uncomfortable, as if they were in control, not him. Also, they knew how to flirt and play games with him. The result? He never knew where he stood. He tried ignoring chicks but sooner or later he'd be suckered into spending his hard-earned cash on taking a girl to a movie or a fancy restaurant. When Mandy asked if he wanted to hang out together, he said sure, and bought her a gold charm to wear around her neck. Two weeks later she dropped him for another guy. Same thing with

Amber. The way she and Mandy had toyed with him knocked Jim off centre, made him feel that when it came to chicks, he was a total wimp. After Amber dropped him, Jim swore he'd never take up with another chick until he was older and knew the kind of girl he wanted. Until then, he'd stick to his imagination.

=

Silas knew he wasn't asleep. He asked Jim if he was calling a girl or home.

"Home," Jim said. "Checked in with Paula." After a pause, he added, "My mother."

"First time you called home?"

"I phoned early this morning and left a message, but she was still worried. Worried enough to phone my father."

"Zack."

"Yeah. They've been separated six years. Sort of."

Jim saw Zack about once a month. Whenever he had a delivery in the city, his father stopped by the condo and took Jim and Carla, if she was around, out for pizza and a movie. Their parents had what Paula called an amicable separation, which was supposed to mean there were no hard feelings between them. There didn't seem to be any as far as Jim could tell. Sometimes Paula joined them for supper, joking with Zack as if he were someone she'd just met. She met people easily, which was important in her job. She sold real estate and for the last three years had been the company's top earner. Paula was smart, smarter, Zack claimed, than he was, and more ambitious. A work horse, he said admiringly. No grass grows under *her* feet. Jim sometimes thought the reason his father had left his mother was to get out of her way so she could get on with her ambition. As far as he could tell, neither one of them showed any interest in marrying anyone else. According to Carla, Ron wasn't a serious boyfriend and Paula had no intention of ever living with him. Jim didn't know if Zack lived with anyone or if he even had a girlfriend—he was close-mouthed about his life. He probably had more than one. Jim and his father couldn't walk down the street without women glancing at Zack's rugged good looks. Once, when Paula was into the wine, she told Jim that Zack was the most charming man she'd ever met, which made the split all the more confusing.

═

"Sort of?" Silas said. "That must be hard for you."

Jim shrugged. "Yeah, it's hard."

"Tell me about Zack," Silas said.

Jim told him that Zack didn't like the city much. He liked the outdoors, fishing, hiking, camping. Before the split their family had gone on camping trips together. He told Silas he remembered his father and himself lying on their backs on top of a picnic table, looking at the stars. While Carla and Paula were asleep inside the tent, his father pointed out the Milky Way and the Big Dipper, Orion's Belt and Cassiopeia. Jim didn't mention how happy he'd been that night, tucked into the crook of Zack's arm in the middle of dark woods. Instead, he said, "With the light pollution in the city, I can't see stars from the condo. But with the power off, I saw them last night."

"Wait until we're on the Prairies. You'll see stars you've never seen before. Planets," Silas said, waving a hand toward the sky. "The whole universe."

Jim didn't see many stars that night, or the next, because when Silas pulled over at the truck stop at the end of the day, the two of them climbed into the box room behind the seats, where Jim slept on the floor at the foot of Silas's bed, next to a small closet and a battery-operated television. Jim fell asleep partway through the news.

Jim's second morning on the road they drove past another gigantic lake, this one so huge that Jim couldn't even see the other side. Passing the lake seemed to take forever, but by late afternoon, it was behind them and the rocky landscape became heavily wooded. By nightfall that had given way to hilly farmland, ponds and small lakes.

By the third day, the trees had become sparse and the land began to flatten into fields of wheat and hay on either side of the road. Jim saw the occasional harvesting machine at work, leaving behind acres of stubble where the crop had been cut and left in giant rolls. Here and there a grain elevator rose straight up from the land. Silas remarked that the grain elevators reminded him of castle towers in Spain, the way they lorded it over everything else. He talked a lot about Spain and all the other countries whose flags were tattooed on his arms. Silas had fought alligators in South America, survived a close encounter with a shark in Australia and nearly been run over by a herd of stampeding elephants in Africa.

Jim asked how long Silas had been away.

"Seven years."

"What did you do for money?"

"I had various jobs. Worked on a freighter. A sheep farm. A coffee plantation. Did all kinds of things. Saved my money and moved on until I'd circled the world."

"Cool."

Jim knew that if he stayed out west he'd need a job. He had money in the bank, but he didn't want to blow it all. He liked having money in the bank, even if he didn't know how he'd spend it. Unlike Carla, who spent every cent she earned, he saved most of what he earned mowing lawns and weeding gardens. Jim asked Silas what the chances were of finding a job out west.

"Pretty good if you go north," Silas said. "No point looking for a job this far south. Southern prairie farmers are being beat up by a drought and won't be hiring any time soon. Your best chance of finding work is farther north. It so happens I'm heading north and if you want to get down and have a look around, I know a good place to drop you off."

"Where's that?"

"Wait and see," Silas said mysteriously. "We'll be there tomorrow."

That evening after turning north, they stopped at a truck stop for the night and, before bedding down, went for a walk alongside a coulee. Jim didn't even know what a coulee was until Silas explained that it was a fold in the land made by an ancient creek bed. It was true that the coulee did fold in the middle where an old creek had once snaked its way across the prairie. "A beautiful sight," Silas said and it was. In the fading light the coulee's sides were soft and furry looking. The school-book pictures he'd seen of the prairie had led Jim to expect it to be entirely empty and flat, but it was often broken by coulees and clumps of trees.

As they drove farther north the next morning, the prairie changed again. The land undulated into gentle wooded hills, and fields grazed by horses and cattle. The fields were dotted with sloughs, where ducks and geese swam. The farmhouses, circled by poplars and set far back from the road, were miles apart. Jim had never seen houses so far apart and figured the distance between them would fill five city blocks.

Shortly before noon, he glimpsed a town ahead. The buildings looked looked like they were floating on the horizon. Silas said the town was almost thirty miles away and it was the distance that made it look like a mirage. After they travelled farther down the road, Silas announced that the town was the place he'd drop off Jim.

"It's a small town," he said, "but it's got one of everything, and that makes it a handy place to live."

"I don't want to live in a town but somewhere in the country," Jim said.

"But you'll need to buy stuff from time to time, like warm clothes." Silas glanced at Jim's bare arms. "It's hot now, but often it's cold out here. Prairie weather can change mighty fast and next week it could be snowing." He paused. "And you'll need food. You can't go long without food."

Closer to town, what had first appeared as a floating mirage took the shape of stores, churches and houses that became clearer the nearer they came. When they reached the main street, Jim saw that Silas had been right: the town seemed to have one of everything. As they drove along the one paved street, he picked out a motel, a hardware store, a video store, a car rental, a barber shop, a general store, a service station, a police station, an elementary school, a high school, a library and four kinds of churches, one of them with a spire, another with a bulbed dome.

Silas pulled off the road and into a parking lot in front of a small strip mall where, Jim noticed, there was a drugstore, a hairdresser, a bank and a café. "Come on," Silas said, "I'll buy you a hamburger at Marilyn's." He nodded toward the café where two cars were parked outside, a white and blue police car and a red Cavalier with a For Sale sign in the back window.

"I have money of my own," Jim said.

"Keep it."

Inside, Silas grinned at the woman who greeted them. She was a heavy-chested woman in a baggy sweatsuit. A plastic clip held a knot of grey hair on top of her head. "Hi Silas," she said. "Good to see you again."

"You too." Silas headed for a booth at the back. The only windows in the café were at the front and it was dark inside, which was why the small copper lamps on the tables were lit even though it was the middle of the day. The tables and booths were made of some kind of light wood with dark swirls in it. Silas slid into the booth next to the washrooms; Jim sat opposite him.

"How's business?" Silas asked when Marilyn appeared with a menu.

Tucking a strand of hair behind an ear, she said, "Not bad. The usual regulars." Jim noticed that her earrings were made of bird feathers.

"Marilyn," Silas said, "this is Jim."

"Hi Jim," Marilyn said. "You going to the coast with Silas?"

"He's getting down here," Silas said and ordered a burger and coffee. Jim ordered a burger and Coke.

"You both want the works?" Marilyn asked Jim, not Silas; she knew what he wanted.

"The works," Jim said.

"Two burgers with the works, Dory," Marilyn shouted into the kitchen.

While Silas was using the washroom, Jim looked around the café, noticing that the only other customers were two police officers, a man and a woman in blue gold-striped uniforms who sat at a front window, where, Jim supposed, they could keep an eye on the road. When Silas returned, Jim took his turn in the washroom. As soon as he sat down again, Silas asked for his home telephone number. "That's so I can call your parents and tell them where I let you down," he said. "When you're a parent, you never stop worrying about your kids."

Jim wrote the numbers on a paper napkin and handed it to Silas. "I might not stick around here, though," he said. "I'll see how it goes."

The burgers arrived and they ate quickly without talking. By now a new awkwardness had settled over Jim. During the past few days he and Silas had become friends and he didn't know how to say goodbye to him. Was this a final goodbye? Would he ever see Silas again?

When he finished eating, Silas got to his feet and said, "One thing I learned in my travels is that you never know when you'll bump into someone you've met on the road. It happens." Reaching across the table, he shook Jim's hand. "See you around."

Jim watched Silas amble to the front, his bald spot catching a wink of copper lamplight.

Minutes later, Marilyn appeared with a Coke. "Silas wanted you to have this," she said and Jim felt a pang of regret. Already he was missing Silas. And weirdly, he was missing Zack now more than he missed him at home. He supposed it was because Silas reminded him of Zack. The two men were alike in a couple of important ways: both knew how to let Jim just be—it was okay with them if Jim didn't feel like talking. But if he did feel like talking they were interested in what he had to say.

A man of few words was how Paula described Zack. Like his father, Jim spoke only when he had something to say. He was comfortable with silence while he chased one thought after another, sort of like he chased notes on the guitar, drifting along in no particular hurry. Jim didn't like to hurry. Zack didn't either. All in good time, he used to say when he took Jim with him on the road. Zack didn't like being hassled. Jim remembered that whenever his mother hassled his father about helping out more around the house—this was before they moved to the condo—Zack would disappear for a couple of hours. When he came back, Paula would have cooled down and everything would go back to normal. Jim loved his mother, but unlike his father she wasn't always easy to be with.

Silas was easy to be with. There'd been times when the two or them were rolling down the highway that Jim felt he could have kept on riding beside Silas forever. Was the feeling mostly for the open road, or was it mostly wanting to be with Zack, or someone who reminded him of Zack? Or was it that riding with Silas had made the journey west seem so easy, like everything was falling into place?

Not anymore, Jim thought. He was on his own and it was possible that from now on nothing would fall easily into place. A scary thought. But at least his life wouldn't be boring. Wasn't this what he had wanted, to take on the excitement and uncertainty of the open road? By the time he'd finished the Coke, Jim had shaken off a case of the jitters. In its place was a surge of elation that came from being pleased with himself for having made it this far. He'd set out for the Prairies and here he was.

4

There was only one road going north from the town and before entering the café Silas had pointed it out. "Best chance of a job would be somewheres up that road," he told Jim, "but you might have to walk a piece to find one." Now Jim stood in the café parking lot thinking that before he walked up that road, he'd better buy some food. Also a pair of sunglasses—his old pair was inside his backpack with his Walkman, and already he was blinking in the strong sunlight. In the strip mall next to the café he bought the cheapest pair of sunglasses he could find before heading for the general store, where he bought peanut butter, cheese, bread, bananas and a large bottle of cold water. Stuffing his tuque into the plastic grocery bag, he continued on to what looked like little more than a dirt track, but was, the woman in the general store assured him, the only road north.

The unpaved road was narrow and straight, and after spending days sitting in the truck, Jim was glad to be walking. It felt good to stretch his legs and suck in the clean prairie air. He heard grasshoppers rustling in the dry grasses close by and saw dozens of hoppers high-jumping onto the road. Beyond the town, fields of ripened wheat soared away like a flock of giant yellow birds with spreading wings. Since arriving on the Prairies, Jim had noticed that wherever he looked, the horizon was smack in the middle, dividing the sky and the land in half. He remembered that when he was a kid and he and Paula had visited his grandfather, who lived on an island, the sea met the sky halfway, like the prairies did here. Living in a big city where tall buildings blocked the sky, he rarely saw the horizon, and now that he was taking in its awesome breadth, he had the feeling that some part of him had been let loose, that something shut up tight inside him had escaped and was flying skyward. He didn't know what that something was, only that the longer he walked, the lighter and freer he felt.

A half-ton truck came toward him, kicking up dust, its white-haired driver waving as he passed. Going by the tall grasses and weeds in the ditch, Jim figured there couldn't be much traffic on the road, because if there were, the plants would be covered with dust. After he'd walked another couple of miles, he came to a stretch of fenced woods on the left hand side of the road. The fence went on for maybe a quarter mile before Jim came to a closed wooden gate with a wooden beam overhead. Burnt into the beam in crude letters were the words MAJESTIC FARM. On the other side of the gate a driveway curved away and disappeared into the woods.

When Jim had gone another quarter mile, he came to an arrow-pointed sign on the same side of the road. The sign was tilted so far down it was close to falling over. Jim squinted at it, trying to read the letters cut into the weathered grey wood. BLISS, the letters spelled. Bliss was the word Paula used when she came home after a day of showing properties non-stop. Kicking off her shoes and stretching out on the couch she'd say, *This is bliss*—meaning there was no better place to be. Curious, Jim followed the arrow farther along the road to a small island of trees that he figured must be Bliss. He was less sure when reaching the trees he glimpsed behind them and saw what appeared to be a small house and a couple of smaller buildings. He looked down the road, but there was only one other building in sight and it was maybe a half mile away on the opposite side of the road, where he saw the tiny figure of a man walking across a wheatfield. Apparently Bliss was nothing more than these three beat-up buildings. One of them was a house set back about fifty feet from the road. It looked deserted, its shutters closed, its front veranda collapsed, not a scrap of paint left on the clapboard, the flowering shrubs at the side and front of the house gone wild.

Jim was standing at the bottom of what looked like it might have been a driveway. Through the thistles and crab-grass he picked out a dirt track sloping upward toward the house. Following the track Jim came to a round stone shape he recognized as a well. On top was a wooden cover cracked with age. A well meant water. By now, Jim's water bottle was almost empty and he'd need water soon. Sweating from exertion, he lifted the wooden cover and looked inside. Six feet down was a scum of brown. Dust. The well water was coated with dust that must have come through the crack in the cover. There was a hook on the inside stone wall and on it a tin pail tied with a rope. If he wanted a drink, he'd have to bail out the scum with the bucket. Was he thirsty enough to do that now, or should he wait until he'd looked around? From his vantage point beside the well, he noticed that with the overgrown trees and shrubs, the dirt road couldn't be seen from where he was standing. It occurred to Jim that the farms were spread so far apart that there were no neighbours close enough to know if he bedded down here for the night. He might just do that.

But first, to make sure the place really was deserted, he'd check it out, starting with the building directly in front of him, which because of its low roof and wide double doors, he guessed was a garage. There was a rusting barrel against the doors, and when Jim took hold of it to shove it away, he noticed it was blackened inside, likely from burning trash. The doors swung open. As he'd thought, the building was a garage. There was no vehicle inside, but there had been once, because Jim smelled oil and there were worn tires on one wall. On the opposite wall was a scythe—Jim didn't know how he recognized what it was but he did—hanging beside a blackened rake and shovel. Leaning against the wall was a hand lawnmower. After he'd looked all this over, Jim closed the doors and went to explore a modest peak-roofed building nearby, in what had been a small orchard. Most of the fruit trees were gnarled and dead, but one of them was healthy, its lower branches so burdened with yellow fruit that they touched the ground. Jim picked an apple and, biting into its freckled skin, was surprised that it tasted sweet. He chomped on two more before approaching the door of the small building with windows down either side. Like the garage door, this door was unlocked. Inside were three rows of four small desks, twelve altogether, and at the front was a large desk with a blackboard behind it. At the back of the room were empty bookshelves and a pot-bellied wood stove. Without doubt this was a schoolhouse. With nobody living close by, it was a weird place for a schoolhouse, but that was what it was. Jim snickered at the thought that though he was in no hurry to return to school, here he was on the Prairies, standing inside one.

Behind the schoolhouse was a rhubarb patch gone to seed and what might have been a henhouse with a small doorway opening into a chicken-wire pen, barely recognizable through the tangle of wild mustard and stinkweed. Beyond the pen was a half-acre field thick with weeds and bordered by half-dead trees and a broken-down fence marking what he guessed was the property line.

Taking a closer look at the house, Jim noticed that it had no back door: the owners must have used the wooden door in the shed attached to the side of the house. Jim gave the door a tentative push. Creaking, the door opened halfway, allowing Jim to peer inside. The half-light was enough for him to make out a stack of wood, a workbench and a plywood cabinet. Beside the cabinet was a step leading to another door. Jim gave the knob a slow turn and the door whispered open, but only an inch. Because the door stopped opening, Jim had the creepy feeling that someone was behind it, that the house was occupied, that its owner was waiting for him inside like a spider waited for a fly. Maybe, he thought, the doors were unlocked because the owner *wanted* someone to open them. The question was why. Rooted to the step, Jim listened for movement on the other side of the door that would indicate a living thing: a shuffle of feet, a ticking clock, a scraping chair. There was nothing but silence.

Still he was wary, and that wariness made him open the door only slightly wider—three inches this time—while he waited, hand on the knob, in case someone inside should suddenly wrench open the door. But no one did, and pushing the door wide, he stepped onto a wooden floor that groaned beneath his weight. Again Jim waited, listening, but still he heard nothing, not even the rustle of a mouse. The room was dark but there was enough light for him to make out a window on the side wall. Reaching out, he tried unhooking the shutters. Only one of them would open—the other was nailed shut. But enough light flooded in for him to pick out the objects in what was obviously a kitchen with a wood stove, a sink, a table, two chairs, a rocker, a cabinet and, beneath a window on the opposite wall, the kind of sofa Paula called a daybed. Jim opened the shutters above the daybed. More light flooded in, and he saw a scrub board hanging beside the sink and a wooden icebox, the kind he remembered seeing in his grandfather's kitchen—the entire room seemed to be from his grandfather's time. In the bright window light he noticed that every surface in the kitchen was coated with a thick layer of dust; even the deserted cobwebs hanging from the ceiling corners were coated with dust.

Although the kitchen hadn't been used for a very long time, Jim couldn't shake the idea that the owner might have died in the house, that the body was still inside, maybe upstairs on a bed. That would explain the unlocked doors. If there *was* a corpse upstairs, wouldn't the flesh be too shrivelled and dry to smell? Maybe not. The dry tomblike odour in the kitchen might come from something deeper inside the house.

None of these thoughts was enough to deter Jim from exploring. Directly in front of him was an open door. Poking his head into the next room, he stood listening before crossing to the window and unhooking the shutters. Again light flooded in, and he realized he was inside a sitting room that in his grandfather's time was called a parlour. Against the front wall was another wood stove, with empty bookshelves on either side. The bookshelves on the opposite wall were also bare. Running a finger along the edge of a shelf, he pushed up a ridge of powdery dust. The room contained a sofa, two rocking chairs, a table and a carpet. As in the kitchen, everything was layered with dust. The carpet dust was so thick that each footstep sent a flurry of dust up Jim's nose, making him sneeze. Tugging the front door open, he stood in the threshold, inhaling fresh air. He noticed that the steps below him had broken loose and were hanging at a precarious angle. Although he couldn't see it because of the overgrown shrubs, he knew the dirt road was directly ahead, beyond the trees. The sneezing stopped, and leaving the front door open, Jim mounted the staircase, climbing slowly, the sound of each step magnified by the silence of the house as he reminded himself that if there really was a corpse anywhere in the house, it would be lying on a bed upstairs.

Of course there wasn't a corpse on the bed or anywhere else, and Jim felt foolish for thinking there might have been, knowing that it was the unlocked doors and the knowledge he was trespassing that had spooked him. Once the bedroom window shutters were open, he saw a rolled mattress on an iron bedstead, two straight-backed chairs and a large clothes cupboard.

The second upstairs room was smaller and contained a washstand, a tin tub and a large chair with a hole in the seat. A potty chair—Jim remembered seeing one during a grade-five visit to the museum. Clearly this room had been used as a bathroom. He closed the window shutters, went downstairs and shut the front door. For the first time, he noticed a kerosene lamp on the parlour table and it struck him—*there was no electricity in Bliss!* Having been caught in the past, he'd accepted the wood stove and the icebox without thinking about the fact that neither one ran on electricity, which was why he hadn't seen an electrical wire or a light switch anywhere. *Perfect!* After being caught in a massive power outage, the last thing he wanted was electricity, and he was excited by the prospect of crashing in a house without it.

The excitement dribbled away and the spooky feeling that he was being led returned, only this time it wasn't because he imagined a corpse upstairs. Now the feeling was that he'd been led to this particular house, that all along someone or something had been leading him away from home so he could find this place named Bliss.

Stop it, Jim told himself, stop creeping yourself out. Nobody was leading him anywhere, nobody but himself had decided to leave the city and head west. Also, before meeting Silas, getting to the Prairies hadn't been easy. There was the four-hour wait on the highway before the house painter picked him up. Then a long sweltering wait sitting on the running board of Silas's truck before he got lucky. It was pure chance that he'd come upon this house. Fact was, he had been such a homebody he didn't know that if you took a chance all kinds of interesting things could happen.

Having shaken off the creepy feeling of being led, Jim decided he might hole up in Bliss for as long as he liked. Why not? Since leaving the city, he'd been on the move and was ready to take a break from travelling and hunker down in a quiet place. He couldn't ask for a quieter place than Bliss and staying here would be a bit like camping. He wouldn't miss all the electronic stuff like the computer and the TV—he remembered that the few times his family had gone camping he never once missed TV. He'd been so turned on by the excitement of living in the wild, close to nature, that watching TV had been the last thing on his mind.

Jim knew that by staying in the house, he'd be what Paula called a squatter—realtors didn't like squatters living in empty houses they were trying to sell. But no one was trying to sell this place, so why would anyone care if he squatted here? On the drive west, whenever Jim had seen an abandoned farmhouse it had struck him as sad that nobody lived in it anymore, that the house was empty, that the people who had probably built it were gone. Did abandoned houses keep the memories of the people who had lived there? The people who moved away had the memories, but did the houses themselves? Was that what ghosts were—memories? Don't go creeping yourself out again, Jim told himself. Get busy and clean this place up. Get rid of the dust in the kitchen. He'd already decided to sleep in the kitchen. He wouldn't use the whole house, only the one room.

Jim carried the daybed mattress outside and whacked it with an old broom he found in the shed, raising dust clouds that went up his nose and started the sneezing again. Leaving the mattress outside to air, he went to the well, lowered the tin pail and began bailing out the scum. He must have dumped thirty buckets of scummy water into the bushes beside the house—he stopped counting after twenty—before the water was clear enough for him to see his reflection.

He was carrying a pail of mostly clear water to the house when he looked up and noticed that the unopened shutter had been nailed shut against a pane of shattered glass with a tiny hole in its centre. A bullet hole. Someone had fired a shot though the window, probably a kid fooling around with a BB gun. Jim continued to the kitchen and set to work wiping down the table and chairs, the cupboard and shutters. Tying a cloth around the broom, he swiped at the cobwebs until they were gone. By the time he finished hours later, he was hungry and made himself a couple of cheese sandwiches, washing them down with cups of cold well water. Then he went to the outhouse he'd noticed behind the shed. Inside was a bucket of lime with a small hand shovel to use when the air stank. The air didn't stink. In fact, it had a dry, perfumy smell. When he finished, Jim washed himself at the well and carried the mattress inside where, stretching himself full length on the daybed, he surrendered to perfect silence. Before his eyes fluttered shut he looked around the kitchen and thought now that the room was clean and he was here, the house wasn't sad anymore.

Early in the morning he awoke to the sound of a bird singing in the shrubbery outside the window above his head. Jim had no idea what kind of bird it was, but its melodious song was thrilling to hear and he lay quietly on the daybed, willing the bird to keep on singing. After a while it flew away and Jim drifted back to sleep.

Later he woke up to a quite different sound, a strange snuffling that, when he came fully awake, he realized was coming from outside the opposite window. Swinging his legs to the floor, he padded across the kitchen and looked through the unboarded half of the window. At first he couldn't tell where the sound was coming from, but when he leaned far out the window he was astonished to see a large black bear gobbling up the apples on the lower branches of the tree, snuffling noisily as it gulped them down. Oblivious to the fact that someone was watching from inside the house, the bear ate greedily, tearing apples from the tree until the lower branches were stripped. Only then did it stand on its hind legs and bat the upper branches with its paws, tumbling apples to the ground. Jim had never seen a bear outside the zoo. *Wow,* he said, but silently, so the bear wouldn't hear. Even after the bear had wandered away, leaving broken branches and busted apples behind, Jim kept chanting, *Wow,* in an incantation of wonder and delight.

5

Having made up his mind to hang out in Bliss, Jim spent the next few days exploring cupboards and drawers, taking only what he needed to make the kitchen his—a blanket folded over the back of the rocker, two pillows on the daybed, a pewter candle holder on the table. He found a canvas bag with *H* stitched on it hooked to the back of the kitchen door. Inside a drawer on top of some tea towels, he found a framed photo of a man and a woman with their arms around each other. Because they looked young and happy, he stood the photo upright inside the cupboard, where he would see it whenever he took out a plate or a cup. He hung the knitted tea towels on a hook beside the sink. He found jars of rice and tea, boxes of matches and candles. To add to the stash, he hiked to town and bought bread and cereal, butter and milk, keeping the dairy items cold by putting them in the bucket and lowering it into the well. He didn't buy anything that required cooking, not because it was too hot—the nights were cool—but because he didn't want to light the stove. Jim remembered the night when his parents were still living under the same roof and their house burned down after the chimney caught fire. No way he was lighting the stove until the chimney was cleaned. Also, smoke would be a dead giveaway that a squatter was inside.

Since coming to Bliss, Jim felt that time had expanded, as if there were more of it here than there had been at home, an illusion created by his being free to choose what he did each day. He went to bed when he felt like it and got up when he felt like it. There was no need to use the alarm on his watch because the melodious bird woke him every morning—sometimes twice, soon after dawn and later as he lay in bed dozing. There was no need to claim the shower before his sister—he washed at the well when he was ready. There was no need to eat at the same time every day, only when he was hungry. He was free to do what he wanted when he wanted. Although he was using only one room, in a burst of energy and enthusiasm he spent his third day in Bliss cleaning the other rooms in the house. The dust crept into his ears and nose and coated his curly hair until it looked like a fuzzy wig. Still he kept on because, as with yardwork, he could see what he had accomplished.

After he'd sluiced the dust from his body, he went for a walk, following the road even farther north, reading the names on the signposts at the end of long driveways leading to farmhouses he couldn't see, concealed as they were behind stands of trees. *Chumnik, Foster, Kurelek, Stenson.* Some of the signs were as much as a mile apart. Hiking along the road, Jim was excited by the space and the silence; even more, he was excited to be on his own. He was alone but he wasn't lonely, and so far he wasn't missing home. Though he thought about Paula and Carla from time to time, he was in no hurry to go back. Being on his own was a turn-on, and this new independence his particular kind of bliss.

Late Sunday morning when he went outside to wash, Jim saw a crow eyeing him from its perch on the well top. His first day in Bliss, he'd seen four or five crows flying over the woods, but unlike this one, they didn't perch close by. This was the biggest crow Jim had ever seen. The crow didn't move when he approached, not even an eye. It was almost as if it was challenging him, daring him to come close. Jim stopped, waiting for the crow to fly away, but it stayed where it was until Jim was beside the well. Only then did it flap away to a nearby tree. Lifting the wooden cover, Jim brought up the pail and, tipping back his head, poured cold water into his mouth and over his face. The morning ritual of washing and drinking at the well did more than wake him up—it made him feel more energetic and strong. At home Jim seldom drank the tepid fluorinated water that came from the condo taps, but here he couldn't drink enough of the well water that tasted of something deep within the earth.

Jim was drying himself with his T-shirt when he felt someone watching. Turning, he saw a boy of maybe four or five standing in the schoolhouse door, staring at him. The boy was dressed in black pants and shirt and a broad-brimmed black hat. He didn't smile or speak but stood serious and still and, like everything in Bliss, seemed to be from the past. Jim nodded to the boy then wondered if he was real. The boy didn't move a muscle. It was as if Jim was looking at a ghost. They stared at each other for maybe half a minute before Jim broke the silence with a "Hi."

Immediately he heard footsteps inside the schoolhouse and a girl appeared behind the boy. She was about Jim's age and was wearing a long white dress. Like the boy, there was something old-fashioned about her. She definitely wasn't a chick. She stood there staring at Jim while he stared back, too astonished to speak.

"We haven't hurt anything," she said. From the apologetic way she spoke, Jim figured that, like him, she was trespassing on Bliss.

"Neither have I," Jim said, and grinned so she'd know it was a joke. "I don't mind you being here. You can come any time you want." Making himself go casual, he ambled toward her and the boy for a closer look.

"I don't come often," the girl said. "Only when I want . . ." She nudged the boy out of the schoolhouse.

The boy still hadn't spoken.

"Is he your brother?"

"Thomas is my sister Rachel's son." She began fidgeting with the boy's hat. Her nervousness made Jim forget his own, and he asked her name.

"Miriam."

"Mine's Jim."

"Good day, Jim," she said, her voice formal and stiff.

Now that he was near her, he saw that she was beautiful, with green eyes and thick black eyebrows. Remembering his sister's advice, he tried not to stare. According to Carla, staring was a dead giveaway that a girl had knocked you over—Carla never used the word *chick,* calling it as sexist as the B-word. His sister claimed that a girl wanted, even expected, to knock a guy over, but that she didn't want to knock him stupid. Making himself go cool, Jim waited for Miriam to speak. Instead she turned around, and he saw thick black hair tumbling down her back. *Don't leave,* he almost said before coming up with the brilliant idea of asking if she'd like an apple. "A bear ate most of them," he said, "but there's still a few left." Reaching up, he picked three apples and gave one to her, another to the boy, and bit into one himself. "They're delicious."

"I know. I already ate one." Miriam smiled and Jim noticed the wide mouth, the two slightly crooked front teeth.

Thomas didn't want the apple and passed it back.

Jim had never seen such a serious kid. Not that he'd seen many little kids, but the ones he had seen were usually holding onto a skipping rope on their way to a city park, jumping out of their skins and laughing with excitement. They weren't at all like this kid, who reminded Jim of a tiny old man.

"You don't like apples?"

He shook his head no and Miriam said quietly, "He doesn't speak, but he understands everything we say."

Jim hauled up a pail of cold water and asked the kid if he'd like a drink. Thomas bobbed his head and Jim handed him the tin cup. Then he asked Miriam where she lived.

"Over there." She pointed toward the trees.

"You mean the place called Majestic Farm?"

"Yes."

"Is your last name Majestic?"

That brought another smile. "No, the farm is named after the mountain where Father was rescued by God."

"Rescued by God?"

"When Father was a young man," Miriam said in a weird singsong voice, "he was chained to the Devil until God broke the chains on Majestic Mountain." There wasn't a speck of doubt in her voice. Jim resisted the urge to say, *Hello, don't you know that being chained to the Devil is so far out it's beyond weird?* Instead he asked what happened to her father after he was rescued. Not because he was interested in her old man, but because he wanted her to continue talking while he studied the soft, firm flesh rising like twin mounds beneath the thin cloth of her dress. "I mean, how did your father end up on the farm?"

"After God saved him, Father was reborn a new man. He changed his name and, vowing to serve God, set himself on the Righteous Path," Miriam chanted. She was looking not at Jim but behind him, as if someone was standing there, hypnotizing her. "To atone for his sins, Father undertook a pilgrimage, trusting God to guide his footsteps, which He did. In that way Father reached the Prairies, where he came upon a deserted farm and knew it to be the place God had chosen for him to live. To honour God, he set about building Him a stone tower. There were few stones hereabouts and, often footsore, Father pushed a wheelbarrow far and wide, picking up stones until he had gathered enough to build the tower."

"Is the tower still on the farm?"

"Yes, it is where Father goes to pray. And as pastor, that is where he receives the instructions from God that guide all of us along the Righteous Path."

Instructions from God? The Righteous Path? Jim didn't know what to say. Instead he asked how many lived on the farm.

"Including the new babies, there are sixty-one: twenty-seven Hamfists and thirty-four Godshawks—that's my family. I have four brothers and sisters and five half-sisters and -brothers," Miriam said proudly. Watching her push away the hair stuck to her cheek, Jim noticed she wore no eye colour or lipstick and that her unplucked eyebrows almost met above her nose. He liked her hooked nose, the way it made her look exotic.

"Wow. I only have one sister."

"When my stepmother died," Miriam explained, "Father took Mother to wife."

To wife, she said, as if she lived in another time. To keep her talking, Jim asked what they did on on the farm.

"We follow the Righteous Path through daily work."

"And what is your work?" Jim expected her to say cleaning and cooking, the kind of work Carla said enslaved women. Miriam told him she worked in the kitchen during mealtimes but her main job was beekeeping. "My bees make so much honey," she said, "there is enough to sell at the market." Again Jim heard the pride in her voice. "In winter I work in the sewing room—we make all our own clothes on Majestic Farm."

While she was talking, Jim noticed that the crow had again perched itself on the well, where it seemed to be watching Thomas dash cupfuls of water against the house. Miriam asked Jim if he minded.

"Why would I?" Jim said. "He's not hurting anything." To keep her talking, he asked Miriam if she came to the schoolhouse every Sunday.

"No, but after Sunday-morning service each of us is allowed to think about God in our way, and sometimes I use the time to come to the schoolhouse. Today is the first time in a month I have been able to come."

Jim asked why that was. He knew he was being pushy, but she didn't seem to mind his asking. She told him that she'd been at a camp in the woods. Jim had in mind a Sunday-school camp where kids played softball and soccer and canoed on a lake, something that as a kid he'd wanted to do but never did. It wasn't that kind of camp at all. The way Miriam described the place, way off in the wilderness, it sounded like some kind of boot camp where you had to punish yourself to stay alive. She told him her father believed that to survive in a wilderness, everyone had to rely on their faith that God would provide. They slept on beds of leaves and grass, hunted for their food and cooked over a fire for which they gathered fuel.

"The mosquitoes were everywhere," Miriam said, scratching the bite marks on her arms.

Jim stopped himself from asking what being eaten alive in the middle of nowhere proved. Instead he asked why Miriam had come to the schoolhouse.

"I like it here." She hesitated and then admitted she'd never been to school.

"Never?"

"On Majestic Farm we are home-schooled. For three years I was home-schooled by Mother and my aunts until Father decided that I had learned enough," Miriam said. "But it was not enough, and ever since I learned to read, I have longed to go to school." Jim heard the wistfulness in her voice.

"If that's what you want, why don't you?"

"I am not allowed. Father says that too much learning is dangerous and that I have received enough schooling, that any more would be wasted on a girl."

If his sister were here, Jim thought, she would be in orbit by now, ranting on about how denying women an education subjugated them to men. He could hear her shrieking, "This is happening all over the world!" Usually Jim tuned Carla out, but now he was thinking that maybe she had a point. Why would schooling be wasted on a girl? If a girl liked school, why not let her get on with it?

Miriam asked if Jim went to school.

He should have seen the question coming, but it caught him off guard. "Sure," he said. "Where I come from most everyone goes to school from the time they're six years old until they finish grade twelve."

"Then you are finished school?"

"No. I'm taking some time off."

"Why?"

"It's hard to explain," Jim said, averting his gaze to cover his embarrassment. How could he explain to someone who longed to go to school that he couldn't see the point of what he'd been taught? Also, admitting that school didn't seem useful to his life might sound like he agreed with her father that schooling would be wasted on a girl. To change the subject, Jim asked if Miriam knew who had built the schoolhouse, the garage and the house.

"I don't know," she said, "but the buildings have been empty for a long time."

"Then whoever built this place won't care about me staying here for a while."

By now Thomas was tugging her hand. "Yes, yes," she told him, "we are leaving." She glanced at Jim. "If we don't leave now, someone will come looking for us."

"And then what?"

Jim noticed Miriam's olive skin grow pale. "Father will know I left the farm without his permission and I will be punished," she said, and holding Thomas's hand, she set off briskly, making her way toward the back of the property, following the trail of flattened grass they had made earlier. Close behind her, Jim noticed she was cutting across the property at a diagonal that ended in the back corner, where the fence had fallen down. He asked if Majestic Farm's land came all the way to Bliss. Without slackening her pace, Miriam said it did, that the two properties were side by side. Then he asked if she would come back next Sunday. At the moment nothing seemed more important than the answer to this question.

Miriam stopped and, turning, said, "I will try, but it is hard to get away." Jim saw her hesitate before she went on. "I am pleased to meet you, Jim," she said in a small, shy voice. A moment later, she and Thomas broke into a run, the crow flapping behind them until they were gone.

For a long time Jim stood wondering if he had really seen a beautiful girl and a little boy vanish into the woods. Had he had really spoken to someone named Miriam, or had he imagined their conversation? Was the abandoned schoolhouse inhabited by lonely ghosts? "No way," Jim said. "They were as real as me." Here he was, talking to himself again.

6

Not long after Miriam and Thomas disappeared into the woods of Majestic Farm, Jim's nose picked up a strong musky stink. It took a few seconds before he realized it was coming from him. It was *his* body, *his* stink. He'd been wearing the same T-shirt, jeans and underwear for over a week and, living on his own, hadn't noticed how much he stank. The thought of Miriam catching a whiff of his body, especially his gaunch, made his cheeks burn with shame. Slouching into the house, he tried to convince himself that when Miriam was camping in the wilderness, she would have smelled even worse. But he doubted it. According to his sister, because of testosterone, guys stank worse than girls. Also, Carla said, girls were cleaner. Remembering how she dried her underwear over the shower rail every night, Jim had to admit that Carla was probably right.

Taking the steps two at a time, Jim galloped upstairs and brought the tin bath outside, filled it with well water and left it in the sun. While the water was warming, he gravitated toward the schoolhouse, curious about what Miriam had been doing inside. The door was still ajar. Pushing it wider, he wandered up the aisle to the front and saw a hat on top of the teacher's desk. Miriam's hat. She'd forgotten her hat. Ghosts don't wear hats, he told himself, feeling foolish for thinking Miriam might not be real. The hat was plain straw with a wide brim frayed at the edges. It was definitely Miriam's because there hadn't been a hat on the desk before today, and Thomas had left wearing his. Come to think of it, he'd never taken it off. In a moment of wishful thinking Jim had the idea that Miriam had left the hat behind on purpose so there would be an excuse for them to meet again. He tossed the idea quickly aside. She didn't seem the kind of girl to play tricks and had left the hat simply because in her hurry to get back to the farm, she'd forgotten it. He grinned, pleased to have an excuse for seeing her again. As soon as he cleaned himself up, he'd head for Majestic Farm with the hat.

Jim noticed the position of the teacher's chair: it wasn't tucked in like he remembered but pulled back, which meant Miriam must have been sitting at the desk. What was she doing there? It was clear enough what Thomas had been doing. Going by the chalked figures on the blackboard behind the desk, the kid had been drawing. Did she bring Thomas here so he could draw? Didn't they have blackboards on Majestic Farm?

Plunking his large frame in the teacher's chair, Jim looked over the rows of desks, wondering if Miriam had been imagining herself sitting in one of them. Was it to daydream about being in school that she'd come to the schoolhouse? Or was she doing something else? He looked around to see what she might have been doing, but the bare walls and shelves offered no clue. Jim opened the top drawer of the desk, but there were no clues there either, only stray pieces of chalk, a scatter of dead flies and dust—everywhere there was dust. The next drawer down was slightly more interesting, if only because it contained a thin black book. Picking it up, Jim opened the dusty cover and read the date at the top of the first page, *September 1950*, and the list of names written in a neat, teacherly hand: *Kirstin Andersson, Barbara Atkins, William Atkins, Lionel Chumnik, Elizabeth Crozier, Teresa Crozier, Charles Dempster, Thomas Dempster, John Jelinek, Walter Kurelek, Frank Stenson, Sandra Summers.* There were tick marks beside the names, one for each day of the week. Except for William Atkins, everyone had near-perfect attendance. Jim was holding an attendance book, what his grade-two teacher used to call the class register. "Roll call," she'd say first thing every morning, making a tick mark beside a name as one by one the class shouted, "Here!"

Putting the register away, Jim opened the second drawer. Inside was a dusty stack of writing exercise books. He picked up the top book, which had *Kirstin Andersson* written on the cover, and turned page after monotonous page of *O*'s and *P*'s, each letter executed in a sturdy, determined slant. Jim riffled through the blank pages, thinking Miriam might have written something on them, but there was nothing to see but row after row of boring letters. He opened the last drawer and saw another book.

Jim picked it up without enthusiasm, until he noticed the cover wasn't dusty—someone had brushed or wiped it free of dust. Miriam. Had she been reading this book? The book had a pale green cover with gold lettering, badly faded but still legible enough for him to read the title, *Treasure Island.* The title rang a bell. Wasn't this the book Paula had read to him at bedtime when he was six or seven? He was holding a real book—not a school register or an exercise book, but a storybook. He hadn't read the book himself and couldn't recall much about the story beyond there being a lot of exciting stuff in it about pirates and treasure. Thumbing through the yellowing, rough-edged pages, Jim noticed that some of them were smudged with fingerprints and that, to mark her place, Miriam had tucked a blade of fresh grass into a chapter, "The Man on the Island." So far she had read ninety pages, which meant she had spent quite a bit of time in the schoolhouse. Interesting. Was reading how she thought about God in her own way?

Jim propped his feet on the desk, leaned back in the teacher's chair and opened *Treasure Island* at chapter one. Never an enthusiastic reader, he was now eager to read, if only to keep up with Miriam. And so while the sun warmed his bath, Jim read about the old buccaneer, Captain Flint, hiding himself away at the Admiral Benbow, the small inn run by Jim Hawkins and his mother. Flint was hiding from another pirate, Old Pew, and his shipmates, who were hunting for the treasure map hidden inside the captain's trunk. About thirty pages into the story Old Pew arrived at the inn, but by then Flint was dead and Jim Hawkins narrowly escaped capture with the treasure map wrapped in oilskin. It was an exciting yarn, and Jim was so caught up in it that more than an hour had slipped past before he returned the book to the bottom drawer and went to check if the bathwater was warm.

Stripping off his clothes, he climbed into the tin tub, soaped himself all over, then washed and rinsed his hair. Although he was alone and there was no chance of being seen from the road, he wrapped himself toga-style in a sheet before stepping out of the tub. He scrubbed his grungy clothes in the scummy water and rinsed them in cold water. Using a piece of old rope, which he'd found in the shed, he strung a line between the house and the garage and hung the clothes over it to dry, telling himself he'd buy a change of clothes in the morning. The warm bath had made him sleepy, and knowing it would be hours before his clothes were dry, he went inside, flopped onto the daybed and was soon asleep.

Eventually hunger woke him, and lurching off the sofa, he tripped on the sheet and slammed onto the floor. Dopey and muzzy-headed, he went outside clutching the sheet around his middle and was startled to see that his clothes were now in shade. Even so, they were mostly dry. He pulled on the T-shirt and damp jeans, and made himself peanut butter and banana sandwiches—three of them, because he was ravenous. Afterwards, he cleaned his teeth with a finger—he'd have to buy a toothbrush—and ran a hand through his hair. Like Paula's, his hair was unruly, and no matter how often it was combed and brushed, it corkscrewed all over his head. When he was twelve, Jim had tried to get rid of the curls by shaving his head but it didn't help, and his hair grew back curlier than ever.

Mostly Jim ignored his appearance, but now he stared at the cracked mirror above the kitchen sink, trying to see himself through Miriam's eyes. Would she think he was good-looking? Maybe. Maybe not. He wasn't ugly, but with his freckled skin, chubby cheeks and pale eyelashes, he wasn't exactly what Carla would call cute. Paula claimed that his reddish-gold eyelashes made his eyes bluer. Once she told him he was handsome, but he didn't believe it. He knew he was no poster boy but an ordinary-looking guy. "Nothing the matter with that," he said to the mirror, and went out to the schoolhouse to pick up the hat.

It was gone. For certain Jim had left the hat on the desk, and for certain it was no longer there. He looked under the desks before accepting the disappointing fact that the hat had vanished. Not by itself, of course. Miriam must have come for it while he was asleep. Jim kicked himself for not taking the hat into the house. Then he remembered Miriam saying she'd be punished if her father found out she'd come to Bliss. She must have come back for the hat so Jim wouldn't try to return it. If he had showed up at the farm with the hat, Miriam's father would have known she'd left Majestic Farm without his permission and she'd be punished. He'd have to figure out another way of getting on the farm. But not today. Better to sleep on it before crashing the place.

Now that he was cleaned up with no place to go, Jim was at loose ends. He supposed he could hike into town—if he went to town he could phone home. It being Sunday, Paula would be there, and he could tell her he'd found a place to stay. With the café closed for the night, nobody would likely be using the pay phone and Jim would have it to himself.

Paula answered after the second ring.

"It's Jim."

"I can still recognize my son's voice," Paula snapped.

"You still mad at me?"

"Of course. What do you expect?" One thing Jim liked about Paula was that she was honest. She didn't mess around.

"You're not still uptight worrying about me?"

"What do *you* think?'

"Don't lay a guilt trip on me, Mom. If you want me to keep phoning, you'll have to get off my case." This was something he would never have said if he were home instead of thousands of miles away.

He could tell she was thinking this over. "Point taken," Paula said. "The fact is, I'm not worrying as much as I was, thanks to a trucker named Silas. He called me a few days ago and told me where he dropped you off. He called your father too. Are you still in the same town?"

"Just a few miles out of town."

"He said you were okay. He sounded like a nice man."

"He is a nice man," Jim said, then added, "for a trucker." For once his mother didn't rise to the bait. Sometimes he baited her like this—he wasn't sure why. Perhaps he wanted to hear her version of why she and Zack had split. "I'm living in an abandoned house named Bliss." Before his mother could remind him he was squatting, he added, "Nobody has lived in the house for years and I'm only using the kitchen. It's like I'm camping. I'm not using the stove."

"Well, that's reassuring," she said. "Are there rats?"

Jim told her that the place was ratless, that so far he hadn't even seen a mouse, but that he'd seen a bear. "There used to be an orchard here and it was cleaning up the apples," he said.

"Weren't you afraid?"

"I was watching from inside the house," Jim said and told her about the schoolhouse, that he'd found a book in the desk drawer and had started reading it.

"Then all is not lost,"Paula said.

"It's a book you read to me. *Treasure Island.* Remember?"

"Of course. You loved it." There was a pause before Paula went on. "That was before you discovered Game Boy, when you still liked being read to, and reading."

Jim squirmed. Since growing out of Game Boy, he didn't want to be reminded he'd ever liked it.

"How long do you plan on staying in the house?"

"Not long if I don't find a job," Jim said. "Which reminds me, can you phone my customers and tell them I'm away?"

Silence.

"Their phone numbers are in my bedroom in the top drawer of the desk."

"The desk I bought for you to do your homework?"

"Right. Thanks, Mom."

"I suppose you expect me to call the principal too, and tell her you won't be starting school next week."

"Thanks."

There was an awkward pause before Jim said that he'd better be going. He wanted to keep talking, but he knew if they kept talking, Paula would get on his case again about school. "I'll call next Sunday," he said and hung up. After buying a Coke and a Mars bar at the service station, he was back on the road to Bliss.

By now the sky had deepened into full night. The moon had not yet risen, and away from the scattered lights of town, the sky was so dark that planets and stars looked like foil cutouts stuck on a giant blackboard. Out here on the prairie, the stars seemed to pulse with waves of light and the planets seemed larger and more luminous than Jim had ever seen them. To the east he saw a faint red glow above the horizon and knew it was Mars safely in its orbit—

Jim was still kicking himself for being sucked in by DJ Buddy's joke. No vehicles passed him on the road, but here and there he saw the distant light of a farmhouse window. He shivered, not from the fear of night but from the chilly air, and also from the exhilaration of walking alone beneath the vast starry sky. With blue sky overhead during the day, outer space seemed little more than the subject of TV shows and movies. An illusion, Jim thought, knowing that it was the other way around, that the illusion was merely the curtain of the day sky, which, now that it had been opened, left him feeling as tiny and helpless as a baby. He remembered overhearing his mother tell his sister about a baby that had been left one night on the church steps not far from their condo. Half listening, Jim hadn't given the baby a second thought, but now he thought how terrified it must have been of the city at night, the jungle of flashing red ambulances and police cars tearing past, sirens wailing. The truth was, the city could be terrifying at night, and sometimes when Solly turned into his own street after they'd been to a late movie and Jim walked the rest of the way back to the condo alone, he was jumpy and afraid. But here on the road to Bliss he wasn't afraid. He was full of wonder at the overwhelming splendour of the universe. Remembering something his science teacher had said, Jim realized that for starlight to be seen from Earth, it had to have travelled trillions of years, which meant that by looking at starlight now, he was looking directly into time. Time wasn't a black hole—it was light. Gigantic, humungous, expanding, mind-blowing light. Light that couldn't be contained by seconds or minutes or hours. Time couldn't be contained by the watch on his wrist. Now that he was thinking about time in a big way, it occurred to Jim that the watch wasn't much more than a stone-age tool.

7

While Jim was having his wake-up wash outside the next morning, he glanced up and saw a moon so faint it looked like it had been chalked on the blue sky. The fading moon was the only thing left of the night sky—the planets had disappeared in Earth's turning and the stars were absorbed by the sunlight now topping the trees circling Bliss. Except for discussions in school science classes, Jim had never given a thought to Earth being transformed by night and day—he had taken this transformation for granted. That's what happened if you were boxed up in a city all your life. Kids who were brought up on farms around here probably knew far more about night and day than he did.

Jim downed a couple of cheese sandwiches and set off for town to buy himself a change of clothes. Slung over his shoulder was the canvas bag with the *H* stitched on it that he'd found hooked on the kitchen door. From now on he'd use it to carry groceries, and today his new clothes. Later, when he visited Majestic Farm, he wanted to be dressed in fresh-smelling clean clothes.

He had spent a restless night, tossing and turning on the narrow daybed, unable and unwilling to stop thinking about Miriam, remembering her shyness when she smiled, the mounds of soft flesh beneath her dress, the slight toss of her dark hair—she had the darkest, shiniest hair he'd ever seen on a girl. By the time he'd rolled out of bed this morning, he'd made up his mind to see more of her, and the only way to do it was to find work on Majestic Farm.

Besides wanting to see Miriam, Jim also had the fact that his cash was running low on his mind. He had a bank card in his pocket, but he didn't want to use it, and the money he'd managed to save wasn't so much that he could coast along without a job. Besides, once he started spending his savings, he'd go through it fast. If he was going to stay in Bliss, he'd have to find work. He couldn't ride a horse or milk a cow, but maybe there was other work on Majestic Farm that needed doing. There was no way he was going to ask his parents to send money—both Paula and Zack had made it clear they'd support him only as long as he was in school.

Jim set off, the early morning air silkily cool on his bare arms and so silent it seemed even the grasshoppers had stopped to listen to the crunch of his feet on the road. As he passed Majestic Farm, the gate didn't look as unfriendly as it had before he met a beautiful girl who lived on the other side.

In town, Jim bought a toothbrush, socks, T-shirt, jeans and, on impulse, a cheap straw hat—he wasn't wearing his tuque anymore and needed more protection from the sun. He also bought bread and milk, cheese and ham, which left him with a ten-dollar bill. By the time he was on the road again, the sun was hammering his head so hard that even the straw hat wasn't enough to keep the sweat from dribbling down his face. Back in Bliss, he stowed the groceries, ate two ham sandwiches, brushed his teeth, washed off the sweat and set out for Majestic Farm wearing new clothes. Swinging his legs over the closed gate, he followed the dirt driveway through the trees. About a quarter mile in, the driveway opened into a huge yard. Directly opposite Jim, on the other side of the yard, was an enormous barn. Over the barn doors were huge letters spelling THOU SHALT NOT WANT, the blackened letters so jagged they looked like they'd been burnt into the wood by lightning. The barn doors were open but Jim couldn't see anyone inside, or outside either, which gave him a chance to size up the place.

To the right and left of the barn were log buildings that ran the length of a courtyard, bringing to mind drawings he'd seen in a school textbook of old forts enclosing a square where soldiers drilled with bayonets and guns. Behind the barn, Jim saw a distant field dotted with grazing horses and cows. The field, which seemed to go on for at least a mile, was edged with thick woods, as if it had been cleared from forest. Majestic Farm was so private and secluded that Jim felt he'd stumbled into another world. There was no sign of Miriam's beehives or of the stone tower she'd mentioned, and curious, Jim set out to explore. He hadn't taken more than half a dozen steps when he heard a shout.

"Hey, where do you think you're going?" Looking sideways, Jim saw a man in black pants and shirt striding toward him. Except for his size and age, the man could have been Thomas's double—the same black clothes, the same blond hair beneath a broad-brimmed black hat. The man was about Jim's height but thicker in the neck and shoulders.

Not far behind him, a large ginger-coloured dog hobbled on three legs, hopefully wagging its tail.

"What do you want?" Beneath the man's hat was a face so blank it was impossible to say if it was friendly or unfriendly.

"I'm looking for work." Jim knew enough not to mention Miriam.

"What kind of work?"

"Whatever you have." Not true. Jim wouldn't chop off a chicken's head or slit a cow's throat. He'd clean out a pigpen before he'd do either chore.

"What's your name?"

"Jim Hobbs."

"You from these parts?"

"No, but I'm staying nearby."

"Where would that be?"

"Along the road."

"The old Bliss place," the man said. He still hadn't cracked a smile, and his questions were making Jim chippy.

"Are you going to tell me if there's work?" Jim said.

Looking him up and down as if he were a prize horse, the man said, "For a big fellow like yourself, there might be something. Most of the time we do all the work ourselves, but sometimes, like now, we're short-handed. We might hire you. Or we might not. It will depend on Father."

The pastor. So this man must be Miriam's brother, though he sure didn't look like her. Also, he was way older, at least middle-aged.

"Ben." Looking sideways, Jim saw that the speaker was an old man sitting in the shade of the veranda. "Bring the visitor to me," the old man said.

Ben led the way to the veranda, where a mongrel napped

in the noon heat, not even even bothering to lift its head. The pastor stood up and Jim realized he wasn't at all what he'd expected, which was a large, imposing man with a fierce, hawkish face. Except for wearing suspenders and being hatless, the pastor was dressed like his son. It was the only similarity. For one thing, the pastor was short—so short that even with inches of springy white hair, the top of his head reached no higher than Jim's shoulders. The old man had more hair than a punk rocker, the way it grew sideways and down, joining a wide, flat beard that lay on his chest like a bath mat.

The pastor tipped his head back, the better to see Jim. "Welcome to Majestic Farm." He smiled, and Jim noticed his teeth were slightly crossed, like Miriam's. The pastor shook Jim's hand and indicated a wooden bench against the wall. "Take a seat," he said. He himself sat in a high-backed wooden chair and, stroking his beard, asked if Jim was a stranger to these parts.

"Yes."

"Remove your hat and sunglasses,"the pastor told him, "so I can have a better look at you." The pastor himself was wearing not sunglasses but wire-rimmed granny glasses. "I don't like talking to someone whose eyes are hidden behind dark glasses." After Jim had done what he was told, the pastor asked where he was from.

Jim said he was from the big city. "There was a huge power failure and the electricity went off. I was trapped in the subway." Something about the pastor told him he'd need an explanation about why he'd left the city. Not wanting to get into anything personal, Jim felt the subway accident was the best way to explain why he'd left home.

"A power failure. Such a thing would never occur on Majestic Farm for one simple reason: we have no electricity." The pastor chuckled as if he'd made a joke.

"And I'm tired of the city," Jim said. But not one word about being tired of school.

"Ah yes, the city," the pastor said. "I was once a city boy myself." He heaved a regretful sigh. "The city was bad for me, Jim. When I lived there, I was a derelict and a no-good, and after I left I never went back."

The pastor a no-good? Jim didn't know what to say. The pastor didn't seem to expect him to say anything, because he went right on talking.

"The fact is, Jim, the world outside Majestic Farm is in a bad way. We have abused God's Will and brought down His Wrath upon us."

Here it comes, Jim thought. Was the old man about to deliver a sermon? But the pastor merely asked if Jim was religious.

"No," Jim said, then added quickly, "but I'm clean-living." He didn't know why he'd added the bit about clean living. It probably had something to do with Miriam telling him that her father had been chained to the Devil. Not that Jim believed in the Devil.

The pastor broke into a hearty laugh that made Ben, who was sitting on the step, look up—all this time he'd been locked in silence beneath his hat. "Then you will fit in with us just fine. We're very clean-living on Majestic Farm."

"Does that mean you're offering me a job?"

"I'm sure Ben can find you a job. He's the slave driver around here." He laughed again. "I'm the moral compass." Placing his hands on the arms of the chair, the pastor pushed himself up, hesitating partway. "Arthritis," he said, "an old man's disease. Time for an old man's nap." He put out his hand, and Jim felt it tremble when it touched his. He decided he liked Miriam's father, who was not at all what he'd expected. Opening the screen door, the pastor looked at Jim and said, "Ben will explain the rules governing Majestic Farm."

Governing Majestic Farm, he said. Had Miriam mentioned rules?

"All of us must abide by the rules, Jim," the pastor said.

The old man went inside, and a girl who looked a few years younger than Miriam appeared with two glasses of cold water. Placing them on the bench, she left without a word. Standing up, Ben picked up a glass, swallowed the water in one long chugalug, then sat down on the step and waited until Jim had done the same. Without looking at him, Ben said, his voice challenging and defiant, "Don't think you're the first person to come around looking for work. We've had others. Some stay a few weeks, maybe a month or more, others only a day or two."

"Why is that?"

"The rules. To work here you have to respect our rules. If you can't or won't respect them, then you're on your way." Ben looked at him, the eyes beneath the hat brim flat as steel. "You got that?"

"I got it," Jim said. This guy was sure different from his father.

"There's a lot of rules, but I'm telling you only the ones you need to know. Rule number one: Keep the body holy and pure. No alcohol or drugs of any kind."

"Not even aspirin? What if I get sick?"

Ignoring the sarcasm, Ben ploughed on. "Rule number two: Women are kept separate from men, except for their husbands, fathers and brothers. Unmarried girls live with their parents. Unmarried men live in dormitories above the workshops. Over there." He nodded toward the log building on the opposite side of the yard. "Our young women are healthy and good-looking, but you are not to look at them lustfully, to talk to them or address them in any way."

No chicks here, Jim felt like saying, but he let it pass. Ben probably didn't know about city chicks. Even without turning his head he could feel Ben staring at him suspiciously, as if he knew this rule would be the hardest to follow. "You got that?" Ben said.

Jim didn't bother replying. He was busy thinking. What was the point of working on Majestic Farm if he couldn't even speak to Miriam?

"Rule number three: We pray four times a day—before each meal and during the evening prayer meeting. When we pray together before each meal, you are to respect our prayers and not interfere with or mock them."

Jim didn't think that would be too hard.

"Rule number four: There are no gadgets on Majestic Farm. I'm talking about radios and games. Don't bring things like that here. On this farm we have our own world, untouched by consumerism and sinful vices, and we will do everything we can to keep it that way."

To lighten things up, Jim waggled his watch.

Ben ignored it. "Rule number five: We work together and help each other out."

Jim kept his silence by telling himself that if he took a job here, he'd need the practice.

"That about covers the main rules," Ben said. "Except there's no profanity, of course."

"Fuck."

Ben ignored this too.

"Before I decide to work here," Jim said, "I want to know how much you pay and what the work is."

"We pay room and board—that's three meals a day. You would sleep in the men's dormitory. We hardly ever pay cash. On Majestic Farm we avoid the temptation of money."

Jim shook his head in disbelief. Did Ben expect him to work his ass off just for the meals? He told him he already had a place to sleep but he'd take the meals. "And I have to be paid in cash."

There was a long pause before Ben asked how much cash Jim had in mind.

"Depends. What's the job?"

"Digging a cistern for a new house. Two houses will be built, but you'll be working on only one."

"Sounds like grunt work. One hundred bucks a week," Jim said. He'd never dug a cistern in his life—he wasn't even sure what a cistern was—but he knew digging was hard work. Take it or leave it, he almost said, because he was losing his appetite for working on the farm, especially now that he knew he'd never get a chance to be alone with Miriam.

"I'll pay you seventy a week," Ben said and eked out a grin. It was narrow and quick, but at least it told Jim he'd be paid in cash. "Come on, I'll show you around." Ben opened the same door his father had, which was one of four doors opening onto the veranda. This door led to a hallway with a kitchen on one side and a much larger room on the other. The larger room was sparsely furnished with long plank tables and benches in rows. "This is our meeting hall," Ben said. "We take all our meals here." At the far end of the hall was a fireplace with a wide stone chimney that went all the way up to the roof. On the roof were wide windows through which sunlight poured down. "Solar heat," Ben said. "There's no heating oil or gas on Majestic Farm. We use wood and the sun, mostly the sun."

There was no shortage of sun, and as he crossed the yard, the three-legged dog hobbling behind, the heat hit Jim like a slap on the face. Halfway across the yard, the dog sat down and watched them, its tongue lolling out as it worked up the energy to return to the shade of the veranda.

"Over here are our workshops," Ben explained. "Sewing and weaving, leather work, carpentry, cabinetmaking. Every piece of furniture on the farm is made right here." Again Jim heard the pride in his voice. "On Majestic Farm, we're completely self-sufficient and depend on no one but ourselves."

Through the screened door Jim noticed two women in white dresses inside a workshop, but Ben passed them without explaining what they were doing. The large carpentry shop at the end of the building was empty. "Most of the carpentry work is done in winter after the harvest is in," he said, to explain the absence of men.

Like its twin, the log building had a veranda running its width. When Ben reached the end, he stepped down and followed a beaten path at the back of the building that ran along a field where potatoes grew in rows all the way to a fence. Beyond the fence was a pen containing sheep and goats, and beyond that, the field Jim had seen earlier, where livestock grazed. The field ended at a faraway belt of trees. The size of the farm surprised him—it was so much larger than he could have guessed from the road.

Ben changed direction, walking behind the barn, pointing out a beetfield while ignoring the women, wearing white dresses and straw hats, who were hoeing. Next to the beetfield were animal paddocks, a chicken run and a pigpen. Beyond them were more grazing and growing fields. On the far side of the first field, where the grass gave way to woods, Jim spied a stack of white boxes. Beehives. He knew what they were because Silas had pointed out similar-looking beehives a couple of times when they were driving west. Jim saw a flash of white move between the hives and what looked like a shack. He knew better than to ask Ben if the flash of white might be his younger sister. Jim was sure it was Miriam. He asked where on the farm he'd be working.

"Behind the orchard," Ben said and lengthened his stride.

Rising above the cherry and apple trees was the tower Miriam had mentioned. It was a tall stone structure that looked like a kind of flattened pyramid. About forty feet high, it had wooden steps built up one side and what looked like a tent on top. Surrounding the tower were seven tiny stone towers, each with a wooden marker carved with a name. Jim stooped for a closer look and made out the names: *Kazir*, *Noah*, *Alie*, *Zeke*, *Lazar*, *Rachel*, *Gila*. Jim asked if they were graves.

"Yes, most of them infants who did not survive. Even here the wind will sometimes blow poisonous gases from oil refineries across our farm and cause the women to birth too soon," Ben said, then added bitterly, "the sheep and cattle too."

"And the giant tower?" Jim wanted to hear how Ben would explain it.

"The tower is where Father communes with God."

Leaving the orchard, they picked up a dirt road winding through more woods, where Jim saw rustic houses half hidden among the trees. They walked in silence as far as the clearing, where Ben told Jim he would be digging the cistern. Jim asked who had built the houses. "We did," Ben said. "Like I told you, we do all the work on the farm ourselves."

"Then how come you're hiring me?"

"I'm hiring you because some of our men are busy working outside."

"Outside?"

"Off the farm," Ben said, and explained that Abel Hamfist and his sons were master house framers and hired themselves out when the farm needed cash to buy supplies they couldn't grow or make themselves. "Right now they're framing a house for Ted Chumnik."

"So they work for money," Jim said.

"That's what I said."

Jim heard the bite in Ben's voice, but he didn't back down. "Then paying me a hundred bucks a week is only fair," he said. It rankled him that Ben had tried to get him to work without paying him cash.

"It's seventy or nothing," Ben said. "Take it or leave it."

"I'll take it," Jim said. Though mowing lawns and gardening paid better than working on this farm, he reminded himself those were city jobs with city wages.

"You start tomorrow. Breakfast at seven. Be on time," Ben said.

They left the woods. Knowing he would never get away with visiting the beehives, Jim made tracks for Bliss, kicking up dirt from the road that coated his runners with brown dust. The hot air bore down on his bare arms, freckling the skin a fiery red. As he loped along, Jim wrestled with the decision of whether or not he'd turn up on the farm for breakfast at seven. He didn't like Ben and wasn't sure he could follow a bunch of stupid rules. Also, there wasn't much chance of seeing Miriam, let alone talking to her. That was the downside. The upside of taking the job was that he'd be working in the woods where it was cooler, and that the farm was only a fifteen-minute walk away. Being fed three meals a day was another plus because it meant he wouldn't have to spend his cash on food.

By the time he'd reached the overgrown driveway leading to the house, Jim had made up his mind to work on the farm for a week and then decide if he'd stay with the job. Reaching Bliss, he went straight to the stone well and doused himself, grinning all the while as he imagined Miriam's surprise when she saw him at breakfast in the morning.

8

In the meeting hall the next morning, Jim sat at a long table, waiting for breakfast and wondering if Miriam knew he was here. Ben had told him to sit halfway along the bench, and with difficulty he'd squeezed his giant self between two small boys. Miriam could hardly miss seeing him towering over them if she were here—which she wasn't. So far there were only boys in the room, all of them sitting at the same table as Jim.

The boys were about seven or eight, Jim guessed, and so shy that they ducked their heads rather than look at him. Introducing himself, Jim asked their names. The straw-haired boy told him his name was Daniel and the dark-haired boy said his was Atta. That was the sum total of their conversation.

As the men filed into the room and were busy seating themselves at the long tables facing Jim, he glanced behind, eager for a glimpse of Miriam, but there still wasn't a female in sight. It was only when the men were seated and the pastor had taken his seat in a high-backed chair at the centre of the head table that Jim heard a rush of movement as the women and girls seated themselves at the long tables behind him, against the wall. Another quick glance over his shoulder rewarded Jim with the sight of Miriam. She was sitting with her back to the wall, but she wasn't looking at Jim. She was looking at her father, who was on his feet intoning, "Let us pray." Jim looked at the pastor. Like the other men, the old man was hatless, and standing there with his granny glasses and his flattened hair—someone must have combed it—he reminded Jim of the giant frog his science teacher had brought to the lab one day. Like the frog, the pastor had a wide, rounded mouth and popping eyes spaced far apart. Jim wondered if he was chinless beneath the matted beard.

There was the scrape of benches as everyone stood. Noticing that the boy opposite him had his head bowed and his hands clasped together, Jim got up and clasped his hands but resisted bowing his head. Except for a baby fussing behind him, the room was silent.

"O God on High," the pastor began, "on this new day, we present ourselves as newborns, our bodies cleansed by a night of rest. We are but vessels, God, carrying Your message to live pure lives untainted by the temptations of sin. Even here on Majestic Farm, where you entrusted your humble servant to be the leader of the Righteous Path, temptation is with us and we must be ever watchful of its ways." Eyes closed, the pastor spoke in a companionable, intimate way, as if God and he were pals. All eyes were shut except Jim's. He was watching the pastor as he listed the blessings of Majestic Farm: the sweet, pure water welling from deep in the earth; the fields of vegetables and the orchards of fruit; the pastures where sheep, goats and cows grazed; the willing hands that nurtured the pigs and the chickens and the bees.

Having listed the animals, the pastor began listing everyone by name, and to Jim's embarrassment he heard his own.

"We have a visitor in our midst," the pastor said. His eyes opened and his gaze fell on Jim. "I bid you all to be welcoming and polite to Jim Hobbs." Though spoken quietly, the pastor's words masked a command. Moments later, the prayer ended and everyone sat down except the women and girls, who crossed the hall to and from the kitchen carrying platters of bacon and eggs, pancakes and toast, which were set in the middle of the tables along with jars of honey and currant jam, jugs of milk and cream. As the platters were passed from hand to hand, Jim heaped the food on his plate—he'd never seen such a spread. If all the meals were as good as breakfast, maybe he'd stick around longer than a week.

There were now two noisy babies behind him, and glancing over his shoulder, Jim saw a young woman holding a fussy baby over her shoulder, rubbing its back while beside her another baby made gulping sounds at its mother's breast. At the sight of the mother's bare breast, Jim felt his cheeks flush. Though he'd seen hundreds, maybe thousands of naked and half-naked breasts, including Carla's, he'd never seen a baby being breastfed, and he felt he was trespassing on something too private and intimate for him to see. Embarrassed and flustered, he did not look behind him again. Instead he looked carefully around the room and saw that nobody was paying the slightest attention to the mother or the feeding baby, so busy were they eating breakfast. They didn't make conversation, perhaps because, like Jim, they were still dozy with sleep. But he wasn't too dozy to notice that every male in the room, including the youngest boys, was dressed entirely in black—black shirts, black pants—while the women he'd glimpsed so far were dressed entirely in white. It occurred to him that he was the only person in the room wearing a T-shirt and jeans, and for that matter, the only person in the room with red hair, because as far as he could see, apart from the two oldest men, everyone was either fair-haired like Ben and Thomas or dark-haired like Miriam.

Behind him, Jim heard the muted conversation of the servers as the women and girls settled down to eat. Turning sideways, he caught Miriam's warning glance just as she was looking up from her food. The warning was, *Don't let on we know each other.* Their glance locked for no more than an instant, but Jim hoped it was enough to assure her that he understood her message and that she understood his, which was that she was the reason he'd come to work on Majestic Farm, that somehow they'd find a way of meeting.

There was a tap on Jim's shoulder, and looking up, he saw Miriam's brother standing behind him. "Time for work," Ben said. Lurching to his feet, Jim lifted one leg and then another over the bench and went into the entryway, where he shrugged on the black jacket Ben insisted he wear before going outside. Behind the house they passed a staircase leading up to a long balcony. Here they followed a path below the kitchen windows through which Jim heard the clatter of dishes. The path ended at a tool shed where two men waited. Ben introduced the men as his brothers, Asa and Ezra Godshawk. It was easy to see that Ben and Ezra were brothers, both of them having big bones and fair hair, but Asa Godshawk didn't look a bit like them, being hollow-chested and stringy, with a face that looked like it had been bashed in and a nose that had healed crooked. "Asa, you work with Jim," Ben said. "Ezra, you work with me."

The four of them set out on the dirt track through the woods, pushing wheelbarrows holding the necessary tools, Ben leading, Jim bringing up the rear, the three-legged dog hobbling far behind. They had passed a couple of houses when Asa, who was in front of Jim, stopped and in a conversational voice, said, "That's my place right there." He pointed to a two-storey house on the right. "I built most of it myself. It started out as one floor, but as the children came along, I added a second floor." He spoke proudly, his voice scratchy like he'd swallowed a wire brush.

"How many children do you have?" Jim asked.

"Six, and another one on the way."

Jim could almost predict what Carla would say about a woman having six children. Carla would say the woman was being used as a baby machine. If his sister was in the mood, she might lecture Jim about how women were similarly used and abused in many places in the world. Carla had graduated from high school last spring and at this very moment might be choosing the courses for her first university term, which would eventually lead to a university degree based on something called Women's Studies, whatever that was.

"Where are they now?" There wasn't a single kid running around outside.

"Helping their mother. As soon as they can walk, children on the farm are taught to do chores."

Asa and Jim continued walking until they came to the clearings where the new houses would be built.

"This is our lot," Asa said of the first one. "Ben and Ezra's is there." He nodded to the lot farther along the road.

Ben had already pointed out the rectangle staked and tied with string to show the cistern's location adjacent to the house. Asa explained that while he worked the cutter along the rectangle marked with string, Jim was to cut sods and put them in the wheelbarrow so they could be moved nearby. "Later we'll pile the sods against the foundation to insulate the house," Asa explained, "like the pioneers used to do."

Edging and cutting sods was easy and they worked steadily, pausing only once to drink from a jug of water. By late morning they had finished the edging and cutting and for a while stood talking while the dog lay nearby. When Jim asked how the dog lost his leg, Asa told him he didn't know, that Mutt was a stray that showed up on the farm one day and decided to stay. "Like you, maybe," he teased. Then he asked about Jim's family and where he was from. Asa wanted to know what a big-city boy was doing on the Prairies. Still touchy about being questioned, Jim didn't answer, but unlike Ben, Asa took his silence in his stride. Taking a swallow of water, he threw Jim a challenging look. "I bet you didn't know a place like this existed," he said. Pointing to the sloping roof of the nearest house, he went on, "There's solar panels at the back of our houses. All our buildings are heated by the sun with help from wood stoves when the sky is overcast. We don't need oil or electricity."

"You might be better off without electricity," Jim said, and for the fourth time told the story about being stuck underground in the city subway during a major electrical failure.

"See, that's why I like it here," Asa said. "The world outside could come crashing down and inside Majestic Farm we'd be safe, because we're a world unto ourselves."

"Don't you care what's happening in the rest of the world?" Jim asked.

"Can't say that I do. I've had a bellyful of it. When I left that world, it was a mess and so was I." Asa waved his hand as if he was pushing away everything he'd left. Looking at Jim straight on, he continued, "See, a long time ago, I was a heroin addict, a guttersnipe living on city streets as Eddy Mudge, so I know a lot about that evil world. But after I was rescued from the Devil, I began a new life as Asa Godshawk, and my feet are on the Righteous Path. I'm a lucky man."

So, Jim thought, the pastor wasn't the only one on the farm to have been rescued from the Devil. Were there others?

He wanted to learn more about Asa's former life, but before he could ask about Eddy Mudge, he heard the ding-dong of a cowbell. "Dinnertime," Asa said. "Leave your tools here." Returning to the dirt track, he and Jim waited for Ben and Ezra to join them. As they made their way through the woods to the meeting hall, Jim listened to the men talking about the morning's work. They talked easily, casually, without any of the anxiousness he'd noticed in Miriam. There was no mention of wives or children, if they had them. Jim supposed that like Asa, the other men were husbands and fathers.

The afternoon's work was harder than the morning's. With the sod removed, Asa and Jim had to dig out the stony undersoil, shovelling it into the wheelbarrow and dumping it off to one side. After an hour's work, Jim could feel his back and arm muscles ache. It wasn't a bad ache, but he knew he'd be sore tonight. When he and Asa encountered a large rock, which was often, they pried it up with the crowbar and a pick before rolling it away. The biggest rocks were left until later, when, Asa told Jim, they'd be harnessed with rope and hitched up to Horse, the enormous draft horse that also pulled the farm wagon. With the sun high overhead, it was hard, sweaty work, and while the no-see-ums hovered in clouds, horseflies swung back and forth, looking for a damp patch of skin.

When they stopped to rest, passing the water jug back and forth, Asa said, "Horseflies like to land on sweat so you don't feel the bite." Batting one away, he went on. "If they keep pestering us like this, we'll have to smear on the bear grease even though it stinks something awful."

"Does bear grease work?"

"You bet it does. I don't know what we would've done without it when we were camping in the wilderness last month. The mosquitoes were so bad we used up all the bear grease we had."

Jim wondered if Miriam had smeared the stinking bear grease on herself to keep the mosquitoes from biting.

"But we shot another bear," Asa went on, "and rendered another tub of grease."

"When was that?" Jim was thinking about the bear that had eaten his apples—already he was thinking of Bliss as his.

Asa lifted his hat and wiped the sweat from his brow. "About a week ago," he said. "Wednesday, I think it was. Every year about this time we can count on at least one bear showing up to clean up the apples and saskatoon berries." He chuckled. "And the beehives."

"Doesn't that make it dangerous for"—Jim hesitated—"the beekeeper?" he said, catching himself on time.

"The beekeeper has a shrill whistle she blows whenever she sees a bear. So far that works pretty good."

Jim said, "Still, it must be dangerous work."

Asa shrugged. "Not when there's a shotgun handy," he said. "Sometimes the whistle will scare off the bear. But it always comes back, so we shoot it the first time it shows up."

"Who shoots it?" Jim couldn't imagine Miriam with a shotgun.

"Ben. He's the best shot on the farm. Never misses."

At the thought of Ben Godshawk with a shotgun, Jim frowned.

Asa misread the frown. "Don't forget that when God made the world," he said, "He gave us dominion over the creatures of the land. One thing you've got to understand, Jim, is that when you run a farm, you can't be sentimental about animals. If you're going to eat them, you have to kill them."

"Do you eat bear meat?"

"Naw." Asa grinned and Jim saw the gaps where teeth had gone missing. "We feed it to the pigs."

In spite of the flies and the aching muscles, Jim was enjoying himself. He'd always enjoyed pushing his body hard to get something done, which was why he liked working outside. Being cooped up inside sapped his energy, made him feel listless and dull, especially in school. Jim had noticed this himself, and when a teacher accused him of being lazy, he didn't disagree. The fact was that school brought out the laziness in him, but when he was given a job outside, he worked as hard as a man.

Later, walking to supper, Asa reminded Jim there was a prayer meeting after the meal. Prayer, he said, was a powerful force in a man's life, and if Jim wanted to join in the evening prayers, he'd ask the pastor's permission. There it was again—the pastor's permission. Nothing, it seemed, could happen on Majestic Farm without the old man's say-so.

Jim might have said he'd attend the prayer meeting, if only to see what it was like, but having to ask the pastor's permission got his back up and he told Asa that he'd clear out after supper.

As he had before breakfast and dinner, the pastor gave a prayer of thanks before they ate their meal. As well as thanking God for the bounty of Majestic Farm, he thanked Abel, Hosea and Enoch Hamfist for the work they had undertaken on the Chumnik house. To Jim's embarrassment, he himself was thanked for helping Asa dig the cistern. He was bothered by the fact that the women weren't thanked for their work in preparing the meal and nor were the girls for carrying in bowls of lamb stew, mashed potatoes, peas and carrots. Jim watched as Miriam set bowls and platters of food on the table, but she never once looked at him and he did his best to pretend she wasn't there. Behind him, at the women's table, he heard a baby fussing. It sounded like the same baby who had fussed through breakfast and dinner. He heard other baby sounds, but they were quieter—there seemed to be a bunch of babies behind him, feeding and cooing.

Since no one talked to Jim, he ate his meal listening to Abel Hamfist tell the pastor about the work on the Chumnik house. Abel was completely bald, but tanned and strong-shouldered, he looked younger than the pastor. Because Abel was the only man sitting at the front table with the pastor, it was obvious that he was the head of the second family. Looking at his grown sons seated at the long table, he said, "The boys and me put in a good day's work, and thanks be to God, we got all the windows framed."

Boys, Jim thought. But they're men.

"Including one of them fancy sliding bedroom doors," his son Enoch put in. "That took us a while."

There was a snigger from Hosea. "If you ask me, the Chumniks are an ungodly lot," he said. "The missus wants the bedroom door opening onto a deck that will go clear around the house." He paused briefly, perhaps deciding if he should continue with the joke. "She must have a hankering to parade outdoors in her nightgown." He smirked, pleased with himself.

The room fell silent; there wasn't so much as the scrape of a fork against a plate. A frown of displeasure appeared between Abel's eyes and he glared at his son. "That's enough careless talk," he said, his voice sharp as broken glass. "You know such talk is offensive to God." Jim watched Hosea hunch over his food like a scolded kid. It surprised him that the man took the scolding lying down, because he looked as old as Zack, who was forty.

"Careless talk also demeans a man," the pastor said. Though his tone was mild, such was his power that no one said another word.

Shoulders hunched to make room for himself on the bench, Jim kept his eyes averted while waiting for the meal to be over. He heard the women moving back and forth, and just as a slice of apple pie and a mug of tea were placed in front of him, he noticed Hosea staring intently at someone. Turning sideways, Jim saw Miriam farther along the table serving pie and tea from a tray a younger girl was holding. Although brief, the stare troubled Jim. According to Ben, unless they were related, men and women on the farm were expected to ignore one another. Also, Miriam wasn't a woman—she was a girl, and Hosea looked old enough to be her father and probably had a wife and kids. Hosea shifted his stare from Miriam. Finishing the pie and tea, Jim left the meeting hall and was soon on the road to Bliss and the comfort of his bed.

9

After a good night's sleep, Jim returned to Majestic Farm rested and energetic, ready to work on the cistern excavation. His muscles were sore, but it was a satisfying soreness that came from pushing his body hard. Reviewing his first day of work, he realized he was looking forward to returning to Majestic Farm, not only so he would be nearer, if not close to, Miriam, but also because in a weird way the farm fascinated him. Except for the strict rules and the fact that the pastor ruled the place, Majestic Farm had a lot going for it. Jim liked the idea that it could run by itself, that it didn't rely on electricity or oil or modern technology. He was impressed that two families, the Godshawks and the Hamfists, could make or grow just about everything they needed without relying on anyone else. It reminded him of the small independent kingdoms in the fairy tales Paula used to read to him when he was a little kid.

As he walked through the cool morning air, Jim thought about the words burnt into the wood above the barn doors: THOU SHALT NOT NEED. *Need* was a word he hadn't thought much about, probably because until he left home, his parents had been supplying everything he needed. Now that he was on his own and looking after himself, he was forced to think about what he needed and what he had to do to in order to get by. He realized that he didn't need much—at least it didn't seem like much, especially compared to what he had at home, like the TV and the computer plus all the other stuff in his bedroom. Since leaving the city, he'd been getting along fine without electronic hardware and didn't even miss the Walkman he'd lost in the subway—he'd been too busy looking after himself to miss what he'd left behind. A good thing he didn't have his cellphone, he thought, because if he had it with him, Paula would be phoning him every day and bugging him about school.

After breakfast, Jim and Asa returned to the house site and resumed digging. Today progress was slow because they kept running into oversized boulders, and it took all morning to dig the hole a foot deeper. Most of their time was spent waiting until Horse was free—Ben and Ezra were running into boulders too, and the men had to take turns using the draft horse. Asa didn't mind the wait. He told Jim that apart from daytime, nighttime, prayertime and mealtime, no one on the farm followed a timetable, but that sooner or later everything got done. "No point tying yourself in a knot for what you can't change," he said, settling himself on a stump while they waited their turn with Horse.

There wasn't another stump close by, so Jim sat on a boulder and asked Asa to tell him about when he was Eddy Mudge.

"Isn't much to tell," Asa said. "I don't remember a lot about them days. Everything back then is a blur to me now." Fanning himself with his hat, he went on, "Eddy was a heroin addict. He was in the hands of the Devil." Asa looked at Jim. "You ever been tempted by the Devil?"

"No," Jim said. The only devil he knew was the Halloween costume he used to wear trick-or-treating—the same costume every year until he was too big to go door to door.

"You want to stay clear of him. The Devil can mess up your life real bad. Once he gets hold of you, it's hard to get away."

"So how did you get away?"

Asa said, "The pastor found me in the ditch near town. I was dead to the world, so I never knew how I come to be there. Anyways, when the pastor saw me, low-down creature that I was, he and Abel loaded me into the wagon and brought me here. When I come to, I had the shakes and screaming fits something terrible and they tied me to a bed. For two weeks, the pastor sat by the bed and prayed over me, prayed so long and hard that the Devil finally give up and let me be."

Asa lapsed into silence, giving Jim space to think about the tale he'd been told. He was impressed that the pastor had rescued a heroin addict from a ditch and sat by his bed for two weeks. The story altered Jim's view of the pastor and he saw not only the dictator who laid down rules he demanded his family to follow, but a man who was kind and helpful to a down-and-out stranger.

In the days that followed, Asa told Jim more about Eddy's misadventures: Eddy had been a member of the Hoop Valley Gang, the famous gang that robbed three banks before being caught; Eddy had done twelve years in the clink, where he became a heroin junkie; Eddy had roughed up a hooker. "She never told the cops, so I never done time," Asa said. "But I should've. She never done me wrong. It was me who done her wrong, and God should've punished me."

Listening to these stories, Jim couldn't help wondering why Ben had asked if he was clean-living then teamed him up with an ex-con. But as Asa was quick to point out, he was no longer Eddy Mudge. That man, Asa said, was gone forever. Jim believed him. He didn't find Asa dangerous or scary. Ben was the tight-lipped, scary one.

Wednesday morning, Jim and Asa were trying to loosen a huge boulder by wedging a long pinch bar beneath it, but the bar bent almost double and neither of them could work it free. The exertion winded Asa and he sat on the stump to catch his breath.

"Want me to borrow Ben and Ezra's pinch bar?" Jim had seen a long one in their wheelbarrow.

"They need it same as us. Better get our own," Asa said. "There's a long pinch bar in the tool shed. You're younger than I am, Jim. Why don't you fetch it?"

Why don't I! Jim almost shouted. This was the kind of break he'd been hoping for, a break that would maybe give him a chance to check out the beehives on the far side of the barn in the hope that Miriam would be there.

"Take your time," Asa said. "There's no hurry."

But Jim set off at a brisk trot, to give himself more time to explore. He'd left the wooded track and was nearing the orchard with its stone tower rising above the apple and cherry trees when he saw her. Draped in black netting that covered her straw hat and shoulders, she stood on top of a wooden table beneath a branch alive with hundreds of buzzing bees. The bees looked like an enormous cluster of noisy grapes hanging from the branch, and even at this distance, Jim noticed the cluster was in constant motion, with bees clinging to and crawling over one another. Not far from the table, a young girl, as fair as Miriam was dark, stood holding a large white box, which Jim recognized as a beehive. Like Miriam, the girl was draped in netting and wore leather gloves and boots.

Too astonished to move or speak, Jim watched silently as Miriam, using both arms, lifted what looked like a pillowcase up and around the cluster until most of the bees were contained inside. Gripping the mouth of the pillowcase tightly, she looked at the younger girl. "Set the hive on the table, Eva," she said, "then take off the cover." Though uncaptured bees were swinging around her, Miriam seemed completely unfazed.

The younger girl did as she was told.

"Back away now, Eva," Miriam said, "while I put my bees in the hive."

My bees. She'd said that before. She was fond of the bees.

By now two or three bees were swinging around Jim, but he stood absolutely still, not from fear but from fascination as he watched Miriam hold the pillowcase over the open hive and gently shake the cluster loose. The bees dropped in a clump, collapsing over the hive in an angry spilling mass, reminding Jim of a TV program he'd seen of a lava flow seeking out every corner and crevice as it moved down the mountainside.

Tossing the pillowcase onto the grass, Miriam peered into the hive and said, "I can see the queen. She's going inside and the workers are around her. The drones will follow." She beckoned to the younger girl and said, "Have a look, Eva."

At that moment the girl noticed Jim. She stood statue still, glancing at him, then looked away as if she was pretending he wasn't there. Though the glance was swift,

Miriam intercepted it, and turning quickly, she looked straight at Jim. Still mesmerized from watching her capture the hive of runaway bees, Jim could only gawk, speechless and amazed. Miriam had more presence of mind. Lifting the veil, she gave him a quick wave and a smile before lowering the veil. Then she turned to the girl and said, "We'll leave the hive here for a day or two. Once the bees have settled down, we'll move the hive closer to the honey shed." Stooping, Miriam picked up the pillowcase and, unperturbed, shook it over the hive before replacing the lid. Then she and the girl left the orchard without a backward glance.

Jim stayed where he was, locked in a spell of amazement and admiration. He was amazed that runaway bees could be stuffed into a pillowcase and more or less dumped into a hive—he hadn't even known there *were* runaway bees. The only bees he saw were rare city bees that followed flight paths to the nearest flowers from wherever they lived. He brimmed with admiration for Miriam. She was so cool, so calm and collected. Terrified of being stung to death, he'd never move a cluster of angry bees.

As if to convince him that his fear was well placed, an angry bee landed on Jim's left cheek and unloaded a stinger. He swore and lifted a hand, but having done its job, the worker bee had already fallen onto the grass, where it curled itself into a death throe. The sting jolted Jim into action, and he continued to the tool shed for the pinch bar. There were two to choose from, one slightly longer than the other, and unable to decide which would do the better job, he carried both of them back to the woods.

Asa was inside the excavation, using the mattock to loosen the stony soil around the boulder. He looked up and grinned when Jim appeared. He didn't ask where he'd been or what had kept him so long. Instead he observed that Jim had a red mark on his cheek. "You got bit," he said.

"Stung. I was watching a couple of girls bag a bunch of bees from a tree in the orchard and stick them into a box," Jim explained, making himself go cool, like watching what Miriam did with the bees was no big deal.

Leaning on the mattock, Asa said, "I've heard about them bee swarms, but I never seen one myself." Lifting his hat he wiped the sweat from his brow. "I'm told a swarm is a sight to behold, and I'm glad you seen one."

It was this quality of open generosity that drew Jim to Asa, and it was this quality that made Asa easy to work with. If Jim had been forced to work with Ben, he didn't think he'd have lasted more than a day.

Using the longer pinch bar, Jim and Asa finally loosened the boulder and rolled it aside. Glancing at his watch, Jim thought, One hour to remove one boulder—now *that* was work.

=

During the next two days they encountered more boulders, but none so large that it couldn't be more easily removed. By late Friday afternoon, they were done excavating the cistern, a twenty-by-fifteen-foot rectangle ten feet deep. Finished, it would be used to store water. Off to the side was a pile of sods that would eventually become a raised flower garden after compost soil was added. Asa explained that although the vegetable fields were communal and shared by everyone on the farm, the women were allowed to grow their own flowers. Jim knew *allowed* was a word Carla would hate. Women, she would say, should be *free to choose* to do what they wanted.

Now that the excavation job was finished, Jim wondered if he'd be let go. He didn't wonder long. As he was picking up the tools and piling them in the wheelbarrow, Asa told him to leave the barrow where it was because they would be using it next week when they were cribbing the cistern. "Turn the wheelbarrow upside down," he said, "and stow the tools underneath."

Standing on the veranda after supper, Ben counted out seven ten-dollar bills and handed them to Jim. "Be here Monday morning, seven sharp."

"You don't work tomorrow?"

"We sell our goods at the town market on Saturday. And prepare for Sunday," Ben said. "We do not work on Sunday."

Ignoring the Sunday bit, Jim asked what they sold at the market. He was thinking he'd buy his weekend supplies there.

"Vegetables. Fruit. Bread. Pies. Honey."

Honey, Jim thought. *Miriam.* She'd be at the market selling her honey, and he'd be there too. Away from the farm, he might even get a chance to talk to her.

"Get there early," Ben said, "before everything sells."

Tired as he was, Jim returned to Bliss with a light step and seventy dollars in his pocket. When he reached the house, completely whacked from the day's hard labour, he went straight to bed like he'd been doing all week, not bothering to set his watch alarm because by now he was used to getting up before six and was certain he'd wake early. Before he fell asleep he thought, *I need my guitar.* He missed making music with Solly and Web on the weekends.

Yet as much as he liked hanging out with his friends, it was his guitar he was missing, not Solly and Web. His guitar was his closest friend, which was why he wanted it in Bliss. That was the last thing Jim remembered thinking before falling into a deep sleep. Not even a throbbing bee sting kept him awake.

10

The pure joyous notes of the songbird woke Jim and he lay in the slatted morning light, a drowsy smile sliding across his face. Music—he was listening to music. Music more beautiful than anything he picked out on the guitar. The bird sounded so close, he pictured it perched in the bush outside the window. Not wanting to frighten it away, he lay absolutely still, anticipating its melodious treble. But it didn't sing again, and hearing wing beats, Jim sat up, opened the shutters and watched the small, brownish-grey bird swooping away above the shrubbery. Such an ordinary-looking bird, he thought, to have such an extraordinary voice.

Now that light flooded the kitchen, Jim saw that his watch registered ten-thirty. Leaping off the bed, he yanked on his clothes, grabbed the canvas bag and jogged into town without eating breakfast. By the time he arrived, he was itchy with sweat and had trouble finding the market, which was on the opposite side of town from the road to Bliss. Worse, when he reached it, the market was just about over. In the parking lot of a rundown motel, long tables had been set up to display pottery mugs and pots, beaded bracelets and earrings, knitted socks and mitts, wooden clocks and bowls. A bag of stale doughnuts was the only item left on the baking table. Jim passed a huddle of townspeople holding Styrofoam cups, gossiping near the coffee urn. He looked around for Miriam.

There was no sign of her, but the Majestic Farm wagon was in plain sight, parked nearby on the edge of a weedy field where Horse grazed, pulling up tufts of dry, dusty grass. Approaching the wagon, Jim saw several girls, none of them Miriam, sitting in the wagon on plank benches, their backs against the plywood sides, their hands folded in their laps. Though her head was bent, Jim thought he recognized Eva, the girl he had seen the day before helping Miriam capture the bees.

Beside the wagon a solid-looking, sturdy woman was picking up tea towels, pot holders and various sewing items from a table and putting them into a cardboard box. She was wearing a long white dress and an apron with *Chana* stitched across the front. During mealtimes Jim had noticed that the women on the farm wore aprons with their names stitched on them. Jim couldn't remember seeing this woman before, but she obviously knew who he was because she smiled at him and said, "Good day, Jim."

Startled that not only had she spoken to him but she knew his name, he looked at the kindly face framed by a white kerchief that covered all but the tips of two long yellow braids. She seemed to be waiting for him to speak, and he hesitated before deciding that the rule about not speaking to women must not apply off the farm, at least in the market. He said, "I've come to buy some bread, but it looks like I'm too late."

The woman named Chana held up a loaf of bread. "I have one loaf left," she said and passed it to him. Jim handed her two loonies, but she pushed them away. "No, you take the bread. It's a gift from me."

"Well, thanks." Pushing his luck, he told her he'd like to buy a jar of honey too. Behind him, he heard a familiar hard-edged voice. "You heard her. There's none left."

Turning, Jim nearly bumped into Ben, who was carrying a box of cabbages and turnips to the wagon. "I told you to get here early," Ben said. "You're too late. The market's over."

It was true. Everywhere Jim looked, people were stowing unsold items in vans and trucks and collapsing their tables. Without Miriam, there seemed no point in hanging around. By now Jim was famished, and leaving the parking lot, he headed for the café.

He was halfway there when the Majestic Farm wagon went past, Ben and Ezra up front, Chana sitting with the girls in the back. She sat straight, staring ahead, but the girls hunched forward, their heads bowed as they ignored the boys taunting them from the roadside, like they were circus freaks.

Marilyn met him at the front counter wearing the same baggy clothes and the same bird-feather earrings. "Hi Jim," she said. He grinned back, pleased that she remembered his name. She handed him a menu but he gave it back. He already knew what he wanted—a Coke and two burgers. Jim made a beeline for the back of the café. Because of his height, he always sought out the edges and backs of rooms. Even in the subway car he'd chosen an end seat, well out of anyone's way.

The place was over half full, but the booth where he and Silas had eaten was empty and Jim again claimed it for himself and Silas—the truck driver was far away on another road, but the memory of him was here. Marilyn brought the food, and in five minutes, Jim had wolfed down the burgers and ordered a second Coke. By the time the Coke was finished, he'd decided to phone home. He'd promised to telephone home on Sunday, but if he did it today he wouldn't have to walk into town again tomorrow. With the time difference, it was afternoon in the city and there was a good chance of reaching Paula. If she'd had an especially hard week, she sometimes stayed home on Saturday and ordered take-out for supper, which she ate sitting on the living-room sofa.

It was Zack who answered the telephone.

"Hey, Dad. It's Jim."

"The wandering son." It wasn't a joke; his father sounded cross, which he rarely was.

"What are you doing there?" Jim said.

"I could ask you the same question."

"I explained all that to Mom."

"What you didn't explain was why you didn't tell her you were leaving. Why didn't you discuss it with her before taking off?"

"I didn't know I was going to take off until I did it."

"We are both disappointed that you're missing school. It's important that you finish school. I regret I never did and went on the road instead. Don't you make the same mistake, Jim."

"I won't."

"Now that we've got that out of the way, I'll hand you over to your mother. She's been having a hard time, what with you leaving and Carla moving out."

"Where's Carla?"

"She's sharing an apartment near the university with two guys."

"She's got two boyfriends?"

"They're not boyfriends. You know your sister," Zack said. "Not all her male friends are boyfriends."

"Is she still hanging out with the creep?"

"I'm the wrong person to ask," Zack said. "Ask your mother. She's here beside me trying to wrench the phone from my hand."

As soon as she came on the line, Jim told her Carla hadn't said a word to him about moving out. "I didn't know you were alone."

"Would it have made a difference?" There was a tinge of bitterness in her voice—not a good start.

During the wordless slump on the line, Jim couldn't think of a single thing to say. If his mother was waiting for him to tell her he'd come home, she'd have to wait a while longer. A kind of stubbornness had taken hold of him, a determination not to cave in. If Carla was tough-minded enough to move out, then so was he. But he wasn't moving out, was he? He was taking time off.

Paula broke the silence. "I phoned your customers like you asked, and I phoned the principal."

Jim didn't ask what the principal had said.

"Solly called, and that girl who kept phoning you last year."

"Amber," Jim said. "What did you tell them?"

"That you were having an early-teen crisis, which Amber thought was cool."

"More like mid-teen, Mom. I'm fifteen."

"So tell me, what have you been doing with yourself all week?"

It sounded like his mother was warming up slightly. Jim told her he had a job on a farm digging a hole for a cistern.

"But isn't there heavy equipment for doing that sort of thing?"

"Not on this farm." He didn't tell her the farm was some kind of a religious cult. He wasn't sure if it *was* a cult—for all he knew it might be a commune. "Besides being paid, I eat three meals a day there. The food's great."

"It sounds like you've settled in."

"And I'm not missing school."

"Not yet," Paula said, "but you will." When Jim didn't reply, she said, "It is temporary, isn't it?"

Jim heard the anxious pitch in her voice. "Yes, Mom," he said. "It's temporary."

"Good. That's what I told the principal."

For a few seconds neither of them said a word. Then Jim said that maybe they'd better say goodbye. He could tell she didn't want to hang up, but with his father there, he didn't feel too bad.

With the groceries and the box of chalk he'd bought at the general store tucked into the canvas bag, Jim was again on the road to Bliss, this time entertaining himself with the picture of his parents sitting side by side on the sofa sharing Peppy's Pizza like they used to do before the split. In the picture they are both happy just hanging out together. Maybe it was a good thing he and Carla weren't there, Jim thought. Maybe their parents would get their act together if their kids weren't around. Maybe they would pretend they've just met and start all over again.

11

Sunday morning, Jim was again wakened by the songbird, whose trebly voice was so fulsome and enthusiastic it might have been announcing that Miriam would soon be here. The bird, Jim decided, was *chirpling*. He didn't think there was such a word and he smiled, pleased with himself for making it up.

After the songbird had flown away, he stayed in bed. Lying in the half light, he had the odd sensation that since leaving home he was slowly being turned inside out, that his thoughts and feelings were no longer bottled inside him but were outside, where he could see them more clearly. He knew this new way of seeing himself came from being far from home, far from his familiar life. Totally alone, he saw himself as a tiny chunk of land that had broken from the continent, an island that for the time being was drifting wherever currents and tides carried it.

Jim knew that working on Majestic Farm had also changed the way he looked at himself. Working on the farm was so different from working in the city. The people he worked for in the city were rich. They lived in mansions and liked their lawns perfectly mowed and their flower beds as perfectly tidy as he pictured their rooms inside. Their owners drove expensive cars and had far more of everything than they needed. While he was working for them, Jim had envied their wealth and liked imagining what it would be like to live in a mansion and drive a Jaguar or a Lamborghini. He no longer envied them, at least not as much. Since he'd begun working with Asa, he'd been thinking that maybe there were better things to aim for than making a pile of money and driving a Lamborghini—things that would challenge him to settle for what he needed instead of being greedy for more. Things that would make him independent. Being wealthy didn't necessarily make a person independent. It didn't prevent the mansion owners from stumbling around in the dark after the electricity hit the skids. Lying there in the natural light of morning, Jim admitted that there was an upside to having been caught beneath the city when the power failed. The way he looked at it now, the electrical crash had woken him from a dream he'd been living—no, not a dream. It was more like he'd been living inside a bubble that burst when he knocked himself out in the subway.

Hungry, Jim got up and slapped together two cheese sandwiches. Spoiled as he was by warm farm breakfasts, the sandwiches were a let-down. One of these days he'd clean the chimney and light the stove so he could make himself toast and eggs. Asa had warned him that the hot weather he called Indian summer wouldn't last, and that when the heatwave passed, it could suddenly turn cold. *Prairie cold cuts through you like a knife,* Asa said. *Don't be fooled by this heat.*

After brushing his teeth and changing into clean clothes, Jim washed the dishes and tucked the blanket around the sofa bed, wanting the kitchen tidy for Miriam.

Remembering the chalk he'd bought in town, he took it out to the schoolhouse and propped it up on the blackboard ledge where Thomas would see it. The Sunday before, Miriam had said she'd come if she could get away from the farm, and encouraged by her smile and wave in the orchard, he was counting on her showing up.

Restless, Jim fetched a pail of water and rags and set to work washing the dust from the desks and windows before wiping the blackboard and sweeping the floor. On impulse he picked a bunch of late-blooming yellow flowers from behind the garage, shoved them into a jar of water and placed them on the teacher's desk for Miriam. Then, plunking himself in the teacher's chair, he opened *Treasure Island* and found his place in the book—he hadn't read a word since the previous Sunday because after a day's work on the farm, he was way too tired to read. But he was rested now, and when Miriam showed up he wanted her to find him reading the book. He wanted to impress her. He wanted her to know that there were interesting thoughts in his head, that there was more to him than what she saw—he didn't agree with Paula's observation that when it came to people, what you saw was what you got. He also liked the idea that he and Miriam were reading the same book—not that there was a choice. The blade of grass she had used as a bookmark was shrivelled and brown, but Jim left it in its place and read about Jim Hawkins meeting Squire Trelawney, who sent him to deliver a note to Long John Silver about arranging a voyage to Treasure Island aboard the *Hispaniola*.

Jim Hawkins was hiding inside an apple barrel aboard the ship when he overheard a conversation and learned that Long John Silver was a pirate and not the ship's cook he was pretending to be. By now Jim was so engrossed in the story that he didn't see Thomas and Miriam standing in the schoolhouse doorway, he in his black suit and she in her white dress and kerchief—no straw hat today. "Good day, Jim," Miriam said in her old-fashioned way, startling him so that he leapt to his feet, knocking over the chair as the book slid to the floor.

"Hi!" he said, a goofy grin on his face. "You made it!"

"Yes." Smiling, Miriam held out a cloth-wrapped parcel. "I brought you some food left from our dinner," she said, then added, "It's cold because today's meals were made yesterday. We do not cook on Sunday."

Unwrapping the cloth, Jim saw two thick egg-salad sandwiches and a hunk of roast chicken. "Thanks," he said. "Like always, I'm starving." He gave Miriam the jar of flowers. "These are for you," he said.

"Thank you, Jim," Miriam said shyly, taking the flowers.

Jim pointed to the box of coloured chalk. "That's for you, Thomas." A small smile skittered across the little boy's face.

Noticing the book on the floor, Miriam picked it up. "Have you been reading *Treasure Island,* Jim?"

He grinned. He liked the way she said *Jim* so that it sounded like *Jem.*

Making himself go cool, he said, "Yeah, but you can take it home if you want. I mean, I know you've been reading it."

"I couldn't take it home!" Miriam said in a shocked voice.

"Why not?"

"Father would not permit me to keep a story about pirates."

"But it's only an adventure story," Jim said. "What's the problem?"

"Father does not approve of adventure stories. He says we must read only real stories. He says made-up stories are frivolous and full of idle thoughts. He doesn't approve of stories unless they in some way improve our minds on our journey along the Righteous Path." Miriam's singsong voice had returned. Jim had the uneasy feeling that she'd chanted the same words hundreds of times. "Father says books are a danger to the mind," she continued, then quickly added, "except for lesson books."

More likely the pastor wanted to keep out any ideas that contradicted his religion. Even though Jim seldom read a newspaper and rarely watched the television news, he knew this kind of religious control was happening big time in other places, and in that respect, Majestic Farm was no different from the big, bad world.

"Now that you've given me your father's opinion of *Treasure Island,*" he asked, "what's yours?"

"Mine!" Miriam burst into laughter.

Were there two Miriams, one the pastor's pious daughter, the other this laughing girl?

"I like the story!" she laughed. "It's so different from anything I know." Jim was fascinated by the way laughing changed the shape of her lips. He had a sudden impulse to kiss those lips but reminded himself that a kiss would probably send her running back to the farm.

"Different from anything I know too," he said, "except in movies. Pirate movies are big right now."

"Movies," Miriam repeated. "You mean moving pictures? Father says—"

"Don't tell me. I can guess. Moving pictures are a danger to the mind," Jim said, and before Miriam could reply, he changed the subject, telling her that he'd gone to the market yesterday hoping to see her. He thought he saw her cheeks change colour.

"It wasn't my turn to go, but Mother told me you were there."

"Is your mother's name Chana?"

"Yes."

"I also saw the girl who was helping you with the bees. She was sitting in the back of the wagon."

"My sister Eva. She's learning to become a beekeeper."

By now both of them had forgotten Thomas, who, having lined up the coloured chalks on the teacher's desk, was making purple mouse squeaks on the blackboard. Remembering the treats he'd bought to keep the kid happy while he captured Miriam for himself, Jim asked Thomas if he'd like some chocolate-chip cookies and was rewarded with another skittering smile.

As they made their way to the house, Thomas scooching ahead, Jim noticed a large crow perched on top of the well and wondered if it was the same crow he'd seen on the well last Sunday. He didn't ask, not wanting to interrupt Miriam, who was telling him about her bees, how she could tell when they were overcrowded and getting ready to swarm. Because her bees had plenty of space, they had swarmed only once before. But just in case, she always made sure she had an extra hive. When bees build swarm cells for new queens, Miriam explained, the old queen will sometimes swarm with the colony, as she had the other day. "I know my bees *very well*," she added proudly.

"I could see that," Jim said. Struck silent by a sudden attack of shyness, he didn't tell her how much he admired the fearless way she had rescued the swarm, the gutsiness she had showed in standing on the table to capture hundreds of bees using nothing more than a pillowcase. Tongue-tied as he was, it came as a relief when the three of them reached the house and he had something to do with himself. Bolting into the kitchen, Jim opened the cupboard, took out the cookies and laid them on a chipped china plate. It was only when his visitors appeared behind him that he realized he'd forgotten to hold the door open for them. What a klutz, Jim thought—he had a habit of beating up on himself.

Miriam didn't seem to notice. Looking around the kitchen, she observed, "You are tidy, Jim."

"Not always," he said, remembering his messy bedroom at home. It was true that the kitchen was tidy. He thought that maybe he kept it that way because—for now, at least—Bliss was completely his. He handed the plate to Thomas and watched while the little boy studied the cookies before choosing one.

Jim told the boy he could take the cookies to the schoolhouse if he wanted, but Miriam had another idea. "We'll take them outside," she said, picking up the plate. "You go to the schoolhouse, Thomas, and Jim and I will sit on the step where you can see us." This was the take-charge side of Miriam that Jim had seen when she had captured the swarm.

Sitting beside her on the step, Jim watched Thomas place a cookie on the well top in front of the crow, which pecked it into pieces then ate them one by one. "That's Blackie," Miriam said, "Thomas's pet crow. He follows him everywhere."

Sure enough, when Blackie had finished the cookie bits, he strutted behind the boy as he made his way to the schoolhouse holding the plate.

At last Jim and Miriam were alone and he got the chance to ask if Thomas went everywhere with her.

"Yes. He's very attached to me and becomes upset if he's out of my sight. Even Father recognizes that, which is why he allows Thomas to sleep in my bedroom. Sometimes Thomas has terrible nightmares." Miriam paused, and when she spoke again, her words came quickly. "They began after Rachel left and he stopped talking."

"Rachel left? Didn't you tell me she died?" Jim told Miriam he'd seen Rachel's name on a marker below the tower.

"When someone leaves the farm, we say she died."

"She? Have others left?"

"Only Rachel and Gila have left. I never knew Gila. She left a long time ago. She was my half-sister, born to Father's first wife."

Upset by what he'd just been told, Jim pushed himself off the step and went to sit on the well. With that distance between them, he told Miriam it was cruel to say they died when all they did was leave the farm. Jim was uneasy with the thought of never being allowed to return home because he would be thought of as dead.

Miriam said nothing to this but sat with her head bowed, fists tightly clenched in her lap.

Jim asked what would happen if Rachel came back.

"She won't come back."

"How can you be so sure? Wouldn't she come back some day for Thomas?"

"She won't come back because she knows she would be shunned forever if she did. It is one of the rules on Majestic Farm that if a woman leaves the farm, she no longer exists."

"A woman. Don't men leave?"

"No."

"Would that be because a woman has a better reason to leave than a man?"

The sing-song voice returned. "Father says that the rules governing the Righteous Path are for our own good and are intended to protect us from the evils and temptations that beset the world."

Jim knew he'd gone too far. Reminding himself to back off—the last thing he wanted was to quarrel with Miriam—he agreed that a few rules were probably needed on Majestic Farm, just as laws were needed to govern the country, but he said that he wouldn't be able to follow most of them. "Like the rule about not being able to talk to you," he said and waited for her reply.

But Miriam didn't say a word. She didn't look at him either. She was looking behind him. Jim glanced over his shoulder, but there was nothing to see but trees. It was obvious that she was miles away, thinking of something else. To bring her back, Jim asked if she had ever thought of leaving the farm. He really didn't expect an answer but Miriam whispered, "Many times, God forgive me."

"God would forgive you," Jim said, and leaving the well, he reached for her hand.

Angrily Miriam snatched it away. "How would you know what God would forgive? No one knows the Almighty's mind."

"Not even your father?" No sooner were the words out of his mouth than Jim wanted to take them back.

"More than anyone, Father knows," Miriam said. "He is the Guardian of the Righteous Path and interprets it for us."

"Can't you interpret it for yourself?"

"Don't you *see,* Jim?" Miriam's voice was pleading with him to understand. "That would contaminate our beliefs and we would not have the one true faith that is the perfect religion."

"Perfect religion for whom?" Jim said. Now that he was back at the well, he could hold his ground.

Miriam looked at him as if he was an idiot. "Perfect for everyone, if only they would believe."

"It wouldn't be perfect for me," Jim said. "I want to think for myself. That's why I was born with a mind of my own."

"But a mind must be trained," Miriam retorted.

"To obey your father."

"You should not mock Father. You should be respectful."

"I'm not mocking your father. I admire him for making the farm a place that can get by on its own," Jim said, choosing his words carefully, wanting to fix what had gone wrong between them. "It takes a strong person to run a farm that can"—Jim groped for the word—"that can produce everything it needs. I admire your father for that."

"I don't care what you admire!" Miriam jumped to her feet.

Feeling awkward and lumpish, Jim pushed himself off the well.

"Sorry." He tried to catch Miriam's eye but she wouldn't look at him.

"It was a mistake coming here today," she said, striding toward the schoolhouse, Jim dogging her heels.

Thomas was at the blackboard, drawing furiously. By standing on the teacher's chair, the little boy had covered the entire blackboard with what Jim recognized as a picture of Majestic Farm. In the middle of the picture he had drawn a huge bearded face with eyes that seemed focused on a distant place, perhaps a mountain top. A row of stick-figure women in long dresses stood to the left of the face. The women's mouths were large O's as if they were singing, their heads tilted back, their eyes looking upward. To the left of the face was a row of men staring straight ahead, and except for one man shouldering a rifle, the men were holding what looked like farm tools. At the top of the picture was a woman in a long white dress, hair streaming behind her and arms outstretched as if she was flying. Thomas was busy drawing what Jim thought were stars in her hair.

"Come, Thomas," Miriam said. "We must to go back."

Usually obedient, the little boy ignored her and, like one obsessed, kept drawing more stars, which made Miriam angrier still. Jerking his arm, she spat, "Stop, Thomas! Stop!" Reluctantly, the little boy allowed himself to be pulled off the chair and out of the schoolhouse, leaving Jim inside, bewildered and dazed. Through the window, he saw Miriam half drag the boy away, and dashing outside, the dripping yellow flowers in one hand, he followed their trail through the woods, trying to think of something to say that would bring them back.

Miriam and Thomas were almost at the edge of the property, Blackie flying behind them, when Jim cupped his hands and shouted, "You forgot the flowers!" Miriam ignored him. Jim tried again. "Did you hear what I said? You forgot the flowers!" Miriam marched on and soon she and Thomas had disappeared into the woods of Majestic Farm, leaving an angry Jim behind. "Girls," he muttered, tossing the flowers aside. Discouraged and disappointed that the visit had taken a disastrous turn, he went into the schoolhouse and slumped in the teacher's chair, feeling sorry for himself. Just his luck to meet a girl he really liked and already she'd dumped him. But it was his own fault, wasn't it, because he should have known better than to try to be friends with a girl who belonged to a narrow-minded religious cult with weird ideas.

Restless, Jim sat on the desk, his feet on the chair, and looked at Thomas's drawing. For a kid his age, he was quite an artist. Now that he was taking a close look at the drawing, Jim saw something sinister in it—the rifle, perhaps, and the sombre expressions on the faces. The only happy face in the picture belonged to the woman flying dreamily overhead. Jim wondered if the woman was Thomas's mother, who was out there somewhere, flying free.

Too upset to pick up *Treasure Island* or eat the food Miriam had brought, Jim decided to go for a walk. It was the hottest part of the day, but he'd wear his sunglasses and hat. He put the bundle of food inside the well, drank a cup of cool water and started walking, but not toward town. If he went to town he might be tempted to phone his parents and be talked into going home. What he needed right now was to think about whether or not he'd work on the farm in the morning. He wanted Miriam to know he was angry. If he didn't show up tomorrow, she'd know that he wouldn't be made a fool of, that she wasn't the only one who could call it quits. When she saw his empty place at the breakfast table, she'd figure out he wasn't coming back; she'd know that as long as he was in Bliss, she wouldn't be welcome here.

12

Not a single vehicle passed Jim on his solitary walk, the road so dry that each step kicked up a puff of dirt. A half mile down the road he passed a wooden arrow sign, *Chumnik,* nailed to a fence on his right. Chumnik was one of the names in the school register. Two miles down the road was another name he recognized from the register, *Summers,* and farther along a third, *Kurelek.* Jim didn't keep track of the distance, but he'd walked far enough for the road to turn from burnt orange to dull brown as the sun made its flaming descent. The trek did nothing to lighten Jim's mood—the heat made him irritable and his mouth was parched. Cursing himself for not bringing a bottle of water, he turned around and headed for Bliss. He hadn't gone far when he heard a vehicle behind him and, turning, saw a half-ton truck crawling toward him. Stepping to one side, he waited for the truck to pass, but the vehicle pulled up beside him and a white-haired woman rolled down the passenger window and asked if he'd like a lift.

"Thanks, but I haven't far to go," Jim said.

The driver, who was as white-haired as the woman, leaned across her and shouted, "Aren't you the young fellow living in Bliss?"

Jim admitted he was.

"Bliss is our haunted house," the woman said nonchalantly, as if a haunted house was common as dust.

"Don't be filling this fellow's head with foolishness," the man chided her. To Jim he said, "You're our neighbour. Hop in. We won't take no for an answer."

The woman opened the door and moved to the middle to make room for Jim. "I'm Barbara," she said. Reaching across her, the man shook Jim's hand. "And I'm Lionel, the better half." He studied Jim for a moment and said, "I passed you on the road a while back. You were coming from town. As I recall you were wearing a tuque." Lionel chuckled. "That's how I knew you weren't from these parts."

Jim asked the woman why she had called the Bliss house haunted. "Is there a ghost?"

"Oh, no, I didn't mean that kind of haunted," she said in a shocked voice. "I just meant—"

Lionel intercepted her. "Barb meant haunted by memories we have of the place." Abruptly, he asked Jim where he was from.

"The city," Jim replied, and before her husband could ask more, Barbara said, "Now, Lionel, don't pepper the young man with questions."

Jim asked how they knew he was he was staying in the Bliss house.

"A little bird told me," Lionel said. "He also told me you've been working on Majestic Farm."

Barbara volunteered the information that one of men from Majestic Farm had told their son, Ted, about Jim. "And Ted told Lionel."

"I myself refuse to have anything to do with that bunch on

Majestic Farm," Lionel said. "Even though they're framing Ted's house."

"You're the Chumniks," Jim said.

"We are," Barbara said. "And you are our closest neighbour, so you must come to the house and have supper with us. There's cold bean salad and ham waiting in the fridge."

Although Jim had food stowed inside the well, the prospect of having supper with the Chumniks appealed to him more than eating Miriam's food and he didn't refuse the invitation.

Lionel turned onto the Chumnik side road, clouds of dust rising on both sides of the truck and spreading over the fields of ripened wheat. Like most of the farmhouses Jim had passed on his walk, the Chumnik house was set far back from the road and partially concealed by poplar trees. But as they came closer, he got a clear glimpse of a white two-storey house with a veranda across the front and along one side. There were steps leading down from the veranda to a lawn where three little kids were running in and out of a plastic wading pool, whooping and hollering. On the lawn a woman watched from the shade of a table umbrella, a large dog beside her. As soon as the truck rolled into the parking space beside the house, the dog sprang to its feet and bounded toward it. Lionel opened the door, and after the dog nosed the old man's hand, it went around to the passenger side and looked inquiringly at Jim. Jim hesitated before opening the door—the dog was a German shepherd.

"That's Nikki," Barbara said. "He won't hurt you."

Jim opened the door and stepped down. His feet had barely touched the ground before he felt Nikki nosing the back of his jeans.

"That's the sniff test," Barbara explained. "Nikki does that the first time he meets someone, to see if they're friend or foe. Come over and meet our daughter-in-law, Darlene."

The dog followed as Jim went to meet Darlene, a skinny woman in shorts and a halter top who looked about Paula's age.

"Darlene, this is our new neighbour, Jim," Barbara said. Her daughter-in-law waved a hand and smiled. With the other hand she fanned herself with a magazine.

"I'll get us some lemonade," Barbara said and bustled into the house. Now that Lionel was out of the truck, Jim saw that he was small and bowlegged, with a lined face and bright blue eyes. The old man nodded toward a chair. "Have a seat, Jim," he said. When he was seated himself, he asked Darlene what Ted was up to.

"He's working at the house." Darlene pointed toward a raw-looking, unfinished building half hidden in the trees farther along the road. Then she asked how Susie was. Apparently Susie was the Chumniks' married daughter who lived on a farm an hour's drive away—Barbara and Lionel had been on the way back from visiting her when they picked up Jim.

Soon Barbara appeared carrying a pitcher of lemonade and glasses down the veranda steps. Watching her, Jim noticed that like her husband, she was small and stocky with a deep-creased, tanned face. Darlene stood up, took the pitcher from her mother-in-law and began pouring lemonade. Having spied the lemonade, the children left the wading pool and dashed across the lawn. Their mother shooed them away. "This isn't for you," she said. "I'll bring you some Kool-Aid."

"But I want Gran's lemonade," whined the oldest boy.

"*Go.*"

Seeing their mother's hands on her hips and her shoulders squared, the children knew she meant business, and reluctantly, they retreated to the wading pool, Nikki following close behind.

"Little monkeys," Barbara Chumnik said fondly, handing Jim a glass of cold lemonade.

"So what's brought you to Bliss?" Lionel asked. "You finished school and come west looking for work?"

"I'm not finished school," Jim said. "I'm taking a break."

Lionel didn't question this. He said, "You know, you're living beside a school. Well, it's not a school anymore, but it used to be. Barb and I spent two and a half years in that school. That's where we first met. Back then she was Barbara Atkins."

"As I recall," Barbara teased, "back then you were sweet on Elizabeth Crozier."

"I was," Lionel admitted and winked at Jim. "My wife never lets me forget Elizabeth Crozier."

After Darlene went inside to make Kool-Aid, Barbara poured another round of lemonade. Jim confessed that he'd seen their names in the school register.

"You mean, it got left behind?" Barbara asked.

"It was in one of the desk drawers."

"I'm surprised," Barbara said. "I assumed the Blisses would have taken it with them."

Lionel said that after the Blisses left, he used to poke around the place, that he'd even gone into the house a few times but had never looked inside the desk. Taking a swallow of lemonade, Jim asked who owned the place now.

"As far as we know, it still belongs to the schoolteachers, Hector and Iris Bliss," Barbara said, "wherever they are."

"They might be dead now, Barb," Lionel said.

"If they had kids," Jim said, "wouldn't the place belong to them?"

"They were childless," Barbara said. "I recall the day Iris Bliss told me that." Barbara shook her head, remembering. "They were an odd pair, those two, but I never had better teachers. I cried my heart out when they left." She went on to explain how she had returned to school after the Christmas recess and found the Blisses gone, the schoolroom empty of books, a note on each desk written in Iris's hand. "She had beautiful penmanship," Barbara said. "I still have her note tucked away somewhere. In it she said she regretted that she and her husband had to leave and that she would always remember—"

"*Our dear faces,*" Lionel finished. "I squirmed when I read that as a kid, but now that I think about it," he continued, grinning at his wife, "I like that at one time someone thought I had a dear face."

Jim asked where the teachers went.

"I don't know," Barbara said, "but I wouldn't be surprised if they returned to Scotland. That's where they were from. I used to love listening to Iris Bliss read aloud in her Scottish accent."

"We all did," Lionel said. "Every afternoon, she'd tell us to put our heads on our desks while she read to us. She didn't seem to mind if we fell asleep."

"The Blisses had an original edition of Robert Burns's first book of poems that had been passed down through her family. She was very proud of the book and often read from it. She also sang Burns's love poems, including the naughty ones, and Hector would accompany her on his mandolin."

Barbara laughed. "What an odd-looking pair they were! Iris Bliss was a big woman, much bigger than her husband. She had straight black hair cut short and wore see-through nylon blouses with a man's jersey underneath. Hector Bliss was a jaunty little man with a beaky nose and hair that stuck up like dandelion seeds. I recall one day during a play when she sat him on her lap! Not many men would let a woman do that."

"I wouldn't." Lionel winked at his wife. "So don't you try it."

"Hector was a small man, but he had a huge heart," Barbara said.

"And a huge memory. Remember, Barb, when he recited the whole of 'Tam o' Shanter' from memory? As I recall it took him the better part of an hour, and he never once glanced at the book."

"They used to act out little plays—skits, Iris called them," Barbara said. "You know, I haven't thought about those teachers for years and didn't realize I remembered so much. When I think about them now, I see them as pioneers, the way they began what would nowadays be called an alternative school."

Lionel chuckled. "They were alternative, all right. In fine weather we spent half our time either inside Hector's workshop or outdoors. I learned about practical science from watching Hector rig up experiments of one kind and another, and although I was brought up on this farm, he was the one who taught me to really look at nature. I never knew anyone who could find so much of interest in a square foot of earth."

"Wonder." Barbara Chumnik said. "They had a sense of wonder like those children." She smiled at her grandchildren, who were holding out their glasses for seconds of Kool-Aid. "We are born with a sense of wonder," Barbara said, "but somewhere along the way, most of us lose it. The Blisses held on to theirs."

Lionel said, "After they left, I was bused to the big regional school and I didn't like it there nearly as much."

"Why did they leave?" Jim asked.

"I don't know, but I have my suspicions. More than once I asked my parents that question," Lionel said. "But they were hush-hush about it and claimed they didn't know why the teachers left. My father said he thought they might not have had the proper teaching licence and were shut down by the provincial authorities, but I think he was ducking the truth. Covering up. I know for a fact that the folks at Majestic Farm had something to do with it." Lionel looked at his wife. "You recall, Barb, the December morning when we came to school and saw the empty shelves where the books had been. The night before, someone had dumped all the books into the burning barrel and set them on fire."

So that's how the barrel got blackened, Jim thought.

Barbara turned to her husband. "Remember the morning we saw Hector's chickens bleeding in the snow, their heads chopped off?"

"How could I forget?" Lionel said. "It was shortly after that we were told we couldn't drink the well water because it was fouled with manure. There's no doubt in my mind that those guerrilla tactics were meant to drive the Blisses away."

Jim asked if the Blisses had reported what happened to the police.

"I assume so. Hector Bliss was small, but he was feisty. Not a man to take something lying down."

Barbara agreed. "Hector knew right from wrong and was passionate about his beliefs."

Jim asked why someone would want to drive the Blisses away. "None of the kids from Majestic Farm attended the school, did they?"

"No," Lionel said. "Those kids aren't allowed to leave the farm."

Barbara said, "It had to do with my older brother, Will."

"William Atkins?" Jim asked. "His name was in the school register too."

"Yes, it would have been there," Barbara said. "He attended the school for a while. You see, in those days our family farm was next door to Bliss. It's gone now, but at that time our farm was on the other side of Majestic Farm, and every day Will and I would walk to school together. Until one morning I woke up and discovered there was no Will. He was gone. No warning. Left a note for my parents in the sugar bowl. Said he was clearing out and wouldn't be back. There was no explanation. I never saw him again." Barbara's lower lip wobbled.

Lionel reached out and patted her hand. "It's all right, Barb," he said. Turning to Jim, he explained, "A few years later, the Atkinses received a letter from Will saying he was working up north on a geophysical survey ship that was mapping the sea bottom. Not long after, they got the news that he'd been killed in a freak accident. Something to do with underwater ice slicing the keel."

"He was twenty-three," Barbara said and sighed. "I adored him. He was funny and kind. And handsome. He looked exactly like Jimmy Dean."

Blank-faced, Jim asked, "Who was Jimmy Dean?"

That brought an indulgent laugh from Lionel, who said, "A movie idol who was all the rage in the time."

"Girls *adored* Will," Barbara said.

"Especially a particular girl from Majestic Farm," Lionel said. "She and Will used to meet in the schoolhouse. Will told me that himself. They were what back then we called *lovers,* a word you don't often hear nowadays. Will told me they used to meet in the schoolhouse at night, after the Blisses had gone to bed."

Jim waited for Lionel to connect the dots. When he didn't, Jim said, "Are you telling me that the Blisses were driven away because Will and the girl from the farm were getting it off in the schoolhouse?"

Lionel looked embarrassed.

Barbara said, "As a child I never knew any of this. At the time I don't think my parents knew about it either. It wasn't until I was grown up that my mother told me that Will had made the girl pregnant."

"So did they go away together?"

"No, she stayed on the farm . . ." Barbara's voice faltered briefly but not for long, and soon she took up the story again. "Later, my mother learned that one day in November, the poor girl came to Iris Bliss and asked for help delivering the baby. The baby died and the pastor blamed Iris for the death. And for the girl's disappearance afterwards."

Lionel took up the story. "As I recall, the guerilla tactics started soon after that, the worst one them being shot at through the kitchen window."

The hole in the kitchen window.

"Iris and Hector were such peaceful people that being shot at must have been the straw that broke the camel's back. They likely thought if they stayed, they'd be burnt in their beds."

"They might have, too," Barbara said, and Jim felt his neck hair stand on end. He asked the Chumniks if they remembered the girl's name.

Lionel shook his head no but Barbara frowned, trying to remember. "I'm not certain," she said, "but I think it was Gina. Or a name like that." She paused. "I must say, Jim, you're a brave young man to set foot on Majestic Farm. Neither of us will go near the farm. It's a scary place."

"Don't try to scare Jim," Lionel said. "We don't go near the place because we don't like their ways, not because we're scared. What happened to the Blisses was a long time ago, when the pastor and Abel were hot-headed firebrands, not old folks like us. Jim will be fine on Majestic Farm." Lionel winked at Jim. "As long as he leaves the girls alone."

Jim shifted in his chair. Lionel's remark was making him squirrely and he stood up. "I'll be going now," he said.

Barbara looked crestfallen. "Won't you stay for supper?"

"I've got to get back," Jim said. What he meant but didn't say was that he wanted to be alone with his thoughts. He wanted to sort out all the stuff he'd been told.

"But—"

"Don't be a mother hen, Barb," Lionel said. "Let the young fellow go."

Now that the sun was dipping low, the trees surrounding the house cast long shadows on the grass. A welcome breeze had come up. As he walked down the road, Jim noticed the wheat rocking gently in the fields, waving tassels of gold. Reaching Bliss, he headed straight for the well, where he'd put the sandwiches and chicken in the tin pail. Yes, he was angry at Miriam, but he wasn't about to throw away good food. With his head down, he'd almost reached the well before he noticed the crow perched on the wooden cover. Blackie. He was sure it was Blackie. He glanced around, looking for Miriam and Thomas, but there was no sign of either one. If the crow was Blackie, why was it here alone?

The crow dipped its beak and something white caught Jim's eye. A piece of folded paper was tucked beneath the handle of the well top. Jim picked it up and immediately the crow flew to a nearby tree, where it perched on a branch and watched Jim open the note and read the large, childishly printed words.

I was not mad at you, Jim, for what you said.

I was mad at what I said. I am afraid.

Please help me, Jim.

Although the note was unsigned, there was no doubt in Jim's mind it was Miriam's, and he read it again. He was puzzled about what she'd said to him that had made her mad, and had no idea what she was afraid of. He wondered if Miriam had delivered the note herself, or if she'd sent Thomas to put it on the well top. Jim supposed it would have been easier for the little boy to slip away. He glanced around, thinking Thomas might still be here, watching. Though he searched behind the schoolhouse and the garage, there was no sign of him. There was no sign of the crow either, and Jim figured that while he'd been looking for the boy, it must have flown away.

While early stars pricked the fading blue, Jim sat on the well top eating his supper and thinking about Miriam's note. What was she afraid of? After hearing her pious, brain-washed views about the perfect religion and the Righteous

Path, Jim didn't think she was frightened of her father, but there must be someone or something on the farm she was afraid of. But who? Whoever or whatever Miriam was afraid of had made her desperate enough to ask a stranger—which he was—to help her. Although they hardly knew each other, she must have seen something in him she felt she could trust. She was right about that. She could trust him. Her trust flattered Jim, made him feel manly and in a strange way honoured. Not to help her would be cowardly and weak, and he wasn't weak. If he'd been weak, he would never have struck out on his own or stood up to his mother or refused to return to school. If he was weak, he wouldn't be sitting on a well top on the Prairies right now. Jim picked up the note, and as he read it again, he felt his resolve not to return to the farm crumble. If he didn't show up for work tomorrow, Miriam would interpret his absence as a refusal to help, and he couldn't stand having her thinking that he'd turned his back on her.

Even after he'd made the decision to return to Majestic Farm, Jim continued to sit on the well top in the cool air, watching the sky blossom into night. For some reason, tonight's sky reminded him of a vast garden: the stars flickering like tiny flowers, the Milky Way winding itself around them like a giant creeper, Venus white as a daisy, Mars poppy red now that its orbit was bringing it closer to Earth.

Jim thought about the fixed position of the sun, the orderly procession of the planets, each in its own orbit. He thought about the chaos of collapsed matter, the rogue comets—the loose cannons of outer space. Order and chaos. The night sky seemed no longer like a garden but like a gigantic brain. He was looking straight up into the Creator's brain. That was how he wanted to think of God, not as a God who dictated rules and gave orders as to how everyone should live and think, but as a Creator with a mind that was forever changing and expanding.

13

The next morning Jim went to work as if everything was the same as it had been on Friday, though he knew that by pledging himself to help Miriam while continuing to work on the farm, he'd be living a double life. Although his feelings for Miriam had nothing to do with Asa, Jim felt like an impostor or a spy, pretending to be one person while he really was another. The real person was so caught up with Miriam that when Jim walked through the gate of Majestic Farm, it took all his concentration to shut down thinking about her and concentrate on the job.

Today he and Asa began building the wood cribbing for the cistern—the parallel sides that would hold the concrete in place after it was poured. The timbers for this job had been used many times before, and once Horse had hauled them to the lot, they only needed to be nailed in place. Compared with the slog of digging the cistern hole, it was easy work and at first Jim enjoyed it, especially with Asa for company. Unlike Ben, Asa treated Jim as an equal.

Mid-morning a slim, blue-eyed girl with pale gold hair showing beneath her kerchief appeared carrying a jug of water and glasses. Jim watched her set them on the stump close by. With a sliding glance she left the clearing. Jim watched the shapely hips moving beneath her dress. When Asa stopped work for a drink, he told Jim the girl was his oldest daughter, Leah.

Jim wanted to know why Asa didn't speak to her. "She's your daughter."

"We didn't speak because you are here. Anyways, Leah and I speak plenty at home. She's a good girl, pure of heart like her mother." Asa gulped down the water and shot Jim a sideways look. "She's also beautiful, like her mother."

"She's a looker all right," Jim said. If Solly were here, he'd say Leah was hot.

There was a pause and then Asa said, "You could do a lot worse."

"Me?" Jim said. What was Asa getting at? Did he leave the water jug behind on purpose so that Leah would bring it to them?

"We have a shortage of young men on the farm," Asa explained, "and in another year Leah will be sixteen and ready to marry."

Was Jim hearing right? Was Asa seriously suggesting that he stick around and marry his daughter?

"I don't get it."

Asa explained that there was a problem on the farm. With only two families breeding—*breeding* was his exact word—there weren't enough men to go around, and there was talk of some men taking two wives. Asa said he didn't want Leah to become a second wife. It would be better if Jim married her instead.

Marry your daughter! Jim thought. Are you out of your mind? "You've got to be kidding," he finally said.

"I'm not kidding. I thought I'd put the idea in your head, is all."

Jim could tell Asa was hurt—well, maybe not hurt, but offended.

They got back to work, but later, when they paused for another break, Jim brought up the subject again. "I thought having two wives was against the law."

"Not on Majestic Farm it isn't. We have our own laws here."

The pastor's laws. "I know," Jim said and, squatting down, rubbed Mutt's ears—Mutt was the one who followed them into the woods every day; the other one, who lay on the veranda like a rug, went by the name of Dog.

Asa leaned toward Jim and said, "You're not a dope head or a druggie, Jim. It would be easy for you to join the Majestic family."

"I don't want to join the Majestic family. I have a family of my own," Jim said. Not your kind of family, with parents living under the same roof, but still a family.

Asa said, "I mean a much larger family—the family of God."

Here we go again, Jim thought. With Miriam's words about the Righteous Path and the one true faith still ringing in his ears, Jim told Asa he didn't know if he believed in the family of God. When Jim was a kid, Paula had taken him to Sunday school, where he was read Bible stories and talked to about the family of God, but that seemed a long time ago. And in school, teachers avoided talking about God for fear of offending someone's religious beliefs.

"At first I didn't believe either. What the family of God means is fellowship, worshipping together," Asa said. "Why don't you attend the evening prayer meeting? You've got nothing to lose."

By now Jim had learned that if he kept his mouth shut, Asa would back off. Which is what happened. Within minutes they got back to work and didn't stop until the cribbing was finished.

In the meeting hall Jim sat in his usual place while supper was brought in; tonight it was roast pork, scalloped potatoes and apple cake. As Miriam leaned forward to place a platter of meat on the table, her arm brushed his. "Meet me afterwards," she whispered. *Meet me afterwards.* Had he heard right? Well, yes, he had, though it was only three words. Jim was elated that she'd taken the risk of speaking to him. He cast a furtive glance on either side for a sign that Daniel or Atta had heard the whisper, but neither boy had, both of them being more interested in elbowing one another than in anything Miriam said. After the meal the girls cleared the tables, carrying the dishes across the hallway to the kitchen while the men sat talking among themselves. Behind him, Jim heard sucking noises and knew the babies were contentedly feeding at their mothers' breasts, except for the one who always cried during mealtimes. Jim didn't know which one it was. From his first and only glimpse at the babies, he knew that all of them were dressed in white, that if he looked around, he wouldn't be able to tell one from the other.

When the women and girls had returned from the kitchen and taken their places behind Jim, the pastor stood up and a hush immediately fell on the room. It was as if the pastor had a kind of saintly power only he possessed. By now Jim had observed that whenever the pastor stood at his chair in the meeting hall, a hush descended. He had also observed that for breakfast and dinner the pastor was dressed like the other men, but that for the evening meal he wore a long black robe and a black cap that sat on his head like a crown. He stood before them now like a king before his obedient subjects.

The pastor lifted his arms and everyone rose in their places. Stumbling to his feet, Jim watched the pastor smile. "My children," the pastor said. "You know that in God's eyes, we are all children." Lifting his arms higher, he asked, "Have we not been blessed?"

A chorus of voices answered, "Yes, Father, we have been blessed."

"My children, how have we been blessed?"

All around him, Jim heard the voices chanting, "We have been blessed by the bounty of food, fellowship and the satisfaction of work."

"And what do we need?" the pastor asked.

"We need nothing we do not have, Father."

Beaming, the pastor shouted, "Yes! Yes!"

Glancing around the meeting hall, Jim thought that everyone except him seemed to be in a trance.

"But we must never take God's bounty and beneficence for granted." The pastor's fist pounded the air. "Never. Never."

"No. Never. Never."

The pastor made a sweeping gesture with his arms and everyone, including Jim, sat down. Removing his cap and holding it against his beard, the pastor said, his voice sad and morose, "When I was a child, I did not know about God's beneficence, and except for this evening's visitor"—the pastor paused to nod at Jim before he continued—"you have all heard the story of my salvation many times." The pastor raised his eyes to the ceiling, and the glint of window light appeared in his glasses. "Even so, God wants me to tell my story for Jim tonight."

For me? What a crock! Jim thought, his face hot with embarrassment and anger. Cool it, he reminded himself. If he was to meet Miriam afterwards, he had to sit through the sermon.

Lowering his head, the pastor looked around the meeting room and said, "Yes, my children, God wants me to tell my story."

Jim heard the cranky baby. Why were the babies here? he fumed. Why weren't they tucked into bed? Probably there was a rule about that too. Looking around the room, Jim observed that no one else seemed bothered by the cranky baby—certainly not the pastor, who had begun his story.

"As a fatherless boy, I lived in a city slum in a mean, squalid hovel with my poor mother, who did piecework at a garment factory, earning a meagre wage that barely kept us alive. There were no bountiful meals, such as we enjoy each and every day on Majestic Farm, and my mother and I subsisted on little more than gruel and boiled potatoes and, once in a long while, a slab of liver, which we ate without the benefit of butter or a sliver of onion."

The pastor paused and, grasping his throat for effect, made a gagging sound. "After my mother died of consumption, I never ate liver again." Jim snickered. He hated liver too and would have passed it up if it had been served on the farm, but it never was. He looked around the room to see if anyone was laughing. There wasn't so much as a grin.

"I was ten years old when she passed on," the pastor

continued, pointing a finger upward, "to her reward above, leaving me forever burdened with the knowledge that she died of a broken heart, knowing that her only son was a thief who stole the last coins in her purse and robbed strangers who crossed his path. From an early age I became an accomplished pickpocket, and more than once the police dragged me by the collar to our door, to show my mother the miserable creature I had become.

"After she passed on, I became a street orphan, sleeping in alleys and doorways, always on the run from the police. Though I had only a sheet of cardboard and a strip of plastic for cover, I was seldom cold, for I usually had a bellyful of liquor, which I obtained through bribery.

"At sixteen, I met a drug guru, a shaggy-haired stick of a fellow by the name of O'Rorke who introduced me to LSD, which he claimed would bend my mind so that I could look through the universe to its very end. A fatherless young man who had lost his way, I was besotted with O'Rorke, and together we took many trips, both on land and above." The pastor pointed to the sky. "We entered a world of night, of stars and black holes. With LSD pulsing in our blood, we were inside the aurora borealis with its shifting colours and mind-bending light."

Caught up in the pastor's mesmerizing tale, Jim was now listening with rapt attention.

"LSD did not come cheap, and because I was better at it than O'Rorke, I procured the cash we needed to buy the drug, robbing ordinary folk as they went about their business. As skilful as I was, the police finally caught up to me, and O'Rorke and I hopped on a freight train heading west, leaving the city far behind.

"We had reached the Rocky Mountains when O'Rorke got it into his head that we should take a trip to the top of the highest mountain. There, he said, we would be able to mind-travel deeper into the universe than we could on flat land. And so began our search for the highest mountain. After weeks of walking, footsore and hungry, we at last came upon the shining sword of Majestic Mountain thrust heavenward."

Here the pastor shook his head, as if bemused and perplexed. He said, "What fools we were. With LSD coursing in our blood, we thought we could reach the peak of Majestic Mountain without the aid of warm clothing or climbing gear. Dressed in stolen trousers and jackets, worn shoes on our feet, we began to climb. With nothing but peeled branches for poles, we followed the snowy track that led up the lower reaches of the mountain, spreading over the valley below like a heavenly cloak. It was early spring, and though the snow was waist deep in places, we struggled on for three days and three nights, taking shelter beneath trees and overhanging rocks. The higher we climbed, the lower were the clouds. At times it seemed we were swaddled in clouds, through which we heard the distant rumble of avalanches. Eventually we came to a wide chasm that lay between us and the peak we sought to climb. By now we were well above the tree line and, with our pitiful sticks, had no way of crossing the chasm. O'Rorke took out the last of the LSD and we shared it together. At length, O'Rorke confided that he could fly across the chasm because wings had begun to sprout on his back; he could feel them growing and soon they would be strong enough for him to fly. He said I could follow him, using my wings." The pastor looked upward again. "Thanks be to God, I had no wings. There was nothing sprouting on my back. I knew I was nothing but a man shackled to the earth. It is God's angels who fly, and I was no angel but a wretched sinner.

"Just as O'Rorke leapt into the chasm, I heard the rumble of God's voice high above the clouds telling me to go down from the mountain and atone for my sins and live a godly life." Lowering his head, the pastor wiped away a tear.

"I will never forget the sound of O'Rorke's voice, the way his scream became fainter and fainter the deeper he fell until finally his voice was swallowed by the chasm of ice. That sound will be with me always. It is a burden I must carry, to atone for my sinful ways." The pastor sighed heavily before continuing.

"Making my way down Majestic Mountain, I rested for three days, finding sustenance from kind folk until I found the strength to leave the mountains and make my way east. For two years I wandered the Prairies, finding such work as farmers would give me, sleeping in barns and sheds until God led me to the deserted farm that is now our Majestic Farm. Still I continued my wanderings, collecting wheelbarrow after wheelbarrow of stones so that I could build Him a tower upon which I could receive His Word. And so it was."

The pastor paused as much for emphasis as for breath and then continued, "I had returned to the farm from one of my wanderings when I found a boy sleeping in the derelict barn. That boy was to become Abel Hamfist." The pastor patted the shoulder of the man sitting beside him. "Like me, the boy was a runaway thief looking for a better life. Together we built the tower to Him and I set about composing the rules we now abide by to keep ourselves on the Righteous Path." The pastor pointed a finger upward. "It is because of those rules that you, my children, will be spared the temptations of a wicked life. Amen." With this final word the pastor bowed his head.

An unearthly silence fell on the meeting hall and even the cranky baby was silent. It was as if the pastor had woven a spell that had hypnotized everyone in the room, including the baby. But not for long. As the pastor left the meeting hall followed by the men and boys, the baby started wailing again. Though eager to meet Miriam, Jim waited until the baby was taken away and the women and girls left the room. Miriam hadn't told him where to wait, so he thought it better to stay where he was. Five minutes passed, then ten. Lifting one long leg and then another over the bench, Jim stood up and, going into the entryway, looked into the kitchen to see if one of the half-dozen white dresses was worn by Miriam. None of them was. Outside he waited at the end of the empty veranda, thinking she might whisper to him from behind the corner of the house. Ten more minutes passed. Fortunately, nobody was around to watch him waiting. Jim knew that if he hung around much longer, Ben would see him and make a big deal of his being here. Maybe, Jim thought, Miriam was waiting for him in the woods by the driveway, where they wouldn't be seen. Walking at a pace that would avoid suspicion—should anyone be looking—Jim made his way to a place in the driveway concealed by the woods and waited for Miriam. Fifteen minutes passed and still she didn't come. She had risked whispering, *Meet me afterwards*, but something or someone must have prevented her from getting away.

Or maybe she had managed to get away and was waiting for him in Bliss. But that didn't make sense because she wouldn't risk telling him to wait if she was planning to come to Bliss, where she knew he'd go after supper. Nothing made sense, and abandoning his wait, Jim returned to Bliss with a heavy, anxious heart.

14

That night Jim dreamed he was falling into a chasm of blue-white ice darkening to grey and then to black the deeper he fell, his mouth locked in a continuous scream that followed him all the way down. The scream woke him before he hit bottom—if there was a bottom—and he sat up, shivering with cold. The blanket had fallen onto the floor and the cool night air flowing through the open shutters had chilled him to the bone. The warm weather Asa called Indian summer was over.

Closing the shutters and pulling on his socks and jeans, Jim wrapped himself in the blanket and lay down again, vowing to clean the chimney so that he could make himself something warm to drink. What he wouldn't do right now for a cup of hot chocolate! Without the comfort of a stove or hot chocolate, he imagined Miriam curled beside him on the narrow sofa bed and after a while was warm enough to fall asleep.

He awoke knowing he would attend the prayer meeting again tonight. Maybe tonight Miriam would find a way of meeting him afterwards, and he'd be there even though it meant having to listen to one of the pastor's sermons. That morning Jim and Asa dug a grave-size hole where the fireplace-oven would be built. It was easy work because the house foundation had already been marked with stakes and twine. Also, the cooler weather had got rid of the blackflies. In the afternoon they dug holes for the cement posts that, as Asa explained, would support the concrete flooring. When they were done, Asa and Jim put down their shovels and went to the meeting hall for a supper of chicken stew and rhubarb pie. After the meal was eaten and dishes cleared away, the women returned to their places. Tonight the unhappy baby was crying in fits and starts. *Shusss,* a woman said, *Shusss,* which only made the baby shriek louder.

The pastor stood up. Right away Jim noticed Miriam's father was in a very different mood from the one he'd been in the night before. Gone was the hypnotic storyteller and in his place was an angry ruler who stood, robed and hatted, a sheaf of paper in his hands. Tonight there was no attempt to hypnotize his listeners—his children—with a tale of a misspent youth and redemption. Tonight the pastor was intent on driving home the rules he demanded his followers obey.

Jabbing the sheaf of paper with a finger, the pastor said in a voice rigid with anger, "Tonight's lesson is based on His first words that in His infinite wisdom, He bid me write down as I sat on His tower." The toadish eyes swelled as he spat out the words "Thou shall not want!" A finger stabbed the air, a reminder of the words burnt into the wood above the barn door. "As you are well aware," the pastor said, "wanting what you do not have is the work of the Devil." He waved toward the window. "Out there is a world consuming itself with greed, which is the Devil's way of tempting people to abandon the Righteous Path, the pure path that leads us, once our earthly toil is done, to Heaven, the place where God sits in majesty with souls who have lived as they should."

The pastor looked from one face to another. "Wanting what we do not need is Vanity, and Vanity is one of the wickedest of temptations." His tongue shot out. "And what is Vanity?" The pastor puffed up his chest. "Vanity is a fascination with oneself. Vanity says I'm the important one around here. I do not have to consider others. *I* do what *I* want." The pastor shook his head sorrowfully. "Such thoughts are sinful and full of pride."

As he listened, Jim felt the lingering spell he'd been under since last night drift away and he began to see the pastor in a different light. What an actor the old man was, changing himself from a storyteller into this angry preacher. Who was the real pastor, last night's man or the man standing before him now?

The pastor began to rant about vanity's twins: admiration and self-love. Now that he was thinking clearly, Jim tuned out—he always tuned out whenever someone started ranting. Carla was a ranter, and because he tuned her out, he didn't know half of what she said. After Jim's watch showed that five minutes had dragged by, the pastor, exhausted by his own performance, stopped ranting and, adopting a regretful tone of voice, announced that he had the unfortunate task of punishing a family member for wrongdoing.

"It has been brought to my attention," he went on, "that someone has been caught in the sin of wanting what she does not need. Being human, each of us is tempted by sin as we endeavour to follow the Righteous Path. But I say again,

Vanity is one of the worst of sins because Vanity says, I know what is best and what *I* want.

"You know who you are," the pastor continued sorrowfully, as if he was in pain. "And I bid you to stand now and confess your wrongdoing." Removing his glasses, he held them against his beard and waited for the woman to speak, and when after a minute or two no one did, he fixed his bulging stare on a woman behind Jim. "Stand up, Faria," he said, "and confess your sin."

Glancing behind, Jim saw a young woman Miriam's age struggle to her feet, shouldering the fretful baby. "I have nothing to confess, Father," she whispered.

"Speak up, Daughter. Speak up."

In a louder voice, Faria said, "I have nothing to confess, Father."

The pastor shook his head. "Do not confound your wrongdoing with the sin of a lie."

Intent on soothing the baby, Faria did not respond, which unleashed the pastor's fury, and his voice became shrill. "Do you deny that you are using a plastic bottle to feed my grandson Isaac?"

"No, Father."

"No, what?"

"I do not deny it."

"You know that the rule on Majestic Farm is that no child is to be fed except by a woman's breast, that if a mother is unable to feed her child, a wet nurse must be used. Yet you have used a forbidden plastic bottle, and in doing so, you have committed a wrongdoing."

"But, Father, I want to feed Isaac myself, and with the help of a bottle, I can do that."

Though the pastor's eyes blazed with fury, he managed to speak calmly. "What you want is Vanity speaking," he said. "You do not make or interpret the rules, Faria."

"I bought the baby bottle, Father." By now Miriam was on her feet. "And I think"—her voice faltered but she carried on—"I think the rule should be changed."

There was a collective gasp in the room.

"Enough!" the pastor roared. "I have heard enough! Hear my words. Faria and Miriam, you are to go straight to your rooms and await your punishment. Under no circumstances are you to leave your rooms." The pastor was on his toes now, bouncing with anger. "Mark my words, when I am finished with you, you will both repent your wrongdoing. I will not countenance the double sin of Vanity and Disobedience."

Jim could hardly believe what he was hearing. What did the pastor mean, *When I am finished with you?* It sounded ominous and frightening. While the others filed from the meeting hall, Jim sat in a state of shock and confusion until he felt a tap on his shoulder and, looking up, saw Ben looming over him. He was pointing at the door. "Go," he said, his voice quiet and lethal as if a weapon were concealed inside. Jim felt the urge to give him a shove, but just in time he reminded himself to keep his cool and leave quietly. Determined not to hurry, he got to his feet and slouched through the entryway and outside, breaking into a run only when he was out of sight. Although his feet automatically followed the road to Bliss, Jim didn't want to return to the house.

Too upset by what he'd seen to be alone with his thoughts, and badly in need of someone to talk to, he struck out for town with the intention of calling Paula. But he hadn't gone far when he realized that he couldn't talk to Paula without telling her about the weird people he was tangled up with. Being his mother, she would advise him to stay away from Majestic Farm, as he'd intended to do before Miriam asked for his help. But tonight Miriam had stood up to her old man and would need his help all the more. Knowing that, Jim couldn't just walk away from the farm.

Lionel Chumnik. He could talk to him. Backtracking, Jim headed for the Chumnik farm and was partway up their drive when he spotted Lionel's dusty truck parked at the side. Closer to the house, Jim spied the old man on the front veranda. He was sitting in a rocker, hunched forward, watching Jim approach. Nikki was watching too, and as soon as Jim stepped off the road and onto the grass, the dog growled and streaked toward him. Lionel said, "It's all right, Nikki. We know Jim. Come back and lie down." Grudgingly, it seemed to Jim, the dog obeyed.

Pulling the empty rocker close to his own, Lionel said, "This is Barb's chair, but she's not here. She and Darlene are at a quilting supper and Ted's upstairs putting the kids to bed." Jim could hear the children's voices through the open windows.

Lionel said, "You look like you have something on your mind."

"I do," Jim admitted, and lowering himself into Barbara's chair, he told Lionel what had taken place in the meeting hall not an hour ago. It was a relief to tell someone, to let it all out. Lionel listened closely, every once in a while shaking his head in disbelief.

When Jim was finished, Lionel said, "It's hard to imagine making a fuss over using a baby bottle. It goes to show what a strange religion they've got going on that farm." He paused. "But from what I know, I'd say it's not the bottle so much as the plastic that the pastor objects to. According to Ted, not even a plastic bag is allowed on Majestic Farm."

"It's not only the plastic. There's a rule that all babies must feed at a woman's breast."

Lionel said, "Well, Pastor Godshawk is a fanatic, and like all fanatics, he goes to extremes." Leaning close to Jim, he continued, now in a conspiratorial voice, "To tell you the truth, I didn't want the Hamfists to work on Ted and Darlene's house, not after what they did to Hector and Iris Bliss. But framers are hard to find in these parts, and Ted was set on having the house framed in before the cold weather sets in. Barb and I don't mind Ted and Darlene and the kids living with us, but they are determined to have their own place."

"How long will the Hamfists will be working on the house?"

"Ted estimates another week, two at the most. Why do you ask?"

"Because I'll only have a job on the farm until the Hamfists are finished up here."

Lionel nodded. "Ted told me they're building two new houses over there, one for Hosea and his wife. Hosea told Ted that he was marrying as soon as the girl comes of age. Over there they marry off the girls as young as sixteen."

Jim felt he'd been kicked in the gut. Hosea. The way he looked at Miriam. "Did Ted say who Hosea was marrying?"

"Nope. Those folks on Majestic Farm are close-mouthed. I'm surprised Hosea even told Ted he was marrying." Lionel gave Jim a canny look. "Any chance it's a girl you have your eye on?"

A deep flush crept up Jim's neck.

Lionel said, "It would be hard not to fall for one of those girls. From the odd glance I've had of them, they're beauties, every one of them."

"Yeah." Resigned to telling Lionel the truth, Jim said, "And one of them is afraid and wants my help."

"Why is she afraid?"

Jim told him he wasn't sure.

"So you don't know what kind of help she wants?"

"Not yet."

"Well, Jim," Lionel said, speaking briskly now, "when you find out and need my help, you know where you can find me." Lionel paused before asking, "You got a cellphone over there?"

Jim shook his head. "It got lost in the subway."

"Feel free to use our phone any time you want," Lionel said.

The screen door banged shut and a little girl wearing a teddy-bear nightgown burst onto the veranda and, thrusting a book at Lionel, climbed onto his lap and asked, "Grandpa, can you read me a story?"

Putting a fond arm around her, Lionel said, "Gracie, you know Jim." He tweaked the little girl's nose. "We don't mind if he stays for the story, do we?"

Gracie wasn't sure.

"That's okay, Gracie, I'm leaving," Jim said.

He was turning the veranda corner when Lionel called after him, "Remember, if you need help, you only have to ask." Lionel opened *Where the Wild Things Are.*

Walking toward Bliss, Jim noticed for the first time that the large wheatfields next to the Chumniks' farm had been harvested, leaving behind a stubble of yellow beard, the brown skin of earth showing through.

Later, lying in bed, Jim was pulled from sleep by a chorus of howls and yips. Coyotes. He knew what they were. Asa had told him about the coyotes trying to kill the calves and lambs on Majestic Farm. Donkeys were kept in the fields with cattle and sheep, Asa said, because they patrolled the fences and kicked any coyote trying to sneak in. These coyote howls were coming not from the direction of Majestic Farm but from the field next to the Chumnik farm. Jim heard Nikki barking wildly, warning them off. According to Asa, at this time of year coyotes mainly went after deer grazing what was left in a field after the crop had been harvested. Although Asa claimed deer were plentiful, Jim hadn't seen a single one, but now he imagined two does standing frightened and alarmed as coyotes moved in for the kill.

15

During breakfast next morning Jim kept looking around the meeting hall, hoping to see Miriam and Faria, but there was no sign of either one. He heard the baby fretting behind him, and when he turned, he thought he glimpsed Isaac quietly feeding at the breast of another woman, but he couldn't be certain it was Faria's baby.

After the meal, Jim helped Asa hitch Horse to the wagon-load of tools and bags of cement, and they spent the morning mixing concrete, shovelling it between the cistern cribbing and tamping it down. It was hard, steady work, and because they had to keep the cement from drying out, they didn't go to the meeting hall for dinner; instead Leah brought their meal in a basket—pork pies and potato salad. As before, Asa's daughter came and went without a word or a smile from her father. Again, Jim was puzzled that a kind man like Asa could ignore his daughter—Jim wasn't allowed to talk to her, but why didn't Asa? They ate their dinner turnabout so one of them could trickle hose water hauled from one of the communal wells into the cement mixing box. "Not too much water," Asa advised, "or the concrete will be weak." Otherwise, he didn't say much. Jim thought of asking Asa's opinion about the fuss the pastor had made over Faria's using a plastic baby bottle but decided against it. Because the pastor had rescued him from the ditch, Asa would go along with whatever the old man said and did, so there was no point asking his opinion, and he and Jim worked in silence, stopping from time to time to swat away flies. Now that nights were cooler the no-see-ums had disappeared, but the horseflies continued swinging past and occasionally landed a bite. Finally, just before supper, the concrete walls were finished, and throwing the tools into the wagon, Asa and Jim led Horse one lot over so Ben and Ezra could use the wagon and mixing box in the morning. Asa told Jim that from now on they'd be working in the barn, making straw bales to put between the walls while Ben and Ezra finished the cisterns.

On his way to the meeting hall, Jim risked a brief look into the kitchen, where the women and girls were readying supper, hoping to catch sight of Miriam, but again there was no sign of her or Faria. And they weren't in the meeting hall, although Thomas was there, sitting at the end of Jim's table. They ignored each other. The kid was smart, Jim thought—he knew they had to pretend they were strangers. As soon as the meal was over, Jim cleared out. He had no intention of sitting through another of the pastor's rants—not after the fuss he'd made over a plastic baby bottle, the frightening way he'd threatened to punish his daughters. The pastor was a phony, and Jim vowed that from now on he wouldn't listen to another word the old man said.

As was usual after a strenuous day working on the farm, Jim was beat. To stop from worrying what was happening to Miriam, he wrapped himself in the blanket, stretched out on the daybed and found his place in *Treasure Island.* When he'd broken off reading, Jim Hawkins had been looking for the chance to leave the ship. Now he was ashore and exploring another part of the island, where he found Ben Gunn, a rusty-voiced pirate who had been marooned on the island for three years and who knew the whereabouts of the treasure. Jim Hawkins was persuading Ben Gunn to accompany him to the palisade when the book slid from Jim's hands and onto the floor. He was fast asleep.

═

Next morning the sisters were again absent from breakfast, but Thomas was there. Walking to the barn to begin work, Jim came close to asking Asa if Miriam was sick, but he stopped himself on time. If he asked about her, Asa would know they were acquainted and had broken the farm rules. Inside the barn, bales of field straw were piled on top of one another, from the barn floor to the loft. Driving across the Prairies, Jim had noticed thousands of bales—what Silas called jelly rolls—scattered across the fields, but he hadn't seen any of them on Majestic Farm and he asked where they had come from.

Asa explained that the bales came from the Kureleks' fields. He said the straw bales would be stacked between the inner and outer walls of the houses, where they would serve as insulation. The straw would keep the place warm and quiet—so quiet that when the windows were closed no one inside would hear a thing outside, not even a plane. Jim told him he'd never heard or seen a plane flying over Bliss. Come to think of it, all he'd seen was jet writing in the sky.

Asa continued explaining that their job was to unroll the straw and repack it into wire bales. Handing Jim a pair of what looked like new leather gloves, he told him to put them on. "My wife made them especially for us," Asa added proudly. "The straw will scratch our hands, and we need gloves for cutting the wire."

Armed with their gloves, Asa and Jim set to work making wire bales and stuffing them with straw. It was hard work, but Jim liked being inside the barn. Although it was huge, there was a coziness about the place that had to do with the smell of straw and warm cows coming from the cattle stalls at the back. Mutt was curled up just inside the door, but there was something missing, and after he'd been working awhile, Jim knew what it was. "Cats," he said. "Where are the barn cats?" For some reason, Jim thought every barn sheltered cats and kittens.

"We don't keep cats on the farm," Asa said. "They interfere with the milking. Strays that show up are drowned."

"What do you do about rats?" Jim asked, although as he'd told Paula, he had yet to see a rat.

"There's no rats hereabouts," Asa said. "Only mice, and they're no bother."

The work was discouragingly slow. Asa claimed they'd be at it all this week and the next, while Ben and Ezra made the concrete foundation pads that would support the concrete floors. By the end of the week the Hamfists would be finished at the Chumniks' and would begin making the concrete walls. Asa said that when the baling was done, he and Jim would cut grass sods for the roof. "The sods keep out the noise. When you're inside a house with a sod roof, you wouldn't hear a tornado coming."

"Wouldn't you want to hear it coming?"

Asa looked sheepish. "I guess you would."

After a rectangle of straw was strapped with wire, the finished bale was placed against an inside wall to keep it dry. "Once we get the hang of it," Asa said, "we'll have a layer a day stacked against the wall."

Jim had noticed a change in Asa. He was still friendly and talkative, but he now seemed guarded, as if he was holding something back. He had stopped mentioning Leah and did not encourage Jim to attend the evening prayer meeting. Remembering the way Ben had hustled him from the meeting hall yesterday, Jim thought it likely that he'd instructed Asa to discourage him from attending another meeting. He could almost hear Ben's voice: *Just make sure he puts in a hard day's work. That's all we want from him before we're finished with him.*

To make conversation, Jim asked whose idea it was to build a straw-bale house. Asa explained that Hosea Hamfist had come across such a house a year ago when he and his brothers had been working next door to a straw-bale house. "Hosea got a close look at it and figured out how it was done so he could build one for himself."

"Doesn't he already have a house?"

"He did, but he didn't need it after Rachel died. So he gave it up."

Hosea was Thomas's father! Why had Miriam never mentioned this?

"So Hosea's unmarried," Jim said.

"Yup," Asa said, "but not for long. The cistern we dug is for his new house."

Forcing his voice to sound casual, Jim asked who Hosea was marrying. He knew where his question was leading, but he couldn't help himself—he had to know.

"Until the pastor makes the announcement, no one knows for sure." Asa gave Jim one of his gap-toothed grins. "But my wife tells me she knows who the girl is. Ezra's girl too. The other house is for him."

Once again, Jim felt he'd been kicked in the gut. Now he knew for sure: *Hosea was going to marry Miriam.* The thought that all this time he'd been working on the cistern of a house intended for Hosea and her made him feel foolish, as if he'd been tricked. Did Miriam want to marry Hosea? Is that what she had wanted to tell Jim? Preoccupied with these thoughts, Jim had trouble concentrating on the work and it took most of the morning for him to learn the knack of baling. By noon he'd made only three bales to Asa's six. He picked at his dinner and left the meeting hall determined to stop thinking about Miriam and Hosea. All afternoon he worked like a zombie and by suppertime twelve of the bales against the wall were his.

Wedged between his seatmates at supper, Jim knew, without even looking around, that Miriam and Faria weren't in the meeting hall. They hadn't been there for dinner either. He thought the sisters must be quarantined someplace apart, where they couldn't talk to anyone else on the farm. Remembering Miriam's telling him that one of the punishments used on Majestic Farm was shunning, Jim wondered if she and her sister were being shunned. They must be. How else to explain their absence? Knowing there was zero chance of seeing Miriam, Jim was back on the road to Bliss as soon as the meal was over.

He didn't see Blackie perched on the wooden cover until he was nearly at the well. The two eyed each other briefly and the crow dipped his beak. Jim saw the note tucked beneath the well handle. "You're one smart crow," Jim said, reaching for the note. As soon as he picked it up, Blackie flapped to the branch of a nearby tree.

Opening the unsigned note, Jim once again read Miriam's blocky printing.

I could not meet you, Jim. Ben saw me waiting.
I am going to leave the farm. Please help me
get away.

Jim sat on the step reading and rereading the note, letting the news sink in. Miriam was leaving Majestic Farm! She didn't want to marry Hosea! He felt a surge of relief. "Way to go, Miriam," he said. "You challenged your old man and now you're standing your ground. Good for you." Jim vowed he would do anything he could to help her get away. If she stayed on the farm, sooner or later she'd be forced to marry Hosea. He had to get Miriam out of there. But how? And where would she go?

"Someplace far away," Jim said, still talking to himself. "Someplace where she can't be found."

Leaping to his feet, he shouted, "Home! I'll take her home. She'll be safe if I take her home. They'll never find her in the city!"

Guided by no other impulse except finding a safe place for Miriam, Jim jogged into town and made straight for the pay phone, taking the chance Paula might be home; if not, he'd call back in an hour, waiting out the time with a Coke in Marilyn's Café. Paula answered after the second ring.

Before she had a chance to say a word, Jim said, "Mom, would it be okay with you if I brought a girl home?"

"You mean you're coming home?"

"If I can bring her, I am."

A bad start. "Are you blackmailing me?" She sounded angry.

"No. I meant I'd come with her."

"She'd come for a visit?" He could tell she was trying to be calm.

"No, she'd stay for a while."

"Why?" Paula said.

"Why?" Now Jim was angry. What was the big deal? "Because she's a friend who has no place to stay."

"How old is she?"

"Fifteen."

"Have I got this right? You want to bring a fifteen-year-old girl home to live with us?"

"To stay with us. And it's not what you think. She could sleep in Carla's room. I know this is a surprise, Mom."

"That's putting it mildly."

"She's in a tough spot and needs help for a while."

"Is she pregnant?"

"No. She's from a religious family."

"Religious people often get pregnant."

"Well, as far as I know she's not pregnant, and I'm asking you ahead of time if I can bring her home so you can think about it for a while." This last was something his mother often said to him.

"I'll think about it," Paula said. "And I'll discuss it with your father and see what he says."

"But it's your condo."

"And he's your father. I want his opinion."

"When will you be talking to him?"

"This weekend. He'll be staying here again."

"You mean sleeping there?"

"That's what *staying* usually means."

"Well, that's great, Mom. Carla and I should have left home sooner," Jim said and slammed down the phone. He was upset. As soon as his mother was alone, his father moved in. Were his sister and him that much trouble? Well, Carla was, but he wasn't. Until now. So why didn't his parents get back together before?

Back on the road, Jim had reached Bliss before noticing a combine being driven by a man, probably Ted, working one of the fields on the other side of the Chumnik house. He stopped to watch. Moving at a slow, stately pace, the combine cut and threshed the crop, shooting speckles of grain up a long green arm that poured a steady flow of golden wheat into the flatbed of an enormous truck. Neat, Jim thought. He waved at the driver, but Lionel was too far away and too busy keeping the truck alongside the combine to notice anyone on the road. Later, when he was hauling water from the well, Jim heard the harvesting machines still at work, moving back and forth the length of the field as his neighbours made the most of the waning summer light.

16

The next two days on Majestic Farm dragged by with no sign of Miriam, and if it hadn't been for her note, Jim wouldn't have known she was alive. She and her sister were definitely hidden away somewhere. Locked away. Jailed. Were they getting by on bread and water? Was starvation part of shunning? Miriam's absence rattled Jim, made him jumpy and uncertain. How could he help her get away if he couldn't talk to her, if he didn't know where she was? He didn't even know where she slept.

Frustrated by the weight of not knowing, on Thursday morning, as he and Asa were heading for the barn after breakfast, Jim decided to root around for information. Keeping his voice super casual, he asked Asa where the pastor's family lived. Asa explained that the pastor's married children lived in houses much the same as his.

"But what about unmarried children? Where do they live?" Jim remembered being told unmarried girls lived with their parents, but Ben hadn't said where that was.

Asa looked startled. "You don't know?"

"I was never told."

"Why do you want to know?"

Jim shrugged. "Just curious. At breakfast I looked around the meeting hall and wondered where everyone slept. I mean, I haven't seen cottages or anything . . ." His voice trailed away. What a liar he'd become. Did other people on the farm lie when they tried to get around the rules?

"Unmarried sons live in the dormitory above the workshops. Unmarried daughters live in a dormitory with the pastor and his wife."

Jim recalled that on his first day of work, when Ben was leading the way to the tool shed, they'd passed a set of long stairs at the back of the house. As Jim remembered it, the stairs led to a balcony running the length of the building. There were doors and windows opening onto the balcony . . . he couldn't remember how many—six or seven, maybe. Windows too. That had to be the dormitory. That was where he'd look for Miriam.

To be certain, Jim asked where the dormitory was.

"Above the kitchen," Asa said. "My wife lived up there before she married me."

Asa was the pastor's son-in-law! Why hadn't he figured that out before?

Jim knew he'd climb those stairs and look for Miriam. And no matter what, he'd do it today. The question was, When? Noon—he'd look for her at noon. With everyone in the meeting hall eating dinner, he'd climb the stairs at the back of the house. If he remembered rightly, the stairs were close to the kitchen windows, so he'd have to wait until the women were in the meeting hall and not rushing back and forth across the entryway with platters and bowls of food, or clearing away dirty dishes. Timing was everything, and he could easily blow it. But it was a chance he would have to take.

By now he and Asa had reached the barn, and pulling on leather gloves, they set to work unrolling wire and twisting it into rectangular bales. The weather had taken another turn and the morning air had gone from cool to sharply cold, even inside the barn. Whenever Asa spoke, his words came out in moist puffs of air. Jim didn't speak. Now that he'd worked out a plan to see Miriam, he tried to concentrate on the job. But it was difficult to concentrate because it had occurred to him that Miriam might not be in a room above the kitchen—that she might be locked inside a small shed, a jail with barred windows hidden away in the woods somewhere. Or maybe in an underground pit, something camouflaged by branches and sods that would make it difficult, if not impossible, for him to find. A man who threatened to punish his daughters for using a plastic baby bottle could have built such a diabolical place. Fortunately for Jim, he had mastered bale making, and though his mind was a dungeon of possible ways of punishment, by now he could do the job with his eyes shut. Monotony set in. Time dragged interminably on. Would noontime never come? Finally the dinner bell rang, and setting down the wire cutters, Jim removed the gloves.

Side by side, he and Asa crossed the yard, and when they reached the veranda, Jim told a second lie. He told Asa he didn't feel too good. He was sick to his stomach, and if it was okay with him, he'd head back to Bliss. Asa's beat-up face crinkled with concern. "You go on now," he said, "and get yourself to bed. I'll see you tomorrow."

Asa disappeared inside and Jim stepped off the veranda, listening to the clomp and shuffle of boots as the others made their way to the meeting hall. His eyes never left his watch. He'd wait fifteen minutes, to make sure that the women had finished serving and the kitchen was empty, that everyone was in the meeting hall eating. It was a long fifteen minutes, much of it spent with Jim half expecting to be seen. Or found. When the pastor noticed his empty place at the table, wouldn't he ask Asa where Jim was? Yes, and Asa would tell him Jim was feeling poorly, and nobody would have a reason to look for him.

Keeping his head down so he wouldn't be seen from the windows above, Jim ducked to the back of the building and hesitated. What if he met someone coming down the stairs? What if there was a straggler late for dinner? Jim couldn't help snickering. Stragglers on Majestic Farm? Forget it. There were a compost bin and a barrel of rainwater outside the kitchen door, and crouching behind them, Jim waited a minute or two before creeping up the stairs. Seven doors and seven windows opened onto the balcony deck. Jim paused to look through the first window and saw a narrow empty room—more cell than bedroom—containing a bed, a dresser and a chair. He looked through the window of the second room. *There was Miriam!*

Or was it Miriam? The girl in the white dress sitting on the bed was completely bald. Although he was being super cautious and hadn't made a sound, the girl sensed some-one was there and turned toward him. Jim's jaw slackened with astonishment. It *was* Miriam, but without her long, glossy hair. Nothing remained on her head except a dark, whiskery shadow.

At the sight of Jim, she left the bed and opened the door. What a relief she wasn't locked in! He slipped inside and stood facing her, his back to the door.

"What happened to your hair?"

Holding a finger to her lips, Miriam whispered, "I have been shorn. My sister too. It is part of our punishment. We have also been shunned for a week and have been forbidden to talk, even to each other." With her head shaved, Miriam's dark eyes looked enormous and sad.

"Your father did this?"

"He ordered Ben's wife, Zelda, to shave Faria's head and mine."

Jim shook his head in disbelief. "And he ordered this because you bought a plastic baby bottle for your sister's baby."

"Yes. And for walking to town without permission. Most of all Father is angry at me for challenging the rule."

"It was brave of you to stand up to him," Jim whispered.

"I was brave because I had already decided to leave the farm rather than marry Hosea Hamfist," she whispered back. "Hosea asked Father's permission to marry me, and Father gave it. That is why I asked you to stay. I wanted to tell you what had happened. But Ben saw me waiting. He is suspicious and watches me closely."

"When did your father give his permission?"

"A week ago Saturday. That was why I was upset last Sunday."

"But you're way too young to marry!" Jim said, forgetting to whisper.

"I will be sixteen next month. Mother married when she was sixteen. But I will not marry Hosea!"

"He's old enough to be your father."

"Yes, but Father says that because Thomas is so attached to me, it is my duty to marry his father, and now that Father has given permission, Hosea is allowed to speak to me. The house you are working on, Jim, is being built for Hosea and me."

"I know. Well, I knew it was for Hosea and somebody, but I didn't know for certain that the somebody was you."

Heedless of her rising voice, Miriam rushed on. "Hosea is a determined man and he's moving quickly. He has told Father that as soon as he finishes the Chumnik house, he will expect me to settle on a marriage date. It's a sin to say it, but I hate him! I hate Hosea!" By now tears were streaking down Miriam's cheeks. "And I hate Father! Please help me get away, Jim."

Jim put his arms around her. "I'll help you," he whispered. "I promise."

"When I leave the farm, Thomas must come with me," Miriam said.

"You can come home with me," Jim said. "Both of you. They'll never find you in the city."

Miriam looked shocked. "I cannot do that, Jim. I must take Thomas to his mother."

"Rachel? But you don't know where she is."

"Mother knows. She has known for some time where Rachel is."

What a weird family. How many other secrets were there on Majestic Farm? Jim asked why Miriam's mother kept Rachel's whereabouts a secret.

"She has told no one on the farm. She confided in me only after I told her I would leave the farm rather than marry Hosea."

Before Jim could ask where Rachel was, Miriam took both his hands in hers and looked at him imploringly. "If you want to help me, Jim, please, please go to the market on

Saturday. There is a potter there named Patsy who will give you a message for me. You can give me the message when I come to Bliss on Sunday and then we will make the getaway plans." Glancing nervously through the window, Miriam said, "You must go now, Jim. Father has a nap after dinner and will soon come upstairs to his bedroom. You must not meet him on the stairs." Taking Jim's hand, she said, "Quickly! I will show you another way down."

Responding to the panic in her voice, Jim allowed Miriam to lead him to the end of the deck, where she pointed to the corner supporting post.

"I have never done it," she whispered, "but Thomas often shimmies down this post. If you do that, you will avoid the staircase and will not be seen leaving. If you are caught, it will be hard for us both. Look for a path in the woods. It will take you to Bliss."

Jim slid down the post, picking up a splinter on the way down. Casting a quick glance at the kitchen windows, he thought he saw a kerchiefed head. He heard the clatter of dishes. The women were clearing the tables! Jim ducked into the woods and looked for the path Miriam had told him to follow. It wasn't easy to find and he went more than a hundred feet before stumbling on a narrow path half hidden in the undergrowth. He'd found it! He'd found the same path Miriam used when she and Thomas slipped away from the farm on Sundays.

Reaching the oasis of Bliss, he headed for the well and, drawing up water, drank straight from the bucket. Then he went inside and ate three peanut butter sandwiches before flopping down on the sofa bed. But it was too cold for him to stay there without heat. Without heat and with the afternoon stretching ahead, he decided to clean the chimney. He needed to keep busy. Keeping busy would help take his mind off Miriam. Having promised he'd help her, he could do nothing now but wait.

Jim had never in his life cleaned a chimney, but as a boy he'd watched his grandfather clean his. If a tottery old man could clean a chimney, there was no reason why he couldn't do it too. He'd need a ladder to get up on the roof, but there was one in the garage. He'd need a long pole to poke down the chimney, but that was also in the garage, no doubt left by Hector Bliss. Leaning Hector's ladder against the house, Jim monkeyed up, pausing at the third rung from the top to survey the steep roof. He could see that to reach the chimney safely he'd either have to lasso a rope around it and hoist himself up or—as his grandfather had done—build steps onto the roof to give himself a foothold. Deciding steps would be safer, he nailed wood chunks onto the roof twelve inches apart and crawled across the shingles, holding Hector's pole with its ingenious bundle of rags tied to one end. Once he reached the chimney, he stood up and held onto it while he removed a framed screen from the top.

Lately, Jim had been paying close attention to ingenious tools Hector had made—the screen was another. A teacher, Jim thought, but a practical do-it-yourself kind of man. As Jim worked the pole up and down, he was impressed that Hector had put a screen over the chimney opening, a screen with holes large enough to let out the smoke but small enough to keep birds from falling in. Nothing to keep out the dust, though, and there was a lot of dust inside the chimney. His first day in Bliss, Jim had removed bucketfuls of dust from the well and the stove. Now, using the pole, he shoved the dust down into the stove. Apart from the dust, there wasn't a lot to clear out, and Jim figured Hector must have cleaned the chimney not long before leaving Bliss. When he was satisfied the chimney was clean, Jim threw down the pole, replaced the screen, backed down the steps and the ladder, and went into the kitchen, where dust was puffing out from inside the stove. Coughing and spluttering, he shovelled dust from the stove into a big pail he'd found in the shed, carried it outside and set it beside the shed door. To avoid the floating kitchen dust, he stayed outside chopping firewood until the haze had settled. Later, after he'd wiped the kitchen table and shelves clean, he took down the tin of matches he'd found weeks ago and lit a fire. Jim was impressed that the matches still worked after being in the tin for so many years. Moving the tub beside the stove, he put a pail of water on to heat—with the warm weather gone, he could no longer rely on the sun to heat the water. It took hours to fill the tub with enough warm water for a bath, but it was worth the wait. Jim lay in the tub, enjoying the satisfaction of knowing that he had figured out how to get up on the roof by himself and how to clean the chimney. It was encouraging to think that there were all kinds of practical jobs he could work out on his own. After the bath, Jim washed his grungy clothes and hung them up to dry behind the stove, where there was another of Hector's inventions: two lines, a short one for socks and underwear and a longer one for pants and shirts.

Some of the dust had sifted into the cupboards, so Jim heated more water and washed the dishes, as well as the pots and pans that hung on hooks on the wall beside the sink. No doubt the hooks were another of Hector's ideas. As he slipped cheese between slices of bread and slapped them in the frying pan, Jim thought that Hector had probably been the tidy one, with a place for everything. Except for her teacherly handwriting in the school register, Jim decided, Iris was the untidy one. The red roosters he was sure she'd painted on the cupboard doors were lopsided—what Paula would call slapdash—and the knitted washcloths had holes in them where mistakes had been made.

Jim ate his supper thinking about the Blisses, wondering if they were still alive. The month his mother, his sister and he had lived with his grandfather was the only time Jim had spent with a grandparent, his grandmother having died before he was born. Because he'd never known Zack's parents, Jim liked to imagine they might have been like Hector and Iris, who he knew from talking to Lionel and Barbara were kind, gentle people who wanted to be free to live as they chose. Like him, the Blisses had headed for the wide-open prairie, thinking there would be plenty of space to live as they wanted. It occurred to Jim that the pastor had chosen the Prairies to build Majestic Farm for the same reason. The problem was his mind wasn't open like the Blisses', or open like the land. Both Majestic Farm and the pastor's mind were closed so that he could control everyone living there, which meant that no one on the farm was free.

Although Asa had told him he'd be kept on after the Hamfists' return, Jim had no intention of sticking around and resolved that tomorrow would be his last day working on the farm. He liked Asa and had enjoyed learning about how to build a straw-bale house, but even if Asa coaxed him to stay on, after he was paid tomorrow Jim would never set foot on Majestic Farm again. The pastor was a self-righteous dictator who treated his daughters like slaves. There was no way Jim was going to hang around and watch Hosea bully Miriam into marrying him, and after he'd helped her get away, he'd clear out of Bliss too. Without Miriam, he didn't want to be anywhere near Majestic Farm; he was returning tomorrow only to be paid for the work he'd done.

Before going to bed, Jim filled a pail of water and set it on the warm stove so the water wouldn't ice over during the night. Then he set the alarm to wake him in the morning—with the cooler weather, the songbird no longer sang in the mornings and, he hoped, was safely on its way to someplace warm.

17

In the morning Jim went to work as if it was a normal workday, though nothing on Majestic Farm seemed normal—if it ever had. Sitting in his usual place in the meeting hall, he went through the motions of eating breakfast, chowing down bacon and eggs, all the while thinking of Miriam confined to her room, wondering if someone was bringing her breakfast. Yesterday's meeting with her had been so rushed there was no time to ask if she was being fed. He couldn't remember seeing dishes or food in her room. Also, there had been no mention of his having to avoid someone delivering food to the sisters. Miriam looked thinner, but maybe it was the baldness, not starvation, that made her appear skinny. Jim told himself that Chana would be sure her daughters were fed.

The sight of the pastor stuffing himself at the head table filled Jim with disgust and he pushed away his half-eaten breakfast and hunched forward, elbows on the table, which was no doubt against the rules.

Ten minutes later, when they were walking to the barn beneath a leaden sky, Asa asked Jim how he was feeling. Having forgotten yesterday's lie, Jim was startled by the question. "What?" he said.

"You weren't feeling too good yesterday."

"I was stomach sick, but I'm better now," Jim said. Another lie, but a small one. The way he looked at it now, his being here on the farm was a bigger lie. It was dishonest to make straw bales for a house Hosea intended to live in with Miriam; it was honest to do what he could to prevent her living in the house with Hosea.

Before entering the barn, Asa glanced at the grey sky, which seemed to have dropped like a ceiling during breakfast. He sniffed the air. "Smells like snow," he said.

"Isn't it early for snow? We're not even close to winter."

"You don't know prairie weather," Asa replied. "On the Prairies, we can get hail, drought, snow, rain just about any time. A few years ago, August was the only month it didn't snow. Fact is, except for the wheat farmers hereabouts, we need snow. There's been no rain all summer, and you know from digging the cistern that the ground is bone dry. We haven't had rain for so long that last night I mistook the sound of my wife taking a shower for rain." He sniffed the air again and said, "Yup, I sure hope it snows."

Moments later, a few desultory flakes drifted down. Jim laughed when Asa held out his hand and lapped up the snow. "Manna from heaven," he said with his gap-toothed grin. Within minutes the snow had stopped and there was no evidence that any had fallen.

Once they were inside the barn, Jim was eager to begin work so that he wouldn't have to talk. He was feeling two-faced about Asa. More than anyone else on the farm, Asa had been kind and helpful, and Jim hadn't told him this was their last day working together. He knew Asa was hoping he might stay on for a while, but there was no way Jim could tell him he was quitting because his father-in-law was about to ruin Miriam's life.

After dinner, the pastor suddenly appeared in the barn as if Jim's thoughts had conjured him up. From time to time Jim had glimpsed the pastor strolling about the farm to watch others going about their chores, but this was the first time the old man had stopped to watch Jim and Asa working. For a long while he stood in the barn entrance, so silent and still that he reminded Jim of the giant marble frog in the middle of a lily pond in one of the mansion gardens where he'd worked. With his granny glasses, the pastor seemed to be looking in two directions at once, like the frog. He stood sideways so that he could see what was going on outside while keeping an eye on Asa and Jim. Jim wondered how long Miriam's father could stand there without speaking.

Finally the pastor spoke. "I came to have a word with you, Jim," he said.

Determined not to fall under the old man's spell, Jim said nothing but continued working, snipping off a length of wire.

"Put down the cutters," the pastor said in the mild-mannered way he'd used on Jim's first day on the farm, when he'd told him to take off his sunglasses and hat.

Reluctantly, Jim set the wire cutters aside. "A word about what?" he asked, keeping his voice neutral. The thought crossed Jim's mind that he'd been seen entering or leaving Miriam's bedroom yesterday and his heart skipped a beat.

"About your future with us," the pastor said.

Was that all? Jim snickered with relief.

"Here on Majestic Farm," the pastor continued. He was watching Jim closely. "Asa tells me you are a hard, steady worker, and that is exactly what we need on the farm—another hard, steady worker."

"It's a job." Jim shrugged.

"If you were to remain with us," the pastor went on, "we might build you a straw-bale house one day." This was the smooth-talking pastor, not the angry patriarch who had sentenced his daughters to baldness and a week's confinement.

Keeping his voice firm, Jim said, "I won't be staying. Today is my last day on the farm." He couldn't look at Asa.

The pastor moved closer and, peering up at Jim with genuine curiosity, asked, "And why is that?"

"It's time I left," Jim said.

"And where will you go?"

"For now, I'll stay in Bliss."

"By yourself?"

"Yes."

"But why would you stay there when you can enjoy the comfort of a well-run farm?

"Why would I stay in Bliss?" *Keep your cool,* Jim told himself. *Keep your cool.* "Because I like it there."

"But alone?"

"I like being alone."

"Bliss is not a suitable place for a young man to live alone. A young man needs the company of others," the pastor said. A preaching tone had crept into his voice. "Moreover, the Bliss house is run-down and in a state of collapse. There's no water system and the place is a fire trap. You would be far better off living in our dormitory with other young men." The mouth opened even wider in what was meant to be an encouraging smile.

Jim knew that the only way to get the old man off his

back was to tell him the truth, or part of it. Putting his height to good use, he looked down at the pastor and said, "I don't want to live in a dormitory and be expected to follow a bunch of stupid rules." The *stupid* was deliberate, intended to offend the pastor, to make him back off.

His words had the opposite effect. "You may think our rules are stupid," the pastor said, his voice unruffled and quietly persistent, "but that is because you do not understand our way of life."

"It grows on you, Jim," Asa said.

"It won't grow on me," Jim said.

"It won't grow on you if you don't open your heart," the pastor replied.

What a joke. Did the old hypocrite think about Miriam's heart when he told her she had to marry Hosea? "I open my heart when *I* decide to," Jim said, "not when someone else decides I should."

At last the pastor got the message. Tilting back his head, he fixed his bulging stare on Jim. "You are a prideful young man," he said, all trace of coaxing and false persuasion gone. "You are at your peril if you do not remember that pride goeth before the fall." When he wanted, the pastor could make his voice as lethal as Ben's.

Jim hadn't intended to say more, but the threat bugged him. "Another thing," he said. "I don't believe all that stuff about you and the LSD guy happened on Majestic Mountain. I think you made up the whole story."

Jim knew he'd hit the mark because for once the pastor had nothing to say. His eyes popped and spit flew out of his mouth as he spluttered, too angry for words. Turning his back on Jim, he left the barn.

"You shouldna done that, Jim."

Out of the corner of his eye, Jim saw a dejected Asa sitting on a straw bale. He knew that he'd offended him, that he was upset by what had been said to his father-in-law.

"Sorry I didn't tell you I was leaving," Jim said.

Asa didn't say a word. He picked up his wire cutters and Jim picked up his. They worked in silence until late afternoon. When they were finished, another row of straw bales was stacked against the barn wall.

The time came to return the gloves. Jim put out his hand. "Thanks, Asa."

But Asa refused to shake hands, and it was only when Jim reached the barn door that he called out to him, "Look after yourself, Jim! It's a dangerous world out there!"

Not as dangerous as it is on Majestic Farm, Jim felt like saying, but he let it go and, head down, crossed the clearing. He was about to mount the veranda steps when he nearly collided with Miriam's brother.

"Didn't see you," Jim said and was making a move to duck around Ben when an arm shot out.

"You have insulted Father and the meeting hall is closed to you. You have been banished from Majestic Farm," Ben said. He shoved a roll of bills into Jim's hand and pointed toward the road. "Now go. I don't want to see you back here. Ever."

"That's two of us."

Ben lifted a fist and for a moment it looked like he was about to throw Jim a punch. Behind him Jim heard someone say, "Let him go." It was Asa's voice. So we're still friends in a way, Jim thought.

As he followed the drive that took him to the road, it occurred to Jim that Asa was more of a man than Ben. He was a human being, and Ben was a robot—a big iron robot with a cold, blank stare. Where Asa had a heart, Ben had a time bomb that could blow up in your face if you made the wrong move.

It was only when he was back in Bliss that Jim discovered the robot had docked him seven dollars for missing an afternoon's work. Jim wasn't surprised. He shrugged with grim satisfaction—no amount of money could persuade him to return to Majestic Farm.

18

Wakened by his watch alarm next morning, Jim dressed quickly in the shivering cold and, pulling on his woollen tuque, jogged to town, thinking that after he'd picked up whatever Patsy had for Miriam, he'd buy himself a warm jacket. He remembered that when he was at the market before, he'd passed a woman standing behind a long table covered with pottery bowls, mugs and pots, on the same side of the parking lot as the Majestic Farm wagon; he hadn't paid any attention to her, but now he figured the woman must have been Patsy.

Though Jim was early, the market was full of early risers like himself, and making his way past them, he went straight to the pottery table. There, smack in the middle of the table, was the sign PATSY'S POTS. Jim couldn't have missed it if he'd tried. He couldn't have missed Patsy, either, because there was only one person behind the table—a bulky, square woman with mashed-potato hair who was talking to a man with a hearing aid and a cane. She was gesturing and laughing, maybe telling a funny story. Two elderly women were also at the table. They looked so much alike Jim thought they must be sisters, maybe even twins. The sisters were picking up various pots and mugs and putting them down, unable to choose. Jim occupied himself by doing the same.

Now that he was looking at the pottery, Jim realized how much he liked the colours—the deep turquoise and a blue the shade of a prairie summer sky. The sky colour was a splash inside the pots, mugs and bowls; the turquoise coated the outsides. There was an assortment of small pots. Two of them had yellow lids with bee knobs on top. Jim picked up one of these.

"You like that honey pot?"

Startled, Jim turned and saw that Patsy was now leaning across the table toward him. The old man and the sisters had moved away.

"I think I'll buy it."

Patsy regarded him through thick bottle-bottomed glasses. "Are you by any chance Jim Hobbs?" Though no one else was at the table, she spoke to him in a hushed, undercover way.

"Yeah, I'm Jim."

"Then I have something for you."

"What?"

Speaking in the same uncover way, Patsy said, "If you give me the honey pot, I'll put something inside it and box it for you."

"Thanks."

"And I'll put in my card for you. It has a little map showing you how to get to my place."

Why did he need a map that showed how to get to her place?

The sisters were back, standing farther along the table, watching closely.

"If you give me the pot," Patsy said again, her voice now crisp and matter-of-fact, "I'll box it for you. Do you want a ribbon?"

"Sure." Jim gave her the pot.

"That will be five dollars."

Jim handed over the money and Patsy began rummaging beneath the table, shifting newspapers and plastic crates, grumbling, "Where did I put that box?" Gone was the businesslike Patsy and in her place was this muddled woman. A glance at the women convinced Jim that Patsy was putting on an act, for the sisters were now watching her, their noses twitching with curiosity. Patsy popped her head above the table and asked, "Did you ladies want something?"

"Oh no!" one of them said. "We haven't decided."

"Let me know when you have," Patsy muttered while continuing to rummage beneath the table. She kept muttering and shifting things around until Jim heard her cry, "Bingo! Here it is!" The sisters looked on while she wrapped the honey pot with tissue, tucked it into the box along with one of her cards and taped the cover shut. Patsy beamed as she handed Jim the box. "There you are, sir!" she said. "I hope you get full use of it."

Full use of it. What exactly did she mean by that?

Putting the box in the canvas bag slung over his shoulder, Jim was about to move away when Patsy clapped a hand to her mouth, "I almost forgot!" she said. Nodding toward the table on the far side of the parking lot, she went on, "There's a woman named Chana at the Majestic Farm table who told me that you are to go over there. She wants to give you something." Patsy winked, as if to say, *You know I'm not a ditzy dame.*

Jim played along, "Okay," he said, and leaving Patsy with the nosy sisters, he found his way through the Saturday crowd. He'd planned to avoid the Majestic Farm table, but if Chana wanted to see him, there must be a good reason. After what had happened yesterday, he didn't think the robot would let him anywhere near his mother, but Ben wasn't there, at least not in sight.

While he waited behind the old man who was talking to Chana, Jim studied the display of baking goods, preserves and knitting. He didn't remember seeing knitted mittens and sweaters being displayed before. Obviously the cooler weather had brought them out.

The old man left with a loaf of bread. Stepping forward, Jim asked for two loaves of bread. "I've got used to your baking," he told Chana.

She gave him a warm smile. "That will be two dollars, Jim."

He handed her the coins and picked up the bread.

Chana said, "I couldn't help but notice that you bought a honey pot and I want to give you this jar of honey."

Miriam's honey. "I can pay for it," Jim said, digging into his pocket.

"But I want to give it to you as a token of my thanks for all your help."

Your help. What kind of help? Did she mean the help he'd be giving Miriam? Jim didn't ask. Although Ben wasn't around, a stern-faced woman with *Zelda* stitched on her white apron was standing close by. Ben's wife. The woman who had shaved Miriam's and Faria's heads. Chana smiled as she placed the jar of honey in Jim's hand. "Take it, please."

"Thanks," Jim said, and stowing the honey and bread in the canvas bag, he left the market and headed straight for Marilyn's Café. The parking lot outside the café was filled with half-ton trucks and two cars, a black Impala and the red Cavalier. Although the café was crowded with Saturday shoppers stopping for coffee, Jim's usual booth near the washrooms was empty, and immediately he claimed it. While he waited for a bacon-and-egg breakfast, he unwrapped the honey pot and, peeling back the tape, lifted the cover. The message he'd expected to find was tucked inside. Pulling out the folded note, Jim hesitated, asking himself if he should read it. He wanted to read it, but the message wasn't for him. It was for Miriam, and she hadn't told him to read it, only to pick it up. Reluctantly he shoved the note into the pot and took out the business card with PATSY'S POTS written in blue letters on one side. Turning the card over, he saw a map printed on the back. A black line followed the highway west for forty miles then went south for eight. A small blue sign, PATSY'S POTS, marked the turn. Pocketing the card, Jim taped the box cover back in place. Miriam's sister Rachel hadn't gone far. She was at Patsy's. Why else would Patsy have given him the card?

Marilyn brought Jim his breakfast. Famished, he ate quickly before heading to the general store, where he picked out the cheapest jacket he could find and a pair of gloves—remembering the idiotic mittens Paula had made him wear when he was a kid, he hadn't been tempted by the knitted mittens displayed at the market. After stowing the groceries with his other purchases, he left town wearing his new clothes, which he kept on even after he was back in Bliss. He lit the stove, and while the kitchen warmed up, he stretched out on the sofa bed beneath the blanket and went to sleep.

═

Hunger woke him late afternoon, and after eating a tin of stew mopped up by a crust of fresh bread, Jim changed back into his old clothes and went outside to split wood. He had a stash of wood in the wood box beside the door, but it wouldn't last longer than a day or two. Having dismissed the pastor's condemnation of the house as a fire trap, Jim intended to keep the stove going until morning. Also, with the biting cold, he'd need enough wood to last him for the next few days. Stepping outside, he noticed the pail of dust he'd shovelled from the stove. This wasn't the tin pail he used for hauling water but another he'd found in the shed. Better dump the dust somewhere, though not too close to the house. Pail in hand, he passed the schoolhouse and continued to a corner at the very back of the property, where he could empty the pail without the dust making its way back to the house. Wading through crabgrass and stinkweed, he'd almost reached the broken-down fence in the back corner when he stumbled into a hole made by an animal of some kind. Because the mouth of the hole was wide and the mound of dirt beside it almost a foot high, the animal who'd dug this hole had to be bigger than a mouse or a gopher. Jim's first thought was to dump the dust into the hole but he changed his mind. The hole must lead to the animal's den. Why block the entrance? He was looking around for another place to empty the pail when something red caught his eye. Parting the crabgrass with his foot, he saw a large rectangular cookie tin, what Paula called a biscuit tin. He set down the pail of dust, picked up the tin and shook it lightly. Something rattled inside. He tried to pry off the lid, but after scraping off the dirt, he saw it had been secured with bands of tightly wound wire. He noticed something was written on the lid, but because of the wire and the caked dirt stuck to it, he couldn't make out what it said.

Back at the well, Jim hauled up one bucket of water after another and poured them over the tin. Fetching a screwdriver from the shed, he scraped away the dirt crusted on the lid. Gradually letters took shape and he saw that words had been painted on with black enamel and that in scraping off the dirt, he'd damaged several letters, which made the words difficult to read. But after an hour's careful work, his hands freezing with cold, he'd freed enough letters to read the inscription: *Herein lies the infant son of Gila Godshawk and Will Atkins. Died Nov. 1966.* The words were crowded together on top of the biscuit tin as if they were on a birthday cake, but this was no birthday cake—this was a coffin that had been buried a long time go and was dug up by the animal living in the den. Inside the tin was the baby Barbara Chumnik's brother, Will, had fathered.

Jim's first impulse was to ditch the tin. The thought of what was inside creeped him out and he wanted to get rid of it fast. After all, it had nothing to do with him. But he couldn't just throw away a biscuit tin containing baby bones, could he? It wasn't something he could carry to town and throw in the garbage bin outside Marilyn's Café.

Jim sat on the step and tried to think what to do with it. He'd have to rebury the tin, but where? It was beginning to grow dark and he'd need plenty of light to dig a grave. There was no way he was keeping the tin inside the house. The garage, he thought. I'll put it on the workbench for the night and bury it in the morning.

Now that the coffin was out of sight, Jim carried a bucket of well water inside and, when the water was warm, thoroughly washed his hands in an effort to rid himself not only of the dirt from the biscuit tin but of the sad knowledge of what was inside. Sitting in front of the stove, sock feet on the open oven door, he considered what was written on the lid. Why was the baby born in Bliss? Why wasn't it buried on Majestic Farm among the other graves near the stone tower? There were women on the farm to help Gila—her mother and aunts—so why wasn't the baby born there? According to Barbara, the pastor had blamed the Blisses, Iris in particular, for the baby's death and had harassed them, burning their books, killing their chickens, dirtying their well water, until they had packed up and left. Something was missing from the story. Why would Gila come to Iris Bliss for help? Was she running away from the farm when the baby started coming? Did she come to Bliss by chance?

Jim had come to Bliss by chance. If the power accident hadn't trapped him inside the subway, if he hadn't knocked himself out and started walking, if he hadn't walked out of the city and been given a lift by Silas, if Silas hadn't dropped him off in town and advised him to follow the road north, he would never have found Bliss, met a girl, fallen in love and set foot on Majestic Farm. Until he became involved with Miriam, everything had fallen into place so easily that he'd had the spooky feeling he was being led. With everything going so smoothly at the market this morning, the feeling of being led had returned.

Finding the baby's coffin had changed all that. Jim was

spooked all right, not by a feeling of ease but by the feeling that—as Barbara Chumnik had said—Bliss was haunted. He told himself it wasn't logical that a dead baby could haunt a house; the baby's bones weren't inside the house but inside the garage. But the baby might have been born inside the house. It was this thought that was creeping Jim out, that made him think the house might be haunted. But where in the house was the baby born? Upstairs on Iris and Hector's bed? Upstairs would have been cold in November. The baby was probably born downstairs. Was it born on a parlour sofa or on the daybed near the stove? It was this question that haunted Jim. Though the heat from the stove made him sleepy, throughout the night he wrestled with the unknown answers.

═

He awoke stiff and sore, battered by the uneasy sleep. The fire had gone out. The kitchen was ice-cold, and he was hungry. First thing after breakfast he was burying the biscuit tin. He wanted it buried before Miriam showed up. He knew she wouldn't go into the garage, but he'd feel better if it wasn't there. Jim had no intention of telling her about the biscuit tin, at least not today. She was so upset about being married off to Hosea and escaping from the farm that she didn't need to know about his finding a dead baby born over forty years ago.

Jim lit the stove and, after breakfast, ventured into the cold morning air, hands deep in his jacket pockets, head down as he searched for a place to dig a grave. He did this systematically, walking back and forth in straight lines behind the schoolhouse and the garage, gradually working his way to the back of the property, on the lookout for an animal hole—with the jungle of grasses and weeds, it would be easy to step into another one.

He was approaching the den when he saw something brown scuttle into the hole and disappear. The animal had a thick, wide body and moved close to the ground. Although Jim didn't know what it was, he knew enough, given its size, to leave it alone. He was backing away from the den when he noticed what looked like a stick of wood lying in the long grass where the animal must have tossed it. Picking it up, he realized it wasn't a stick but a small cross whittled from a single piece of wood. There was nothing marked on it, no writing or inscription of any kind; if there had ever been words, they had long since weathered away. He slipped the cross into his pocket.

Abandoning the jungle growth, Jim made his way to the garden. The weeds were thick here, too, but less so, and not as deeply rooted because the decaying wood border kept them at bay.

The place he chose for the grave was beside a huge rhubarb plant gone to seed, its plumed stalks towering over the giant leaves. Fetching the shovel and biscuit tin from the garage, Jim began digging. The first foot was easy going, but as he'd discovered when excavating the cistern, when he dug deeper he encountered large rocks. But he persevered, wanting the tin coffin to be well buried. When the grave was deep enough, he put the biscuit tin on the bottom and shovelled in the dirt, tamping it down with the shovel. Then he piled rocks on the grave, anchoring the wooden cross on top. He stood, uncertain what to do next. The only thing he'd buried before in his life was a pet gerbil that died when he was six. This was different. He was burying the remains of a human baby. Should he pray, and if so, who would he pray to? To God? Jim's idea of God wasn't in the earth but in the universe, somewhere in the mind that created it. Should he pray for the baby? But the baby had died a long time ago and it didn't make sense to pray for him now, or for the baby's father, Will, who was also dead. He decided to pray for the baby's mother, who might be alive somewhere. Feeling awkward and inadequate, Jim mumbled, "I hope you're okay, Gila, wherever you are."

He put the shovel back in the garage. Then, returning to the grave, he pulled a large rhubarb leaf over the pile of rocks to conceal it.

By now it was mid-morning, which left Jim with just enough time to clean the pot-bellied schoolhouse stove. The stove was so ancient that Jim figured it must have been old when the Blisses bought it. On the stove door was a round window with metal lacework circling the handle that adjusted the draft. It took a while to clean the blackened window. Before he cleaned the stovepipe he had to empty the pail of dust from the kitchen stove, but he did that now, dumping it down the outhouse hole. Why hadn't he thought of dumping it down there before?

Another if, Jim thought. If he'd thought about the outhouse hole earlier, he wouldn't have found the biscuit tin, and if he hadn't found that, there wouldn't be proof of Barbara Chumnik's story. And if he hadn't heard the story, he wouldn't have known the connection between Bliss and Majestic Farm. Taken together, the if's boggled his mind.

19

Jim was eating more toast and honey when he looked out the kitchen window, saw Blackie on top of the well and knew Miriam and Thomas were on their way. Moments later they appeared, Miriam with a white shawl wrapped around her head, Thomas in the farm uniform of black jacket and hat. Rushing out to meet them, Jim was quick to notice that Miriam was shivering with cold—now that she was bald, she was probably feeling the cold more than when she'd had hair. She allowed him to put an arm on her shoulder and guide her toward the house. "It's warm in the kitchen," he said.

"I noticed smoke coming from the schoolhouse stove-pipe. It was thoughtful of you, Jim," Miriam said, giving him a shy smile, "to light the stove so Thomas could use the blackboard."

Shrugging off the praise, Jim looked at the little boy. "You want to draw?" Jim put out his hand and was pleased when Thomas took it. It felt good to be trusted by a kid who seemed not to trust anyone besides his aunt. Jim saw Miriam watching from the kitchen window as, hand in hand, he and Thomas walked to the schoolhouse. A secret grin tugged the corners of the little boy's mouth. Jim thought it was a grin of delight that came from Thomas's knowing that the stove had been lit especially for him. As soon as Jim opened the schoolhouse door, the kid made a beeline for the desk and, taking out several chalks, immediately began to draw, almost in a frenzy, as if he already knew the picture he wanted to make.

Jim found Miriam sitting in the rocker by the stove. She had unwrapped the shawl and now it draped her shoulders, soft as snow. "I didn't bring any food," she said. "Yesterday was the first day I was allowed out of my room."

"Did anyone bring you food, or were you expected to get by on bread and water?"

"Bread and water."

How could the old man be so heartless?

"Mother brought us food. And I always keep a jar of honey in my room."

"Yesterday at the market your mother gave me a bottle of your honey." Knowing Miriam was desperate to ask if he'd picked up the message from Patsy, Jim couldn't resist a bit of teasing. "It's the best honey I've ever tasted." He nodded to the honey pot on the table. "Whenever I help myself to a spoonful, I think of you capturing bees in—"

"Did you pick up the message?"

"Let's see." Jim opened the cupboard door and, holding up the box, said, "Do you mean this?" He waved the box tantalizingly in front of Miriam. Wordlessly, she snatched it, opened the lid and took out a piece of folded paper.

Jim watched her unfold the note. She read slowly, mouthing the words, as if she couldn't quite decipher their meaning. Without warning, she began rocking back and forth. "I didn't know," she sobbed, over and over. "I didn't know."

"What didn't you know?" Did the message contain what he'd already guessed?

Miriam wiped her eyes with her shawl and handed him the note.

"*I am not far away. I am living at Patsy's,*" the note read. "*Patsy says you and Thomas can stay here.*"

"*Rachel.*"

Beneath her name Rachel had written, "*Destroy this message.*"

Miriam's printed notes looked like a grade-two kid had made them, but right away Jim noticed this note was written in a neatly slanted hand. He returned it to Miriam. "Your sister," he said.

"Yes. My dead sister," Miriam answered with a smile, and Jim realized she'd made a joke.

"Well, that's good," Jim said. "All this time she's been living close by. It's amazing."

Miriam looked dazed, as if the news of her sister's closeness hadn't really sunk in.

Jim told her that Patsy had given him a card with a map on the back showing how to get to her place, that he figured it was no more than an hour's drive. "Why didn't Rachel go farther away?"

"Thomas. He must have been the reason she didn't go far," Miriam said thoughtfully, her voice becoming more certain as she went on. "She must have been waiting for a way to get him off the farm."

"I can see it wouldn't be easy to find a way," Jim said. Unable to communicate with anyone on the farm who might help her—Miriam, for instance—Rachel couldn't just show up one night without warning and whisk Thomas away.

There would be confusion and noise, and for sure she'd be caught. She'd need to work out a foolproof plan.

"Who told you about picking up the note from Patsy?"

"Mother."

Chana. Jim thought Chana probably knew far more than she ever let on. He said, "Then she must have known Rachel was living at Patsy's. Why didn't she tell you before now?"

"I don't know," Miriam said.

You know what other people want you to know—Jim remembered Zack saying that to him. "So that's where you'll go when you leave the farm," Jim said.

"Yes. That is where Thomas and I will go. He must be with his mother."

"No question." Unfortunately, Jim didn't stop there but went on. "Sounds to me like Chana set the whole thing up." He heard the bitterness in his voice, the *what's in it for me.* Lovesick, he was disappointed Miriam wouldn't be accompanying him home, where he could have her to himself—and Thomas, of course. What had he been thinking? As Carla would say, *Grow up!* Digusted with himself for being childish at a time when Miriam was desperate for help, Jim resolved to concentrate on being helpful. "So you want me to drive to Patsy's," he said. Because of the secrecy, Jim knew he would have to drive them to Patsy's himself.

"Yes. I could go there on foot, but it's too far for Thomas to walk quickly. If we aren't quick, we'll be tracked down."

Jim asked when she planned to leave.

"Tomorrow night, when everyone is asleep."

Jim yelped. "Tomorrow night! Why so soon?" He'd expected her to say a few days, even a week. With so little time, how could he find a way of getting the two of them to Patsy's?

But Miriam didn't seem to notice his panic. "Now that my mind's made up," she said, "I want to leave right away. Father will have told Ben that I'm unhappy about marrying Hosea, and now that I am allowed out of my room, Ben will keep a close eye on me. Hosea too. Rachel's leaving is never far from their minds."

"How did Rachel leave the farm?"

"She went off one day and never came back. No one looked for her. If it weren't for Thomas, no one would bother looking for me either, but Ben and Hosea will do everything they can to track down Thomas and bring him back."

"Wouldn't Hosea track you down?"

"Only to find Thomas. Hosea might decide he wants another young woman instead of me. Ben and Zelda have a fourteen-year-old daughter who would suit him better—if he can wait two years." The sarcasm in Miriam's voice was unmistakeable.

Abruptly, Jim asked a question that had been bugging him. "What about Gila?" he said. "What happened to her?"

"I've already told you, I don't know much about Gila," Miriam said impatiently, reminding Jim of Paula's I-don't-have-time-for-this voice. "She died long before I was born. She was my mother's older sister, born to Ruth, Father's first wife. Mother was a child when Gila died."

Jim knew Miriam was annoyed that he was talking about a dead aunt when there were more important things to talk about. Though he couldn't or wouldn't tell her why he'd asked the question, at least now not, Jim's mind was busy with wanting to know. He wanted to know the reason Gila had come to Bliss to have her baby. He wanted to know if, when she was older, Chana had seen the grave marker by the stone tower and had asked how her older sister had died. He wanted to know the secrets Chana kept. With her friendly, open face, she didn't look as if she had many secrets, but Jim was convinced she knew far more than she let on. He was intrigued that Chana was helping her daughter and grandson leave the farm but wasn't leaving herself.

Impulsively, Miriam reached out and took Jim's hand. "We *must* make a getaway plan, Jim. We must."

If anything could take his mind off Chana, it was having Miriam's warm hand in his. Holding it firmly, he agreed that they had to make a plan. "But I'm warning you that I may not be able to get hold of wheels by tomorrow night. It might take longer."

"Wheels?"

"A car or a truck of some kind." Jim felt a flutter of panic in his chest and his mind went totally blank. He hadn't a clue how he could get his hands on a vehicle and was upset that Miriam thought he could get hold of one so fast. Did she think he could just snap his fingers and a vehicle would appear? She had no idea how difficult it would be to get hold of a truck or car. Did she think someone would just hand him a vehicle? *Excuse me, but would you mind if I borrowed your truck for a while? I don't have a driver's licence, but I only want to use it for a few hours.* Reminding himself that Miriam knew next to nothing about the way things were outside Majestic Farm, Jim forced himself to chill out. "I'll work on it," he said.

For a while they sat silently holding hands, the only sound in the kitchen the pot of water steaming on the stove. Jim knew that by promising to help Miriam, he had, as Zack would put it, bitten off more than he could chew. If only he could talk to his father right now. Zack might not have an answer, but at least he would listen. To take the pressure off having to find a getaway vehicle so fast, Jim told Miriam that they had to find a way of keeping in touch in case he couldn't get hold of a vehicle by tomorrow night.

Miriam nodded. "I will send Thomas here tomorrow after supper and you can tell him yes or no."

"But he doesn't speak."

"He'll understand what you say." Miriam smiled. "Thomas is a smart boy, and yes or no isn't very hard." She stood up. "I'd better see how he is."

"I'll make some hot chocolate," Jim said, reluctantly letting go of Miriam's hand. While she went to the schoolhouse, the shawl wrapped around her head, Jim spooned dark powder into three cups, stirred in hot water and, when his visitors returned, handed the cups around. Preoccupied with thoughts of tomorrow, neither Jim nor Miriam spoke, sipping their drinks in silence, Jim standing near the window, staring at Blackie perched on the well. When Thomas had drained his cup, Miriam stood up and the shawl slid to her shoulders. Impulsively, Jim reached out and stroking her bare head, asked if it was sore.

Miriam smiled. "No, but it's itchy. Mother says it will itch until it grows in. She's been shorn several times."

"Why?"

"As you know, Father does not tolerate disobedience, and Mother stands up to him sometimes."

Jim wasn't surprised. Before he could ask how Chana had disobeyed her husband, Miriam began speaking to Thomas. "Listen closely, Thomas," she was saying. "After supper tomorrow, I want you to come here, and Jim will tell you yes or no. You are to come straight back to me and tell me which it is. Do you understand?"

Thomas nodded solemnly and Miriam looked at Jim as if to say, *He understands.*

"One last thing," Jim said. "If I'm lucky enough to get hold of a vehicle by tomorrow night, you and Thomas are to meet me at the farm gate at midnight. Okay?"

"Okay," Miriam said. Jim laughed—it was the first time he'd heard her use the word. "Midnight," she said.

"Give me your hand," Jim said.

Obediently, Miriam gave him her right hand.

"The left hand."

Miriam gave him her left hand. Peeling back her fingers, Jim took Rachel's note and, lifting the stove cover, wordlessly fed it to the fire. A while back Jim had noticed that all this time Miriam had been holding the note in her clenched fist. He wasn't the only one whose thoughts were scattered.

Moments later, he was following Miriam and Thomas past the garage to the edge of the property, Blackie flapping ahead of them. When the three of them had disappeared into the woods of Majestic Farm, Jim turned back, went into the schoolhouse and damped down the fire in the stove. Then he looked at the blackboard, where Thomas had drawn a row of people with sad, mournful faces, the men in their suits and the women in their dresses. They stood shoulder to shoulder, staring out of the picture with hollow eyes. Without exception, every woman in the picture was bald.

20

Jim sat beside the kitchen stove thinking that if he were home now, he'd be making music with Solly and Web in Solly's basement, away from his sister and her friends, who, according to Solly, were hanging out upstairs in her bedroom, painting their nails pink, fooling around with their hair and talking on their pink cellphones. That was the kind of stuff Carla used to do, though pink was never her colour. His sister painted her nails black and dyed her hair screaming look-at-me colour combinations like purple and orange. Jim wished he had his guitar with him now. Making music would calm him down, take his mind off the Big Problem, which of course was getting hold of a truck or car. But he couldn't get his mind off it, could he, until he had solved the problem. There was only one person Jim could think of who might help find a vehicle: Lionel Chumnik. Lionel knew the situation on Majestic Farm, how they treated women and kept too much to themselves. Jim knew if he told him that Miriam wanted to get away, Lionel would help. He might even offer the use of his truck. Didn't he tell Jim that if he ever wanted help, all he had to do was ask? Well, Jim would ask.

Come to think of it, he might also tell Lionel about finding the biscuit tin the animal had dug up. Tell him what was painted on the cover and what was inside. Jim had the overwhelming urge to tell someone about the infant grave, and the only people he could think to tell were Lionel and Barbara. He'd thought of telephoning home and telling Paula or Zack but had dismissed the idea. He'd been living a totally different life from the one his parents knew, a life he couldn't begin to explain, at least not on the telephone.

Zipping up his jacket, Jim struck out for the Chumnik farm at a brisk pace. When he reached their road, he looked over the harvested fields. He could see they weren't totally bare. There was a coarse stubble of wheat poking up from the brown soil, like a memory of the golden crop that only days ago had swayed gently in the slightest breeze. The fields made him think him of the whiskery shadow on Miriam's shaved head, a reminder of the bountiful hair no longer there.

Approaching the farmhouse, Jim first noticed that Lionel's truck was gone. Because of the cooler weather, he hadn't expected to see the old man sitting on the veranda, but he'd expected to see his truck parked beside the blue half-ton and the grey van. If Lionel isn't here, Jim thought, I'll come back later. He was crossing the grass toward the back door when Nikki bounded off the back step and stood barking a few feet away, challenging him to come closer. Jim hesitated, trying to decide what to do, when the door opened and there stood Ted. Although they'd never met, Jim immediately recognized Ted as Lionel's son. They had the same small build, the same bright blue eyes.

Ted knew who Jim was, because right away he said, "You're the young fellow living in Bliss."

"Yeah."

"What can I do for you?"

Jim asked to speak to Lionel.

"He's not here," Ted said, and holding the door open, he invited Jim to come in for a bite of supper. "We always eat early on Sunday," Ted said, "so the kids have time to watch a video before going to bed."

Lured by the prospect of a warm meal, Jim followed Ted through the porch and into the kitchen, where Darlene stood at the stove in a pair of patched jeans, her hair in a ponytail. "Hi," she said. "Are you up for some mac and cheese?"

"Sure, if there's enough."

While Darlene set him a place at the table and served up the food, Ted introduced the kids—Peter, Danny and Gracie—who sat with their knives and forks upright, ready to dive in as soon as their plates landed on the table.

Ted pulled out a chair and Jim sat down. He looked around the cluttered kitchen, at its wooden shelves crowded with stuffed animals, books, family photographs. Postcards were tacked to the wall above.

Jim asked Ted when Lionel would be back.

"End of next week. He and Mom left last Monday on a trip. Won't be back until after the harvest is done. That'll be another week," Ted said between mouthfuls of macaroni. "We still have a large canola crop to bring in."

"But I thought I saw him driving the grain truck," Jim said in an aggrieved voice. "Tuesday night, I think it was."

Darlene grinned. "That was me," she said. "I was driving the truck, and Ted the combine." Getting up from the table, she carried the pot from the stove and spooned out second helpings.

Ted said, "Since his heart attack a few years ago, Dad hasn't been able to help with the harvest. Doctor's orders. Dad did it for so many years that it's hard for him to sit by and do nothing while we work. That's why Mom takes him away."

Jim stopped eating, letting the news set in. Lionel wasn't here. When Jim had visited the old man last Sunday, Lionel hadn't said a word about leaving the very next day. Why had he offered to help if he wasn't going to be here? So much for Lionel's help. Jim knew he had no right to be angry at an old man he hardly knew. It was just that he was in a tight spot right now and the one person he thought he could count on had gone away.

"Grandpa and Grandma are gamblers," Peter piped up. "They're staying at a casino."

"Barb likes to play the one-armed bandits," Darlene explained. "She saves up all year so she can play the gambling machines."

"She often wins," Ted said. "Mom has a way of coming up with the numbers that's downright spooky—picking them off billboards and road signs they pass on the way—and believe it or not, every year she makes enough money gaming to pay for the trip."

Jim couldn't think of a thing to say that wasn't angry, and like the others, he kept his head down while he cleaned up his plate. After the children had left the table, Ted asked Jim if there was a special reason why he wanted to see Lionel. "I mean," Ted said, "is there anything we can do to for you?"

"No," Jim said, "but thanks." Although Ted and Darlene were warm and welcoming, he was wary of asking if one of them would be willing to drive Miriam and Thomas to Patsy's. There was a chance they might be friendly with

Hosea, who had been framing their new house the past few weeks. Also, Ted already knew Hosea was planning on marrying soon, and if he found out he was marrying Miriam, he wouldn't want to become involved. Even if Ted agreed to drive her and Thomas to Patsy's, how could Jim be sure he wouldn't tell Hosea where he'd taken them? There was no way Jim could be sure, no way he could risk asking Ted for help.

"Well, why don't you hang out with us for a while?" Darlene said.

Why not? It would be good to take his mind off the Big Problem.

After eating a bowl of fresh peaches and cream, Jim sat on the living-room floor with the family, his back against the sofa, watching *The Lion King* and taking a handful of potato chips whenever the bowl was passed, like he used to do before Zack left, when he was Peter's age and their family watched television together on Saturday nights. The Chumniks made him homesick for the way his family used to be. They were casual and laid-back, and Jim realized how much he was enjoying himself. They were a normal family—that was what he enjoyed most about them. There was nothing preachy or weird about them. They were friendly and open and didn't live by a bunch of rules. Even though they couldn't help him with wheels, Jim felt better just knowing that Ted, Darlene and their kids were his closest neighbours.

When the video was over, Jim offered to help clean up the kitchen, something he almost never did at home. "I'll do it after the kids are in bed," Darlene said. "I make their school lunches then too. I do them up the night before because we leave so early in the morning." She'd already told Jim she worked as a teacher's aid at the children's school.

Jim said he'd be heading back to Bliss. Ted followed him to the porch and opened the door. "Move, Nikki," he said. Reluctantly the dog got up from the outdoor mat.

From the doorway, Ted nodded toward the house under construction behind a stand of poplar trees. "If you want to see through the new house," he said, "come on over some day and I'll show you around."

Outside, walking past the truck and the van, Jim realized that he might be able to use either one as a getaway vehicle by driving it himself. He knew how to drive. Two summers ago, Zack had rented a Jeep so they could hang out together at a fishing camp north of the city. They didn't catch any fish, but Zack taught him how to canoe and how to drive the Jeep. Zack's teaching method was to hand Jim the keys to the car and tell him to drive while he sat on the passenger side, a long arm draped over the seat. Occasionally he offered some instruction or made a comment about the clutch or the brake; other than that he said little except to tell Jim he was doing fine. Although he hadn't driven since, Jim figured he could manage to drive as far as Patsy's. The problem was that he was too young to qualify for a driver's licence, and without one, he couldn't borrow either the truck or the van. And how could he get hold of the keys without alerting Nikki? The dog would definitely wake Ted and Darlene, who would call the police. Without a driver's licence, he couldn't rent a vehicle from the small car rental business he'd seen near the service station. By expecting him to help her get away from the farm, Miriam had put him in an impossible position. But he wasn't about to give up. Finding the biscuit tin had fired up his determination to help her escape from Hosea. If she stayed on Majestic

Farm, Miriam would have a miserable life. Somehow he would find a way to help free her from being forced to live with Hosea.

The red Cavalier for sale in the parking lot outside Marilyn's Café. Why hadn't he thought of it before? He couldn't buy it, but if he found out who the seller was, maybe he could talk the owner into renting it to him for a few hours. It was worth a try.

With the heavy cloud cover overhead, it was already getting dark when Jim hoofed it to the café, as usual not a single vehicle passing him on the road. Marilyn's Café was closed on Sundays, but after picking off the telephone number on the For Sale sign in the Cavalier window, Jim went to the pay phone and dialled. A familiar voice answered.

"Is that you, Marilyn?"

There was a rich throaty laugh. "Yes, Jim, it's me," she said—she knew who he was right away. "What can I do for you?"

"I'm interested in the Cavalier that's for sale."

"You want to buy it?"

"Sort of."

"Sort of? You'd better come upstairs."

"Upstairs?"

"My apartment is above the café," she said. "Look up!"

Jim did and saw her waving at him from a window above—he'd known there were offices on the second floor, but he hadn't known anyone lived up there.

"The door's open. I'm at the top of the stairs."

Marilyn was waiting for him in the apartment doorway. Soon Jim found himself in a living room where pictures of horses and buffalo hung on the walls.

"Take a seat," she said, pointing to a beat-up leather sofa. She sat on the other side of a low table that was the same kind of knotty pine as the café booths. She was wearing the now-familiar black sweats and bird-feather earrings. She said, "Am I to understand you're serious about buying the Cavalier?"

"Does it work?" Jim asked. He couldn't risk driving a car that was likely to break down.

"It wouldn't be for sale if it didn't," Marilyn said. "The muffler's starting to go, but for a ten-year-old car it's in good shape."

"How much do you want for it?"

"It's my son Jeff's car and he's open to offers."

"The thing is, I want to use it only once."

"You mean you want to rent it?"

"Yeah. I want to rent it for tomorrow night."

"Then you don't plan on going far."

Jim had worked out the distance. "No more than an hour's drive."

Marilyn fingered an earring in silence before asking Jim his age.

"Fifteen. But I'm close to sixteen."

"And you want me to rent the car to someone underage."

Jim rushed on before he lost his nerve. "I'm too young to have a driver's licence, but I know how to drive. Like I said, I don't want to keep the car. I only want to use it for tomorrow night."

"Do you have a girlfriend? Is that why you want it for tomorrow night?"

"I don't exactly have a girlfriend," Jim said, "but there's this girl who needs to get from one place to another. I said I'd help her, and she's depending on me."

"Is she in some sort of trouble?"

Jim thought this over before answering. "I guess you could say that. She's . . ." Jim hesitated, wanting to tell Marilyn the truth about Miriam's situation but stopping himself on time.

"She wouldn't happen to be from Majestic Farm, would she?" Marilyn knew Jim worked on the farm.

Jim felt Marilyn's eyes on him. *Don't answer. Nobody, but nobody, can know the plan.*

"I'll tell you what," Marilyn said, getting to her feet. "We'll go for a drive and then I'll decide what I'll do about the car."

Outside, she unlocked the Cavalier, handed him the keys and got in on the passenger side. Remembering Zack's advice, Jim sat in the driver's seat and took a close look at the car, which was a standard shift like the Jeep. He remembered Zack telling him that he'd failed his first driver's test because he hadn't taken the time to examine the car closely and had turned on the windshield wipers instead of the lights. Zack said that most cars were more or less alike but had small differences that could confuse a driver if they weren't checked out.

Jim asked Marilyn where she wanted him to drive. Waving a hand toward the general store she said, "Hang a right just past the store, follow the road to the end and hang another right."

Jim followed her instructions while she sat with her hands in her lap. Like Zack, she seemed completely relaxed with him at the wheel of the car, which made him feel good.

After they circled the town in the half dark, Marilyn had Jim drive on the highway, five miles one way and five miles the other before they returned to the parking lot in front of the café and he switched off the engine. Jim knew his driving was better than okay, but he also knew that if Marilyn let him use the car, she'd be breaking the law. He waited for her to tell him if he could rent the car. When she didn't say anything one way or another, he handed Marilyn the keys.

She waved them back. "You keep them, Jim. Give them back to me when you've finished—" she paused— "being the Good Samaritan."

"You're trusting me," Jim said, amazed and relieved. Marilyn hardly knew him, but she was lending him the Cavalier.

"To a point. I'm willing to give you a break. But," she said, her voice hardening with a warning, "if you don't return the car after you're done your"— she paused—"your mission, I will call the police and report a missing vehicle. You'll be charged with driving a stolen car without a licence. The police, Cathy and Greg, are friends as well as regular customers of mine. They won't buy the line that I loaned you the car."

Jim understood that Marilyn was making it clear that *he* was taking the risk, not her. She said, "You understand?"

"Yeah. I understand."

Marilyn gave one of her throaty laughs. "I'm a tough old bird," she said and opened the door partway. "Now I have to skedaddle. My boyfriend always cooks me supper on Sunday."

She got out of the car holding the For Sale sign, and leaning across the seat, she said, "Don't drive on testosterone and you won't be stopped. Cathy and Greg are too busy to bother with the likes of you. When you're finished, leave the keys under the floor mat."

Marilyn had gone inside before Jim realized he'd said nothing about paying for the use of the car. Not wanting to bug her anymore, he told himself he'd settle up later on. He drove slowly past the service station without stopping. The gas tank was three-quarters full and he'd top it up tomorrow night, after he'd finished delivering Miriam and Thomas to Patsy's. Easing the car onto the dirt road, he followed it to Bliss, where he put the Cavalier in the garage and closed the doors, satisfied that the borrowed car was safely hidden.

It was only when he was heating a tin of beans for a late snack that Jim remembered he'd forgotten to phone home. Though he knew Paula and Zack would be expecting his call, he was unwilling to leave Bliss. Unlikely as it was that anyone would come snooping, he didn't want to risk leaving the Cavalier unguarded. Only hours ago he'd been at a loss as to how to get his hands on a getaway vehicle, and he couldn't quite believe there was one hidden away in the garage. There was no way he was going to push his luck by returning to town tonight. Again he was spooked by the thought that things were falling into place so easily that it was as if he was being led.

21

Even with the Cavalier safely stowed in the garage for tomorrow night's rescue, Jim lay on the daybed anxious and awake, his mind doing somersaults as he went through the getaway plan. Over and over he repeated the directions to Patsy's, which he'd read and reread before feeding her card to the fire: forty miles west on the highway, eight miles south from the turn. Simple directions. An easy drive. He'd be driving in the dark, but he'd checked the car lights and they worked okay. Once again he reminded himself that, as Marilyn said, if he didn't do anything stupid, the police wouldn't stop him. So why was he panicking? He was panicking because Miriam's escape depended entirely on him, and if he failed to deliver, he'd be letting her down. The directions was simple, but the job of delivering her and Thomas safely to Patsy's was anything but, and it loomed on the horizon like an impossible mission. It was the possibility that the mission might fail that was keeping him tense and awake. It wasn't until the stars disappeared into the dawn that he finally fell asleep.

Cold feet woke him at noon. He'd worn socks to bed, but the blanket had slid to the floor and the stove had long since gone out. With a nightmare of a vanished car fresh in his mind, he pulled on his clothes, dashed outside and opened the garage doors. The car keys were inside his jeans pocket; but even so he had to make sure the Cavalier was inside the garage, which it was. Closing the doors, Jim returned to the house under a brooding sky. He kindled the fire, heated water and made himself a breakfast of hot chocolate and honeyed toast, which he ate sitting beside the stove, sock feet propped up on the open oven door.

Licking his fingers clean, he picked up *Treasure Island.* With the rest of the day to put in, he was glad to have something to read that would take his mind off the escape. Flicking through the book, he found his place in the story, which had now shifted to Jim Hawkins's friends: Doctor Livesey, Squire Trelawny and Captain Smollett. The three men had decided that their chances were better if they abandoned ship and went ashore, where there was a spring of fresh water inside a stockade. The pirates were already camped on the island, waiting for the chance to capture Jim and his friends—they didn't know Jim was at the other end of the island with Ben Gunn.

A slow, careful reader, Jim took a break every few pages to add wood to the fire or make a snack, and it was the middle of the afternoon when he reached the part of the story where Jim Hawkins turned up at the stockade with Ben Gunn. Not long after, the one-legged pirate, Long John Silver, came to the stockade and tried to persuade Captain Smollett to hand over the treasure map. Long John Silver was two-sided, a dictator one minute and a soft talker the next, but the captain saw through him and sent him packing. Soon open war was declared, and the pirates, as agile as monkeys, climbed the stockade; but after a fierce fight they were forced to withdraw.

Late afternoon, Jim put on his jacket and tuque and went outside to split more wood. By now the woolly clouds were thickly packed with unfallen snow. It was windless, the air eerily still. The thwack of the axe biting the wood echoed in Jim's ears. As he worked, it began to snow, but slowly, the flakes intermittent, as if they were being shaken through a strainer. The flakes were so small they left no mark on the ground, and it was only when bigger flakes gathered on his jacket that Jim knew the snow was serious and he cast a worried look at the clouds. If it kept on snowing like this, the roads would be slippery tonight. Setting aside the axe, he opened the garage door and rechecked the Cavalier's tires. They were worn smooth, which meant they would slip and slide on a snowy road, and if the snow continued, he'd have to be extra careful driving. Closing the garage door, he picked up the axe and went on splitting wood. To his relief, by the time he had stacked the wood inside the shed it had stopped snowing.

Jim was making himself grilled cheese sandwiches for supper when through the kitchen window he saw Blackie alight on top of the well. Soon Thomas was crossing the yard, every so often glancing over his shoulder as if he was fearful of being followed. Immediately Jim went out and led him inside while the crow stayed on the well top, where he could keep an eye on the little boy. When Jim asked if he was hungry, Thomas shook his head no.

"I have a car in the garage," Jim said. "I'll meet you tonight at midnight. The car will be on the road in front of the farm gate. Come on, I'll show it to you." Hand in hand they crossed the yard.

Jim opened the garage doors and for the second time was rewarded by a skittery smile, this one lighting up half of Thomas's face. Probably the kid has never been in a car before, Jim thought. He opened the door and watched the little boy run his hand over the worn vinyl upholstery.

"This car will be on the road in front of the farm gate at midnight," Jim said. "You understand?" He was repeating himself, but he wanted to make sure the kid got it right. Thomas bobbed his head enthusiastically and it occurred to Jim that he wanted to leave the farm as much as Miriam did. Confident the little boy had got the message straight, Jim dismissed the earlier thought of having him deliver a note to Miriam. Thomas was smart. And he could draw. If necessary, he could draw her a picture of the car. Far better to rely on a drawing than to risk giving Thomas a note. If a note was intercepted, their plan would crash and Miriam would never get away. Her life would be totally ruined.

Closing the garage door, Jim walked Thomas to the end of the property, where he watched until the boy and his crow had disappeared into the woods. Luckily, any snow that had fallen had melted away Thomas's footprints. Passing the schoolhouse, Jim remembered the drawing on the blackboard and, picking up the brush, wiped the board clean, but not before taking a last look at the row of hollow-eyed men and women with sad, mournful faces, the women with their bald heads. The kid didn't speak, but his imagination was awesome. Too bad he had to get rid of the drawing, Jim thought. Wetting a rag at the well, he wiped away the evidence that Thomas had been there.

After supper, he added wood to the stove, found his place in *Treasure Island* and again settled down to read. Jim

Hawkins had slipped away from the stockade, found a hidden jolly boat and paddled out to the *Hispaniola,* where two drunken pirates were now guarding the ship. Under the cover of night, Jim was able to cut the hawsers without being seen, and he set the ship adrift. The story was exciting and Jim read on, pausing only to light the kerosene lamp as night drew in. He was so engrossed in the story that he forgot the time. He also forgot the fire. And to look out the window. It was only when he went outside to use the outhouse that he realized he was walking through snow. All the while he'd been reading about a tropical island, the snow had been quietly, stealthily falling, and it was already deep enough to make footprints. The snow was alarming: not only would it make driving more dangerous, but it meant he would leave tire tracks behind. Jim stared anxiously at the falling snow, willing it to stop, but it continued its steady descent.

Inside the kitchen, he added more wood to the fire and looked at his watch: eleven o'clock—one hour to go. He made himself a cup of hot chocolate and sat thinking about the risk he was about to take. Here he was, a long way from home, squatting in an abandoned house and about to drive someone else's car without a licence to a place he'd never been in order to help two people disappear from a weird religious cult. Just the thought of the rescue made Jim's stomach churn and his neck hair stand on end. But his determination to help Miriam never wavered, even for a second. He'd promised to help her, and he would honour that promise. Carla could say what she wanted about him, that he was unreliable, irresponsible and lazy. Sometimes he had been those things, mainly because he was bored. Well, he wasn't bored now. Even Carla would be impressed if she knew what he was about to do.

22

Well before midnight, Jim was standing beside the Cavalier on the snowy road in front of Majestic Farm, the motor turned off to kill the engine noise while he used a beat-up scraper he'd found in the trunk to keep the snow from piling on the windows. With the headlights turned off and the snow coming thick and fast, he couldn't see farther than thirty feet in any direction. The Chumnik farm was completely wiped out, as were the woods beyond the fence. Though he could barely make out the farm gate, he kept staring at it, expecting to see Miriam and Thomas come through it at any second. He willed them to hurry. At this time of night it was unlikely a vehicle would drive past, especially in the snow, but if one happened along, he didn't want them to witness Miriam and Thomas's escape. It was important they vanish without a trace.

As the minutes crawled past, he kept glancing at his watch, trying to hurry up the time. Ten minutes dragged by, fifteen. By the time twenty minutes had passed, Jim was sweating beneath his jacket. What if someone had caught Miriam and Thomas trying to escape? What if they were locked inside her room? What if Miriam had changed her mind and for some reason decided she wouldn't leave? By the time thirty minutes had passed, Jim had convinced himself that she'd chickened out and wasn't coming, and he was angry at her and at himself for agreeing to help her out. To calm himself down, he began talking aloud. "Don't panic. Give them thirty more minutes. Thirty more minutes and if they don't show up, I'm out of here." Since meeting Miriam he'd spent hours and hours waiting for her and now he was fed up, especially at himself. Stomping his feet against the ground to keep them warm, he felt like a geek standing on a prairie road in the middle of the night in a snowstorm, waiting for a girl he hardly knew to show up with her nephew. The longer he waited, the geekier he felt. Only the king of geeks would freeze to death waiting for a girl who belonged to a wacko cult run by a man who followed some crazy drug guru up a mountainside. "You're crazy too," Jim told himself, "to have let yourself get mixed up with that bunch of weirdos."

He continued talking to himself and stomping his feet until a strange and wonderful thing happened. Abruptly, at one o'clock, the snow stopped, the clouds opened and, tilting his head, Jim looked straight up into the universe, where the stars pulsed and shimmered with light. He stood there gazing at the stars as if they were the most miraculous thing in the world. He'd been standing there maybe five minutes when movement to the left caught his eye, and looking toward the farm gate, he saw Miriam and Thomas hurrying down the driveway toward the car. He was so relieved and happy to see them that he looked into the vastness above him and thought, Thank you, God. It didn't matter to Jim whether God was the universe or the universe was God's idea. What mattered was that Miriam and

Thomas were here at last. A big fat grin cracked Jim's ice-cold face.

Miriam's white shawl was wrapped around her head. One hand held Thomas's, the other a black cloth bag. When they were close, Miriam whispered hoarsely, "I'm sorry, Jim. Mutt began to bark, which he never does. Father wouldn't settle and Mother bid us wait until he'd gone back to sleep. Maybe he knew . . ." Miriam's words trailed off and she began to sob. "I never got a chance to say goodbye to Faria or Mother. All I got to do was wave at Mother and she waved back." Miriam's sobs became full-blown weeping, and putting an arm around her, Jim guided her and then Thomas into the back seat. "It's better for you to sit in the back," he said, having already thought this out. "That way you can duck down if we pass another vehicle. Okay?" He was surprised by his gentleness and felt guilty that he had ever doubted her.

Sliding into the driver's seat, he turned the heat on full blast and eased the car forward. In the rearview mirror, he saw Miriam and Thomas huddled together while she continued to sob. He drove turtle slow, knowing that the last thing they needed was to brake quickly on the snowy road and end up in the ditch. As he went on, he noticed the clouds continuing to lift, and by the time they had reached the edge of town, the cleared sky was spangled with stars. Jim thought he saw the reddish glow of Mars among the stars, but not wanting to take his eyes off the road, he couldn't be sure.

At the intersection where the road met the highway, he saw a truck coming from the east and told Miriam and Thomas to duck down. Jim waited until the truck was well past before turning onto the highway, wanting to keep a long distance between himself and any vehicle travelling on his side of the road. He didn't want a driver's headlights shining into the back seat of the Cavalier, or to be forced to brake suddenly if he was passed. The highway hadn't been cleared of snow, and easing his foot against the brakes to test them, he felt the car slew on the slippery road. Jim checked the mileage so that he could keep track of the distance they would travel west before reaching the turnoff to Patsy's, and braced himself for a long, slow drive. Miriam had stopped crying. To help pass the time and to satisfy his curiosity, he asked her how long Chana had known Rachel was living at Patsy's.

"About a year. Rachel asked Patsy to tell Mother not to reveal her whereabouts to anyone. Mother kept her whereabouts a secret until I told her I was unhappy and had made up my mind to leave the farm. Mother asked if I was certain I was making the right decision for myself—she has always wanted my happiness. I told her I was sure, that I would never be happy married to Hosea. She said she'd do what she could to help me get away. It would be a comfort to her, she said, to know that Rachel, Thomas and I would be together."

"Would Chana ever leave the farm?"

"No," Miriam said, her voice muffled with a sob, and Jim knew that for Miriam the hardest part of leaving Majestic Farm was leaving her mother. "She won't leave my younger sisters and brothers." Miriam's words sounded like they were being strangled from her throat. "And she won't leave the young mothers who depend on her to help deliver their babies. I'll never see her again. Or Faria or Eva. At least I know Eva will take good care of my bees."

This brought another rush of tears and Jim gave up conversation altogether. Too bad the car radio didn't work, he thought, because it would help pass the time. He had fiddled with it earlier but all he could get out of it was static.

The Cavalier had gone thirty-seven miles when a half-ton truck suddenly appeared behind them, travelling fast. "Get down!" Jim shouted, and Miriam and Thomas crouched so low that even he couldn't see them. The truck was tailgating, its headlights flooding the Cavalier. Jim hung onto the wheel and struggled to keep cool, wondering who the driver was and why he didn't pass on the straight stretch of road. Was he trying to see who was inside the car, or was he tailgating for kicks? Jim could see well enough to know that the driver behind him was a man. Improbable as it was, he had to fight down the idea that Ben or Hosea had discovered that Miriam and Thomas had left the farm, had borrowed a truck to hunt them down and that very truck was right behind him, waiting for the chance to force him to stop. Jim was close to convincing himself this was the truth when the driver pulled out and, passing the Cavalier, raced ahead.

Jim noticed that only one of the truck's tailights was working. He waited until it looked like a cigarette glow before telling Miriam and Thomas they could sit up. Checking the mileage, Jim figured they were about three miles from the turnoff. By now it was two o'clock and at this hour of the morning, it was unlikely they would pass another vehicle before reaching the turn.

"Look for a sign saying PATSY'S POTS," Jim said. Although the starlight reflecting off snow allowed him to see when he reached the turn, he couldn't read the sign nailed to a fence post because blown snow had obliterated the words. Telling himself that the sign had to be Patsy's, Jim turned onto the side road, crawling along because there were dips where the land became more hilly. The farther they went down the road, the more wooded it became, and widely spaced lights appeared through the trees where driveways branched off. "We're getting close," Jim said. "Keep your eyes glued." He couldn't remember Patsy's mentioning another sign, but he figured there would probably be one at the entrance to her place.

And just as the map showed, when they'd gone a total of eight miles from the turnoff, Jim spotted a driveway and a second sign nailed to a fence. It too was snow-covered. Leaving the engine running, he got out of the car and brushed the snow from the sign. PATSY'S POTS appeared in the car headlights.

"We're here," he said, though by now his words were unnecessary because Miriam had read the sign and she and Thomas were bouncing with excitement.

For a quarter mile Jim followed the winding drive through the trees until it opened into a clearing where a low, sprawling house suddenly loomed in the darkness.

"Are they expecting us?" Jim said, disappointed that a door didn't immediately open to welcome them.

"Mother said they are expecting us sometime," Miriam said, "but they wouldn't know for sure when that would be." She didn't sound at all let down, and Jim felt foolish that considering all the risks they'd taken, he had expected Patsy and Rachel to know when they would arrive.

But the dog knew they'd arrived. Jim could hear it barking somewhere inside. It could hardly miss hearing an engine rumbling like an ancient tank in a war movie.

Getting out of the car, Jim marched to the house and thumped on the door with Miriam and Thomas at his heels, the three of them shivering in the cold night air. Seconds stretched into minutes before an outside light came on. The door opened and Jim saw the second miracle of the night: a slender, dark-haired woman rushing outside and into the arms of her younger sister, both of them laughing and crying, holding Thomas between them while a little white dog ran in circles of excitement.

"You came! You came!" Rachel cried, and kneeling down, she picked up her bewildered son and carried him inside, Miriam following, the dog trotting behind, leaving Jim alone outside.

"Mission accomplished," he said, grinning from ear to ear, happy that the sisters were together and Thomas was with his mother. But as the minutes went by and he seemed to have been forgotten, the smile faded and he stood there feeling more forlorn than pleased. Five minutes passed and still no one appeared to ask him inside. Jim was sure he'd been totally forgotten. After all he'd done to bring Miriam and Thomas here, they had left him standing out here in the cold. How could Miriam forget him so easily?

Thomas's hat. Jim picked it up and, brushing off the snow, wondered if he should take it inside. Undecided, he shifted from foot to foot beneath the glare of the outdoor light, feeling clumsy and out of place and homesick, overwhelmed by the sudden and lonely desire to be at home with his family. He was about to turn around and get into the Cavalier when Patsy appeared in a bulky red bathrobe, her hair so tangled and every which way that it looked like it had been caught in an egg beater.

"Are you going to stand there, or are you coming in?" she said, her voice a mix of kindness and exasperation. "You're cooling off the house."

"I was thinking of leaving," Jim said, putting a hand on his chest—the thought that Miriam had abandoned him had broken his heart.

"Well, you certainly can't leave before you have something to eat," Patsy said bossily. "You look like you could do with a hot meal." She was an entirely different woman from the one he'd met at the market.

Jim shivered. "I'll come in for a while," he said, and still feeling rejected, he added miserably, "but I won't stay long."

23

Taking off his runners as Patsy instructed, Jim stood awkwardly in the hallway. To his left was an open doorway through which he saw Miriam and her sister huddled together on a sofa, arms looped around one another, talking a mile a minute. Neither of them noticed Jim, but Thomas saw him. The little boy sat on the edge of the sofa, his hand in Miriam's. He seemed dazed, as if he couldn't quite believe that the woman beside Miriam was his mother. Jim knew that everything was moving so fast, the poor kid was probably trying to figure out what was going on.

"This way, Jim," Patsy said and he padded after her in his sock feet toward the kitchen at the back of the house. It was a huge room with a mattress-size chopping block in the middle, shelves stacked with pottery dishes and a plank table in front of a large window facing a tangle of trees. There was enough light from the kitchen to see snow-roofed bird feeders hanging from the branches.

"Will you settle for bacon and eggs?" Patsy said.

"Sure."

While Patsy busied herself with the food, she peppered Jim with questions: How was the drive? Were the roads slippery? Was there any traffic? Jim told her there was no other vehicle on the road except one truck heading west.

"Good." She dropped two slices of bread into the toaster. "Then you weren't seen by the locals."

"I don't think so," Jim said and asked if she thought Miriam and Thomas would be safe here.

"They should be," Patsy said, "because the only person besides you who knows where they are is Chana Godshawk. She is a strong woman and will never tell."

From the front room Jim heard excited voices and bursts of laughter.

Patsy slid the bacon and eggs onto a sky blue pottery plate and put it on the table along with a knife and fork. "Eat," she commanded in her no-nonsense way.

Swallowing a forkful of egg, Jim asked a question that had been bugging him for a while. "How come Rachel is staying with you?"

"Well, if you think I'm running a refugee camp, I assure you, I'm not," Patsy said with a grin. "One day a couple of years ago, Rachel showed up on my doorstep, exhausted and starving. She'd been on the run for several days, hiding out in barns and such, so I took her in and taught her how to use the computer. She's become a kind of secretary, handling my email, doing basic bookkeeping, that sort of thing. But she never answers the telephone."

"Why did she come to you?"

"I didn't ask. I guess she came to me because she'd seen me at the market and knew who I was. Also, she knew I was on friendly terms with Chana."

Patsy put a plate of buttered toast on the table, poured two mugs of tea and sat down. "Now, Jim," she said in a way that warned him a lecture was coming. "Now that you're involved with Miriam and Thomas's running away, once you leave here you must not come back. Ever."

"I know."

"And you must not go back to Bliss either. This morning, when they discover Miriam and Thomas have flown the coop, the folks on Majestic Farm will be as nasty as a nest of stirred-up hornets and they'll be all over your place. Bliss will be the first place they'll look. They'll see the car tracks plain as day."

"But they don't know about Miriam and me."

"The car tracks will speak for themselves. Also, you're not one of them and for that reason alone they will suspect you." Placing her elbows on the table, Patsy leaned toward Jim. "Listen closely," she said, "because I'm going to tell you a story Rachel told me. A few years ago, a journalist who was writing a magazine article on religious cults started poking around Majestic Farm. He was very persistent, and when he refused to leave the farm, Rachel said that one of her brothers—Ben, it was—used the hunting rifle to scare him off. Afterwards the journalist reported Ben to the police and they went to the farm to gather evidence, but no one would talk and they couldn't find the rifle."

Jim squirmed in his chair.

"With Miriam and Thomas's disappearance, the folks on Majestic Farm will be out of their minds with rage," Patsy continued, "and if you go back to Bliss, there's no telling what they might do to you."

Until now, Jim had been too busy rescuing Miriam and Thomas to give much thought to being a suspect, but now he was thinking about it big time.

"The fact is, Jim, you're in danger."

Patsy's words upset him and he pushed his plate of uneaten toast aside. He heard a yip and, looking down, saw the fluffy white dog wagging her tail, hoping to persuade Jim to put his plate on the floor.

"That's enough, Mitzi," Patsy said sharply, and the dog retreated beneath the table. "I don't know much about you, Jim, but I know it took a lot of courage to bring these two here tonight. By helping them, you put yourself at risk, and from now on you must think about your own safety. You have to protect yourself." Removing her elbows from the table, Patsy drank her tea, giving Jim time to think.

Though he knew she was right, he was too tired to work out exactly how to protect himself.

Patsy asked him where he was from and he told her the city, and about being knocked out in the subway during the electrical failure and the nurse telling him to stay awake in case he had a severe concussion. "So I started walking west and kept on going."

"Were you unhappy at home?"

"Not especially. But I didn't like the idea of going back to school. And I wanted to take off by myself. Be more independent. See how I could make out on my own."

"Do your parents know where you are?"

"More or less."

Removing her glasses, Patsy looked at Jim, her eyes wonky with fatigue. "They must be worried sick, and if you ask me, when you leave here you should go straight home." There was no denying the concern in her voice. "Do you hear that? *Straight home!*"

"I hear you."

"But for now, you'd better get some sleep. You look dog-tired. How long since you've slept?"

"About fifteen hours. Yeah, I'm beat." Jim had been so revved up he'd ignored his fatigue and was surprised that when he stood up, he had to steady himself against the table. "But I've got to return the car," he said. "I'm driving without a licence and I promised I'd get the Cavalier back as soon as I finished with it."

"A few hours won't make a difference," Patsy said. "The snowplows don't begin work until six and it'll be a lot safer and easier to drive back when the main road has been cleared and sanded. Besides, you shouldn't do any more driving tonight. The plows neglect the side roads and it'll be easier to see in the daylight."

She offered Jim a bed. "I have three grown sons. None of them are here, but their beds still are and you can use one of them to get a few hours' sleep. I promise to wake you at seven." Pushing herself from the table, she said, "Finish your tea while I make up a bed."

Jim wandered into the front room and stood awkwardly in the doorway, still feeling like an outsider. Miriam and Rachel were huddled together at one end of the sofa; at the other end Thomas was fast asleep beneath a blanket, only his pale hair showing. The sisters were speaking quietly, their heads turned toward one another, and it took a while for Miriam to notice Jim. When she did, he said, "I'll be leaving in a few hours. Until then I'm going to crash."

"Crash?"

"I'm going to get some sleep. Patsy's making up a bed." As he turned away, Miriam got up from the sofa and followed him into the kitchen.

"Are you coming back, Jim?" she said, sounding so hopeful that his heart skipped a beat.

"It would be dangerous for you and Thomas if I came back," he said. "I might be followed."

"What will you do? Where will you go?"

"First I'll return the car to Marilyn."

"Who is Marilyn?"

On the drive to Patsy's, Miriam had been so upset about leaving her mother that she hadn't asked a single question about the car, like how he had managed to get hold of it or who it belonged to.

He said, "Marilyn owns the café in town. I borrowed her son's car to bring you and Thomas here."

Miriam looked frightened. "Does she know we're here?"

"No, and I won't tell her. You can trust me."

"I do trust you, Jim. I do."

"After I return the car, I'll be heading home," Jim said.

"Back to the city?"

"Yeah. Back to the city."

"That means I won't see you again," Miriam said. She sounded so forlorn that again his heart skipped a beat.

It was clear that until now Miriam had never given a thought to what would happen to him after he had delivered Thomas and her to Patsy's. But she was thinking about it now. Placing a hand on his arm, she said, "Be careful." Then she kissed him on the cheek. It was a quick, shy kiss, but enough for him to feel the warmth of her lips. "Thank you, Jim. You are my true friend," she said.

True friend. Is that all he was, a true friend?

He was about to tell Miriam he wanted to be more than a true friend when Patsy appeared and announced that the bed was ready. Miriam returned to her sister, and Jim followed Patsy to a narrow room at the end of the hall. "You won't hear a thing in here," she said. Jim must have looked worried because she added, "I promise to wake you at seven."

Jim flopped onto the bed without bothering to remove his clothes and within seconds was out cold.

He didn't come awake until he felt a hand on his shoulder and heard a familiar voice say, "Seven o'clock. Time to get up, Jim." Groaning, he opened his eyes. Patsy was standing beside the bed in her bathrobe. "I've got coffee on, and there's porridge."

She left and Jim staggered out of bed and, after using the washroom, made his way to the kitchen, where his breakfast waited on the table. He ate in silence, the only sounds in the sleeping house the ticking of the pottery clock and the snap of the fire in the wood stove. Even Mitzi was silent, asleep beneath the table, and Patsy herself seemed only half awake. When Jim finished eating, she said, "Don't forget what I told you last night."

"As if I could," he said with a grin. The grin was intended to make light of Patsy's fears but it did nothing to lighten his own. Gulping down the last mouthful of oatmeal, Jim stood up, and thanking Patsy for the bed and the food, he went out into the inhospitable, bleary morning and got into the Cavalier.

24

At the end of Patsy's driveway, where the trees tapered off, the sky was an opaque, milky haze, but there was enough light to see by, and Jim switched off the car lights. He noticed that the only tracks on the road were those he'd made a few hours ago, which meant no one else had driven this road since him. There wasn't much snow on the road, five inches maybe. According to Patsy, the plows cleared the side roads only when blizzards drifted them in. She said most often farmers cleared their own driveways, using snow blades attached to their pickups. The road wasn't all that slippery, but Jim drove slowly, past ghostly white fields bristling with pale stubble.

At the stop sign he looked both ways. To his left was the flashing yellow light of a sanding truck approaching on his side of the road. He decided to follow it all the way to town. What safer place to drive than on a freshly sanded road? The sanding truck was moving at a slow, stately pace, which suited Jim fine because now that he'd accomplished his mission, he was in no particular hurry, having only forty miles to go before gassing up and returning the Cavalier safely to Marilyn. Once that was done, he'd phone Paula and tell her he was on his way home.

Jim couldn't pinpoint the exact moment when he'd decided to go back, but it was definitely before Patsy advised him to go home. It might have been when he had watched Miriam being reunited with her sister, and Thomas with his mother. He didn't know which affected him more, seeing how confused the little boy was to be with a mother he didn't know or seeing the joyfulness of Miriam and Rachel now that the three of them were together.

Or it might have been earlier, when he listened to Miriam weeping in the car because she would never see her mother or sisters again. The cruel finality of that fact affected Jim deeply. Fortunately, he'd never been forced to choose one parent over the other, not even when they split. When Zack left home, he would never have been considered dead, and when he showed up he was always welcome. Although his parents were upset that he'd taken off without warning, Jim knew that when he too returned home, he'd be welcomed with open arms, whereas Miriam would never again be welcome on Majestic Farm.

After a month on his own, Jim was finally admitting how much he was missing home. If he hadn't been so determined to get along on his own, he might have admitted it sooner; instead he'd pushed aside any thoughts of homesickness. He missed Paula, and as always, he missed Zack. He even missed know-it-all Carla. He missed sitting beside her on the sofa watching DVDs and munching popcorn. They didn't watch DVDs very often, but Jim liked it when they did. He missed the way Carla came up to him sometimes and gave him a bear hug. But he didn't miss the way she got on his case about how he should work harder at school. He didn't miss her ragging him about being unreliable, or the way she always ended her rants with an impatient *Why don't you grow up?* Well, he was growing up, and growing up fast. These past weeks he'd proved that he could look after himself, and that when he enjoyed what he was doing, he could work as hard as a man. And as he'd proved last night, he was far from unreliable. As he followed the sanding truck, Jim grinned to himself, thinking how Carla would approve of his rescuing Miriam and Thomas from the farm, from what she would describe as a patriarchal cult.

Although the highway was arrow straight, the truck was moving slowly and the vehicles coming behind didn't take long to pass both it and the Cavalier. So far six half-ton trucks and two cars had passed him. Jim was relieved there wasn't a police car in sight and he didn't have to worry about being stopped and asked to produce a driver's licence.

It was past eight-thirty when he finally reached town and, leaving the shelter of the sanding truck, pulled into the service station. His was the only car at the gas pump. After he'd paid for the gas, he drove to the café, where the unplowed parking lot was criss-crossed with snowy tire marks. On the drive in, Jim had decided he'd hand the keys to Marilyn himself, maybe have a cup of coffee, but as he was getting out of the car, he caught sight of the Majestic Farm wagon at the far end of the lot, Horse's reins hanging loose—the old horse was so obedient, he didn't need to be tied to a railing or post. Jim blinked. Was he seeing things? He felt his heart clench inside his chest. He'd never seen anyone from the farm inside the café. As far as he knew, except for Saturday's market, the Godshawks and the Hamfists seldom came to town. But they were in Marilyn's Café now. *And he was just about to go inside!*

The close call freaked him out, and shoving the car keys beneath the floor mat as Marilyn had instructed, he walked away from the Cavalier with his head down. Slipping into the narrow lane between the beauty parlour and the general store, he leaned against the back wall of the minimall, where he wouldn't be seen. Now that he was out of sight, he forced himself to chill out so he could think clearly. Unless Marilyn had told someone he'd borrowed the Cavalier, there was no reason for anyone on Majestic Farm to suspect him of helping Miriam and Thomas get away. Then he remembered Patsy's words: *You're not one of them, and for that reason alone they will suspect you.* Whether or not that was true, he had to avoid running into Ben or Hosea, or whoever had brought the wagon to town. One thing was for sure: every square inch of town would be searched in an effort to find the missing pair. It was a small town, and with nowhere to hide, Jim knew it would be next to impossible for him not to be seen. He thought of hitching a ride out of town but dismissed the idea. Until now he'd been lucky, but there was no way he'd be lucky enough for Silas Stamps to drive past and pick him up. The highway was easily seen from the town; red-haired and tall, he'd be easy to spot standing on the highway shoulder waiting for a drive. If someone from Majestic Farm saw him hitching, they'd want to know why he was leaving town, and for sure they'd question him about Miriam and Thomas. He'd deny helping them escape but that didn't mean they'd believe him.

The smart thing do to while the town was being searched was to lie low in Bliss until it was time to catch the bus. He'd seen the bus stopping at the general store and he headed there now to read the schedule taped to the store window. He was reading it when he heard his name being called, and looking up, he saw Ted Chumnik waving at him from the service station, where he was gassing up. Ted asked if he wanted a lift. "Sure," Jim called back. Perfect timing. If he went to Bliss in Ted's truck, he wouldn't be seen on the road. Jim reminded himself that Patsy had said Bliss was one of the first places the people from Majestic Farm would look. Yes, he thought, but the farm wagon was already in town, wasn't it, and that meant Bliss had already been searched, which made it a safer place to hang out than town, especially if he hid upstairs in the bedroom. He'd hide in the closet until it was time to catch the four o'clock bus.

Inside the truck, Ted turned to Jim. "I'm surprised to see you in town at this hour," he said. "Thought you'd be working on Majestic Farm."

"I quit," Jim said in a way that didn't invite questions.

"I'm not usually in town at this hour," Ted said, "but my sister, Susie, phoned me in a panic to tell me she'd left her purse at the service station yesterday. Because of the roads she didn't want to come back for it, so I promised I'd come into town first thing this morning and pick it up." He held up a scratched leather bag as if it were a trophy. "Here it is." He grinned. "If you ask me, it looks more like a horse's feed bag than a woman's purse."

Once they had cleared town, Ted said that he might as well deliver the purse, because until the canola fields dried out after the snowfall, he couldn't finish harvesting. But when he got back from Susie's in a couple of hours, he'd get to work on the house. Jim said nothing. If he asked about the new house, Ted might say something about the Hamfists. Did he know a search for Miriam and Thomas was under way? Probably not. Even so, Jim wasn't taking any chances.

Neither of them spoke again until Ted stopped in front of Bliss. Jim got out of the truck. "Thanks for the ride," he said.

"No problem," Ted sped off.

Jim tramped up the snowy driveway. He'd reached the well when his attention was drawn to the garage doors. Did he close them last night? He couldn't remember. But they were closed now. With escape on his mind, he'd probably closed them without thinking.

On his way to the back door, the pattern of footprints caught his eye. There were at least two sets of footprints in the snow besides his own. But wasn't he expecting this? Because the footprints were smudged into one another, he couldn't tell exactly how many prints there were, but he could see that some were newer than his. No surprise, he thought. Didn't Patsy tell him that the folks on Majestic Farm would be all over Bliss, that it was the first place they'd look? Okay, then, the searchers had come and gone. Jim opened the shed door.

As soon as he stepped into the kitchen, he realized his mistake. Immediately he was face to face with the pastor, who was sitting in the rocker that he'd cagily moved from beside the stove to the corner near the boarded-up window so he wouldn't be seen from outside. Jim looked around to see if anyone else was in the room.

"Come in, come in," the pastor said amiably, as if it was his house and Jim was his visitor.

"Why am I being honoured by a visit?" Jim asked, borrowing Paula's sarcasm to camouflage his fear.

"I think you know," the pastor said. Making a show of rubbing his hands together, he went on. "Brrr. It's cold in here, and I've been waiting for you to light the stove so we can talk in comfort."

Why didn't you light it yourself, you old phony? Jim wanted to say, though he knew the answer. If the stove had been lit, he would have noticed smoke rising from the chimney and slipped away.

Jim brought kindling from the shed and, once the stove was going, went back for logs. He took his time about it, delaying the moment when he would have to talk to the old man, who watched every move until, impatient with waiting, he ordered Jim to sit. Moving a chair close the stove, Jim sat down and, telling himself to play it cool, asked Miriam's father what there was to talk about.

"The kidnapping of my grandson."

Kidnapping? The man was crazy.

"Abducting a child is against the law," the pastor went on, "and you have broken the law."

Was that true? Had he abducted Thomas?

"I know that during the night you drove a car from here to our driveway, where you stopped and picked up my grandson and daughter. The evidence is recorded in the snow, so there is no point telling me a needless lie."

The bulging eyes fixed on Jim as the pastor waited for him to confirm what he'd said. Jim sat in silent shock and alarm, his eyes averted, knowing that, as the pastor said, the evidence against him was so clearly written in the snow that denial was useless.

The pastor said, "I trusted you, Jim. I took you in, gave you food and work, and you betrayed me." His voice rose in pitch. "You have betrayed all of us on Majestic Farm: Miriam's sisters and brothers; Asa, with whom you worked. He is most distressed because, like me, he trusted you, Jim. We all trusted you, except Ben. He thought you were sly and cunning, and you are, Jim—you are sly and cunning, two traits that do not win favour with God."

All of this was spoken in a pained voice as if the pastor believed that Jim had not only committed a serious crime but had inflicted a grave injury on the pastor and everyone on the farm.

"But God will seek justice," the pastor went on. "Make no mistake: if you do not tell me where you took my grandson and daughter, you will be punished for your wrongdoing."

From somewhere inside Jim's head, he heard Patsy's voice again. *The folks on Majestic Farm will be out of their minds with rage. . . . There's no telling what they might do.* Fearing what sort of punishment the pastor had in mind, Jim went on the offensive. In a loud voice, he challenged the old man: "Exactly how will I be punished?" *Would you shave my head?* he almost said, but stopped himself on time. He wasn't supposed to know that Miriam's hair had been shorn.

The pastor looked at Jim pityingly as if he was too simple-minded to grasp the most obvious truth. He said, "Surely, Jim, you know that in God's eyes punishment can take many forms. For instance . . ." The pastor's gaze travelled the room and landed on *Treasure Island* face down on the floor beside the daybed. With difficulty the old man got himself out of the rocker and, crossing the room, stooped for the book. Opening the stove lid, he threw *Treasure Island* into the fire. "Ungodly trash should be consigned to the fires of Hell where it belongs," he said and sat down.

Satisfied that he had made a point that even someone as stubborn-minded and proud as Jim couldn't fail to miss, the pastor continued. "You see, Jim, the punishment must always fit the crime." He gestured to the stove, where the book was burning, the corners of its pages curling into black-ridged flames. "Unless you confess about kidnapping my grandson and daughter, your punishment will be much more severe than the burning of a godless, frivolous story about pirates."

This was too much for Jim and he said, "What did the schoolteachers do wrong to deserve having their books burnt? Why did you kill their chickens and dirty their well?" Pointing at the boarded-up half of the window, he asked, "Why did you shoot at them?" The accusation hung like a giant billboard between the pastor and himself. Jim knew that it had been rash to have blurted all this out, and that by doing so he had probably made his situation worse.

There was a prolonged sigh before the pastor said, "That was a long time ago. How did you come by the information about those so-called teachers?"

"People have long memories," Jim said, quoting his mother—it was a remark Paula often made. Using his own words, Jim added, "And they're not as stupid as you think."

For once the pastor was at a loss for words.

"I also know why your daughter Gila came to the teachers for help," Jim said. This was as far as he would go. He wouldn't mention the remains of the baby inside the biscuit tin. He could see that for all his bluff and acting, the old man was upset, that above the matted beard, the pastor's lips were trembling. Jim thought he heard the old man mumble, "May God forgive me," but he couldn't be sure. For a while the two of them sat quietly, the only sounds the hiss of burning paper and the snap of red-hot coals.

Finally, the pastor spoke, his voice heavy with regret but bedrock hard in its intent to obtain what he was determined to have. "I underestimated you, Jim. You are a formidable enemy and have cleverly deflected my purpose in coming here, but you will not deflect me again. You are guilty of kidnapping my grandson and my daughter, and to absolve your sin you must admit your wrongdoing." He paused, waiting for an admission that didn't come. "It isn't too late," the pastor said, "If you tell me the whereabouts of Thomas and Miriam, God will forgive your crime. Think about it."

But Jim didn't need to think about it. For the first time in his life he had taken a stand against wrongdoing—the pastor's, not his—and he wasn't going to back down now. He said nothing of this to Miriam's father but maintained a steadfast silence, which further enraged the old man. The pastor's eyes bulged and his tongue flicked out. On his feet now, he put a hand on the doorknob and shouted, "You are to stay here until you confess! Until then, I forbid you to leave this house! That is my last word on the matter."

Though badly shaken, Jim heard himself saying, "Can I count on that?" But it was said to the closed door. Through the window, Jim watched the old man pass the well and continue down the driveway. For the first time he noticed the pastor's bowed legs, and that he walked with a limp. The limp wasn't so severe that he needed a walking stick or a crutch like Long John Silver, but it was noticeable enough to bring the pirate to mind. In some ways the two men were alike, Jim thought. Both of them knew how to manipulate people in order to get their own way; both knew how to change the way they spoke, blustering and bullying one minute, sly and coaxing the next—a dangerous combination that often gave them what they wanted. But unlike the pirate, the pastor wasn't used to disappointment, and when bluster and coaxing didn't work, he resorted to threats. Did he really expect Jim to stay here until he confessed? And how could he make him stay? Well, Jim *wasn't* staying. He'd gather up his stuff and clear out of here. He'd head for the Chumniks'. Once he got to their house, he'd be safe.

25

The canvas bag. He'd carry his stuff in Hector's canvas bag. The bee pot containing the last of Miriam's honey was tucked inside the tuque—he was ditching the straw hat. Bread and cheese. Two bananas. The bag was only a quarter full and Jim looked around for something else, something that would remind him of Bliss, a keepsake, because once he left, he'd never be back. What he really wanted as a keepsake was *Treasure Island,* but that had gone up in smoke. What about the wavy mirror? No. What about the chipped cup he used for dipping water? Maybe. He opened the cupboard and there, right behind the cups, was the framed picture of Hector and Iris Bliss he'd put there a month ago. Yes. Bundling the picture in his old T-shirt, he added it to the canvas bag.

Jim knew his plan to hang out at the Chumniks' until it was time to catch the four o'clock bus had a couple of possible snags. Snag Number One: Would Ted mind his hiding inside the house until he returned from his sister's? Snag Number Two: In the time it took to reach the house, would Jim be seen crossing the road and hoofing up the Chumniks' drive? Both were chances he'd have to take. There wasn't a minute to lose and he'd have to move fast.

Slinging the canvas bag over his shoulder, he stepped into the shed and opened the door. He was partway outside when—crack!—a bullet slammed into the doorframe beside his head and he heard a shouted command: "Come out with your hands up or stay inside!" Jim banged the door shut, locked it and, head down, scrabbled on all fours through the kitchen and into the front room, where he crouched beneath the staircase to catch his breath. His heart was pounding so hard it was difficult to think beyond the fact that he'd been shot at and his life was in danger. One thing he knew for sure was that it was the robot who'd shouted—Jim recognized the voice. That meant that another man, probably Hosea, had taken the wagon to town. Ben, and maybe someone else, was outside with a rifle and would stay there as long as Jim was inside the house. The shot was meant to corner him. It occurred to Jim that Ben must have been outside all the time his father had been inside trying to persuade Jim to confess. He must have been lurking in the woods, watching Jim get out of Ted's truck and follow the drive. He must have watched him look at the garage doors. It was Ben who had closed the doors. The pastor had probably planned it so that if Jim didn't tell him where Miriam and Thomas were, Ben would force him to stay inside until he confessed.

Trying to rein in his runaway heart, Jim concentrated on working out a way to save his skin. He knew he had no choice but to try to escape, because if he didn't, the robot would break in, and then what? As Patsy said, there was no telling what they might do. Shoot him? Torture him? The fact that Ben would be breaking the law wouldn't stop him. After all, over forty years ago, using terrorist tactics, the pastor and Abel Hamfist had got away with hounding Hector and Iris Bliss off their own property. The Godshawks and Hamfists knew that without neighbours close by to stop them, they could do whatever they wanted with Jim. For the first time since leaving the city, Jim was desperate to use a telephone so that he could call 911. Trapped, cut off from another human being, he felt himself being squeezed by a kind of fear he'd never known. He'd known fear when he was trapped in the subway, but at least there he'd shared the fear with other passengers. He'd known fear when, as a kid, he awoke inside a burning house, but his parents and sister had shared his fear and got him safely outside. The fear that gripped him now was a thousand times worse, magnified as it was by the fact that there was no one here to share it or to help him to safety.

Remembering the fire that had turned his parents' house into a blackened shell, Jim realized that if he refused to give himself up, Ben might try to smoke him out by setting the Bliss house on fire. Hadn't the pastor called the house a fire trap? Ben wouldn't set fire to it during the day, when the smoke would be seen from miles away. He'd set fire to it at night, when flames would have overtaken the house before anyone noticed. Jim had just about convinced himself that fire was the tactic Ben and the pastor would use when it came to him that he wouldn't be much help to them if he was half dead with smoke inhalation.

More likely the pastor would order Ben to break down the door and capture him. Jim didn't like to think what would be done to him to make him confess. Anyone who would shave his daughters' heads probably had some fiendish methods of torture in mind to break down his resistance. Why wasn't Ben breaking in now? Knowing the pastor was too old to help, Jim figured Ben must be waiting for someone else to help him break in. If Ben was alone out there, now was the time to escape.

But how to escape without being seen? Crouched beneath the staircase, Jim tried to figure out a way. One thing for sure—it was impossible to leave by the front door, which he remembered was jammed tight when he'd opened it his first day here. If he tried to wrench it open now, Ben would hear it for sure. Also, the door was at the front corner of the house and easily seen from the woods beyond the well—which was where Ben's shot had come from.

The only possible way of escape was through one of the two shuttered windows on the wall facing him. Scrabbling across the floor on all fours, Jim opened a shutter partway, keeping his head down in case Ben had shifted to this side of the house and saw the shutter move. Jim eased the shutter wider and, when nothing happened, lifted his head above the sill so he could see out. The first thing he did was look for footprints in the snow. He was relieved to find there were none, either close to the house or in the poplar woods sloping down to the road. Though the deep woods beyond were tempting, Jim dismissed their refuge. In deep woods he would be easily tracked, and in deep woods there would be no phone and he *had* to reach a phone.

Because the poplars outside the window were spaced far apart, a single glance confirmed that no one was out there; even so, Jim's gaze slid from tree to tree until he was satisfied no one was watching this side of the house. As he'd guessed, so far Ben was on the other side alone. To make doubly sure, Jim stood at the window, looking left and right before opening it wide enough to throw the canvas bag outside. He heard it plop in the snow about five feet below and ducked down, waiting to see if Ben or someone else heard the plop or the faint groan of the window being opened wider and came to investigate. Jim waited, listening for the sound of footsteps, but he heard nothing except the caw of a faraway crow, and the thought that it might be Blackie flitted through his mind. Once he was outside, Jim intended to slip through the woods to the road and from there to the Chumniks'. The Chumniks' drive couldn't be seen from the well side of Bliss, and if he hurried, he had a chance of reaching their house unseen.

Now that he had an escape route worked out, some of the fear eased away, changing into hard-edged resolve mixed with cunning. Returning to the kitchen, Jim had the presence of mind to lift the stove lid, and banging it hard to make sure it could be heard outside, he poked more wood into the fire to convince Ben that the smoke coming from the chimney meant that Jim intended to remain holed up inside. Next, he filled the kettle with water and slammed it down on the stove. To make himself visible outside, he walked back and forth in front of the undamaged half of the kitchen window, where Ben could see him. Then, moving to a chair, he made himself sit in it long enough to be noticed from outside.

From the chair, he slid to the floor and crawled across the front room to the window, and easing himself through the opening, he hung onto the sill and lowered himself down until his feet were inches above the ground. There was a slight thud when he let go of the sill and landed in the snow. He didn't wait to find out if he'd been heard but picked up Hector's canvas bag and made his way through the poplar woods to the road. By now the melting snow on the road was mixed with dirt, leaving muddy tracks behind. Thinking Ben might hear the crunch of his feet on the road. Jim moved onto the snowy shoulder, where his feet made a faint swishing noise. Remembering Snag Number Two, when he turned into the long Chumnik drive, he broke into a trot, glancing over his shoulder to check if he was being followed. So far so good. He continued running and was now halfway up the drive. In a few minutes he would reach the safety of the house and the telephone.

When he came to the end of the drive, Jim ran smack into Snag Number Three: Nikki. While Darlene and the kids were at school and Ted was at his sister's, the German shepherd's job was to guard the place, a job he took seriously. With a yip the dog bounded off the back step and streaked toward Jim, growling. Jim backed up, fear squeezing tighter with each step. Glancing at his watch, he saw that more than an hour had gone by since Ted had dropped him off. Didn't Ted say he'd be home in a couple of hours? That meant Jim had less than an hour to wait. Until then he was alone—well, not completely alone, because there was a telephone he could use inside the house. The back door was probably unlocked, but if it wasn't, he was sure to find a window he could jimmy open. Once he was inside the house, he'd phone the police and tell them Ben Godshawk had fired a rifle at him. It was crucial that someone besides Jim know that Ben was after him. He'd also phone Marilyn and tell her too. He might even phone Paula and tell her he was coming home. Once he'd made the phone calls, he'd be safe.

Problem was, Nikki wouldn't let him inside the house. When Jim had visited the Chumniks before, the dog had checked him over and, deciding he was harmless, had ignored him, which was why Jim had assumed that Nikki was following him back to the house because he had nothing better to do. Wrong. As Jim neared the back step, the German shepherd bounded ahead and, bracing himself on all fours in front of the door, stared at Jim with his yellow eyes and growled deep in his throat. "Let me in, Nikki," Jim said encouragingly as he took a step forward. The dog's lips flared, and baring his teeth, he refused to let Jim near the door.

When Jim was a little kid, he had lived next door to a family who had a spaniel named Sassy. She was a good watchdog until Jim said her name. As soon as she heard "Sassy," she wagged her tail and forgot all about being a watchdog.

"Nikki," Jim said again. Unimpressed that Jim knew his name, the dog barked out a sharp warning. Jim put one foot on the step and Nikki exploded in fury, leaping off the step, showing his fangs, forcing him to back away. "It's okay, boy," Jim said. "It's okay." But the dog wasn't going to back down, and it became clear that with no one at home, Jim wouldn't be allowed anywhere near the door, or, for that matter, the house. Jim resigned himself to having to wait until Ted came back before he could use the phone. Looking around for someplace to sit, he saw a chopping block beside the woodpile about twenty feet from the house. He backed up slowly, Nikki watching his movements, a steady growl rumbling in the dog's throat like an idling car engine. Keeping his eye on the dog, Jim moved toward the woodpile. Every step he took, Nikki gave a yip of annoyance, and only when he was satisfied that Jim was sitting on the chopping block did he stop growling and settle down on the mat, where he kept a mistrustful eye on Jim.

Thinking he might be able to bribe the dog, Jim dug out some bread and cheese and tossed it on the ground between them. Nikki looked at the food with disgust, scornful that Jim thought he could be bribed. With a sigh of distain, the dog stretched out on the step, now warmed by the sun.

The sun had melted much of the snow, and what was left lay patchily on the grass and in the crevices and hollows of the woodpile. At another time Jim would have enjoyed sitting on a chopping block in the sun, but now, rattled and anxious, he couldn't stop thinking about about how long it would be before Ben broke into the Bliss house and, spotting the open window, tracked him here. Torn between staying where he was and making another attempt to enter the house, Jim was consumed by uncertainty. It spread like a forest wildfire, leaping from one treetop to another, from dread to fear to anger, where it made its way deep into the roots of his being and he found himself angry at everyone, beginning with himself. He was angry at himself for ever setting foot on Majestic Farm, for becoming involved with Miriam and for caring enough about her to help her and Thomas escape. They had met only a few times, yet he had taken chances and risked his life to do what she'd asked. And why had he done that? Did he think of himself as a some kind of hero come to rescue a girl in distress? Some hero. Jim felt his anger snaking its way toward the girl. What did Miriam care about him? Safely hidden away at Patsy's, she would never know if he was captured and tortured unless he ratted on her. And he'd never rat. He was certain of that. He thought of Jim Hawkins, how he'd risked his life to rescue his friends from the pirates. Although it was never mentioned in the story, Jim Hawkins must have been angry. You couldn't be scared and not be angry. The other Jim must have been scared shitless when he was hiding inside the apple barrel, and later when he cut the hawsers on the *Hispaniola* and set it adrift. But he'd done it—he'd stayed true to his purpose.

Stranded helplessly next to the woodpile, Jim directed his anger to Majestic Farm. Although he'd once admired the farm for its self-sufficiency and determination to use only what was needed, Jim was totally convinced that it was an evil, controlling place. All the talk about the Righteous Path was a scam to build a tiny kingdom ruled by the pastor, a kingdom in which women were treated no better than slaves. Before he had begun working on the farm, Jim hadn't taken Carla's rants about women's rights seriously, but he was taking them seriously now. He was thinking that the women on Majestic Farm had no rights except those dictated to them by the pastor. Why didn't more women just walk away like Rachel? They had babies and children—that was why they stayed.

By now the second hour had gone by and there was still no sign of Ted. Was he was planning to stay at his sister's for the afternoon? Anger had made Jim more determined and he decided to have one more try at getting in the back door. He told himself that the worst thing that could happen was that Nikki would bite his arm or leg. As if he'd read Jim's mind, the dog sat up, pricked his ears and bounded off the step. But the German shepherd didn't head toward Jim. Instead he ran toward the side of the house.

Moments later, hearing the sound of a wagon rumbling up the drive, Jim leapt off the woodpile. He knew the sound of one wagon, and it belonged to Majestic Farm. Glancing at the Chumniks' drive, Jim felt his worst fears realized: *Hosea Hamfist was driving Horse!* Sitting beside him was the robot. Jim had figured that right—Ben had delayed breaking into the house until Hosea returned from town. While Nikki shot out to meet the wagon, Jim seized his chance and raced toward the back door, which, as he'd guessed, was unlocked—with a guard dog like Nikki, there was no need to lock a door. Locking it now, Jim leaned against the door while the dog flung himself against the other side, barking furiously and clawing at the wood.

Jim heard the wagon rumble to a stop and a voice ask, "Somebody inside you don't want to be there?" The dog whimpered, and Jim knew that the voice must be Hosea's and that it would be familiar to Nikki, who knew Hosea from the framing job. "Don't you worry, fella," the voice went on. "We'll catch him for you."

Jim couldn't move. It was as if he'd been given a shot of a paralyzing drug. But a moment later he was on full alert. *Lock the front door!* Streaking down the hallway, he secured the lock, and flattening himself against the wall so he wouldn't be seen by the men outside, he lifted the phone off the hook and dialled 911.

26

The operator put Jim through to the police and a woman answered the phone.

"Corporal Foster here," she said. "State your name and the reason for your call."

Jim gave his name and told her he was locked inside the Chumniks' house. "They're not home," he said in a rush of panic, "but I'm hiding in here because two men from Majestic Farm, Hosea Hamfist and Ben Godshawk, are after me and they're outside. Ben fired a rifle at me when I tried to leave the Bliss house. He was trying to keep me prisoner inside but I escaped through a window and came here. Please help me."

"Keep away from the windows. Fifteen minutes and we'll be there. Stay calm," Corporal Foster said and clicked off.

We, she said. *Fifteen minutes.* All Jim had to do was hold on for fifteen minutes.

As soon as he hung up the hall phone, Jim noticed that he was in full view of the living-room picture window, where he could be seen by anyone on the veranda. Beside the front door was a coat closet. Ducking inside, he closed the door and squatted on a pile of boots and shoes beneath a row of coats and jackets. There was a pungent odour of leather and dirt and something else—a coarse, grainy smell. If only he had a cellphone. Although he couldn't use a cellphone without being heard, he'd feel safer with one in his hand. The pastor had gone on and on about the evils of technology, but right now, more than anything else, Jim needed technology.

Someone was on the veranda. From inside the closet, Jim heard the tread of footsteps approaching from the side of the house, and his mind's eye saw a man, Ben or Hosea, turn the corner and pause to look through the picture window before continuing on. Now only a few feet away from Jim, the footsteps stopped and the front doorknob rattled. Closing his eyes, Jim concentrated on the footsteps, willing them to move away. But they didn't move away. Instead he heard a jangling sound, as if a key ring was being shaken. There was a harsh scrape of metal being forced into the keyhole. Either Ben or Hosea was using some sort of tool to pick the lock. *They were breaking in!* There was a click, and Jim heard the door open and someone step inside. *He was right there on the other side of the closet door. Would he open it?* The policewoman had told Jim to stay calm, but how could he with his heart pounding like a sledgehammer?

He held his breath, expecting that any second the closet door would open and whoever had picked the lock would see him sitting beneath the jackets and coats. To his relief, the footsteps passed the closet door and climbed the stairs. One by one he counted the stairs until he heard someone above his head, going from room to room, pausing to open closet doors and no doubt checking beneath the beds. It was tempting to burst out of the closet and dash outside, but he reminded himself that if he made a run for it, Nikki would chase him down. Escape was impossible. And so he waited, knowing it was only minutes, maybe seconds, until he was discovered.

Jim heard another pair of footsteps come through the front door. Then he heard a bark. *Nikki.* The dog was outside the closet, barking and pawing at the door. *Back off, you idiot dog. Back off!* The dog kept on barking and pawing and soon the closet door opened and Hosea yelled, "I got him!" Reaching down, he took hold of Jim's feet and pulled. Determined not to cower or to make it easy for his captor, Jim gathered an armful of boots and shoes, holding onto them while Hosea hauled him from the closet by his ankles, yanking them with such force Jim thought his legs were being wrenched from his hips. Ben came downstairs with the hunting rifle and used the butt end to dislodge the boots and shoes, he grabbed one of Jim's arms, Hosea the other, and together they dragged him through the doorway and across the veranda, a dead weight, Jim's backside bumping against the wooden planks and bouncing down the steps. Nikki whining, confused now about what was going on. Dragging Jim across grass and muddy snow to the wagon, the two men heaved him onto the flatbed as if he were a side of beef and bound his ankles and hands with rope. Another length of rope was forced between his teeth and knotted behind his head. Not a word was spoken, not a look exchanged.

By now Jim's brain was numb, and because he'd been too rattled to look at his watch, he had no sense of how much time had passed since he'd called 911. It seemed like an hour had gone by, but it might have been only fifteen minutes. If the police didn't turn up soon, Jim knew it would be too late, because once Ben and Hosea got him to Majestic Farm, they would hide him in a place where no one would find him. If they could hide a rifle from the police, they could hide him where he couldn't be found.

Living in a big city, Jim had come to regard police sirens wailing outside the condo at all hours of the day as a nuisance, but now that he was lying, bound and helpless, on the flatbed of a farm wagon, the sound of the wailing siren was so welcome that tears of relief pricked his eyes. *The police were here! They had come!*

Halfway down the Chumnik drive, the wagon was forced to a stop, blocked by the police car. Trussed up on the floor of the flatbed, Jim couldn't see the police, but he heard a car door slam and a woman who identified herself as Corporal Foster speak. "Constable Alford and I had a call from a Jim Hobbs reporting that you were confining him inside the Chumnik house," she said. "Where is he now?"

Grunting, Jim banged his bound feet against the wagon boards and a policeman in a navy uniform with yellow stripes leapt onto the flatbed and, untying the rope gagging his mouth, asked if he was Jim Hobbs.

"Yeah. I made the call from inside the house but those men broke in and tied me up."

The policeman untied the hand and ankle ropes and helped Jim to his feet, where he wobbled unsteadily before regaining his balance. Pointing to Ben Godshawk, Jim said, "That man fired a rifle at me when I tried to leave the Bliss house, and I escaped and hid over here."

Neither Ben nor Hosea said a word, but each stood

beside the wagon with a look of disgust that a policewoman, of all people, should be pointing a gun at them. A stocky woman about Paula's age, with cropped brown hair, Corporal Foster stood, legs astride, the handgun braced on her palm.

"The rifle, Constable," she said in a low, deliberate voice. Reaching beneath the wagon seat, the policeman seized the gun and, holding it gingerly by the barrel end, put it in the trunk of the police car. "We'll be fingerprinting the gun for evidence," Corporal Foster said. She looked at Ben. "Do you have a gun licence?"

When Ben didn't reply, Constable Alford said, "You heard Corporal Foster. Answer the question." His voice wobbled slightly, betraying the fact that he was a rookie and no match for the robot, who maintained a stony silence. At a nod from Corporal Foster, the constable took out a notebook and jotted something down. From watching television police shows, Jim thought he knew what he had written: *Suspect refuses to co-operate.*

With the handgun still braced on her palm, Corporal Foster said, "Cuff that one, Constable." She nodded toward Ben. "He'll be locked up until charged."

Ben stood rigid as wood while the constable forced one wrist and then the other into the handcuffs.

"Put him in the car."

Once Ben was in the back seat, Corporal Foster pointed the handgun at Hosea. "Take the wagon back to Majestic Farm," she said. "Under no circumstances are you to leave the farm." Jim saw a look of contempt cross Hosea's face as he climbed onto the wagon. He slapped the reins, and the obedient Horse pulled the wagon down the drive.

Holstering the handgun, Corporal Foster said, "You come with us, Jim."

Reluctantly, he got into the back seat, wishing that instead of the corporal, he was sitting up front, away from the prisoner. Sitting beside the robot was like sitting beside someone wearing a suicide bomber's explosive vest that would denotate at any second. They drove to Bliss, and leaving Ben inside the car, guarded by the constable, Jim showed the corporal the bullet embedded in the doorframe.

Corporal Foster asked if Jim lived here.

"Not anymore. I was just leaving when Ben fired the shot. I've been staying here the past few weeks," Jim said, then quickly added, "but I'm going home." The corporal asked where home was and, when Jim told her, asked if he was in trouble with the law.

"Not yet." Jim grinned nervously, trying to make a joke of it because it had occurred to him that having driven the Cavalier without a licence, he might be in trouble now. The corporal suggested they go inside for a chat, and they went into the kitchen, which was still warm from the stove. Telling him to take a seat, the corporal remained standing. She asked Jim if he knew why Ben Godshawk had shot at him.

"His sister asked me to help her and her nephew leave Majestic Farm and I did," Jim said. "They have a lot of strict rules on the farm and she didn't want to live there anymore. She used to come here on Sundays to get away."

"How old is Ben's sister?"

"Fifteen."

"How old are you, Jim?"

"The same."

Jim knew that she was going to ask how he helped

Miriam escape and that he would be forced to admit that he'd been driving a vehicle without a licence.

"What exactly did you do to help her?"

"I drove her to a place where her sister is staying," Jim explained. "I can't say where that is because if Ben and Hosea find out where she and Thomas are, they'll go after them." Jim knew he was babbling, giving more information than the police needed to know, but he couldn't stop himself. "Hosea wants to marry Miriam and he wants Thomas back. Thomas is his son and Miriam's sister is his mother. Thomas is with his mother now." Speaking passionately, Jim went on, "You can put me in jail, but I'll never tell where they are."

"It's Ben Godshawk we're putting in jail, not you, Jim," Corporal Foster said. "And you can be sure we won't be telling the folks on Majestic Farm anything. We've had dealings with them before." She paused before going on. "But I will ask what vehicle you used."

"I borrowed someone's."

"Not stole?"

"No. Borrowed."

"A Cavalier." It was a statement, not a question. Being a regular customer of Marilyn's, she must have seen him in the café and figured it out. "It's a small town," she added as if that explained everything. She didn't say a word about Jim driving without a licence.

"You'll have to come to the police station," she said. "I assume you are prepared to lay a charge against Ben Godshawk for firing a gun at you."

"I am." Jim glanced at his watch; it was three o'clock. "How long will it take?"

"About an hour." She paused before adding, "That is, if no more altercations are called in."

"I was planning on taking the four o'clock bus."

"You'll have to take it tomorrow," Corporal Foster said. "The paperwork won't be finalized before then. Once that's done, you can get on your bus, and we can lay formal charges against Ben and let him go."

"I'll be on the bus before you let him go?"

"You can be sure of that."

Jim looked around the kitchen. "I don't want to stay here tonight. Not with Hosea up the road."

"We'll find you a place to stay in town. I'm sure Marilyn can put you up." When Jim looked dubious, she continued briskly, "If not, you can spend the night in one of our jail cells."

With the robot? Jim thought. She must be kidding. He looked at the corporal to see if she was kidding, but she didn't crack a smile. "Either place you'll be safe." Jim must have looked worried because she added, "Don't worry, we'll keep a close eye on you until you board the bus."

At Jim's request, on their way to town they stopped at the Chumniks' for Hector's canvas bag, which he'd left near the woodpile when he'd run into the house. No one was home, and although Nikki was stretched out on the back step, he was either too tired or too defeated to move when Jim got out of the police car and went to the woodpile to pick up the canvas bag. The dog lifted his head and glanced at Jim, then, with a heavy sigh, put it down again. Maybe he was bored. Maybe he was exhausted. Maybe discouragement had got him down. Maybe he was disappointed that he'd failed to prevent intruders from breaking into the house he was bound to protect. Whatever the reason, it was abundantly clear that the treacherous and confusing ways of humans were too much for the brave and simple heart of a dog who had tried to do his job and now wanted to be left in peace.

27

Marilyn told Jim he was welcome to use her spare bedroom, and after a couple of hours hanging out at the police station, where he answered questions and signed a report, he went to the café and bought himself two hamburgers and two Cokes before going upstairs to Marilyn's apartment and locking himself inside. In spite of Corporal Foster's assurances, Jim was totally freaked out and far from convinced that one or more of the Godshawks or Hamfists wouldn't show up and demand that he tell them where he'd taken Miriam and Thomas. With Marilyn busy in the café downstairs, he wanted lots of warning in case someone—maybe the pastor himself—came upstairs and broke into the apartment by picking the lock.

Earlier, before he left the café, Marilyn had urged Jim to phone home. And earlier still, Corporal Foster had offered the use of the police station telephone if Jim wanted to call home. But he'd said no, reluctant to call with the police listening in. He didn't mind them listening while he'd talked to Darlene Chumnik, but some conversations were private. Now he picked up Marilyn's kitchen telephone and dialled home.

Because it was a weekday, Jim wasn't expecting Zack to answer the phone.

"Hey, Dad."

"Hey, son." His father almost never called him "son." Jim heard him call, "Paula! It's Jim!" The voice was muffled, as if a hand was being held over the receiver. The hand was removed and his father asked Jim where he was.

"The same place I've been the past few weeks."

"When you didn't call on the weekend, we thought you might have moved somewhere else. We've been worried about you."

"I didn't call yesterday because there was a lot of stuff going on."

"What kind of stuff?"

"I'll tell you all about it when I get home."

"And when will that be, son?"

"I plan on leaving here tomorrow on the four o'clock bus."

"Hold on a minute." This time Zack didn't bother muffling the receiver and Jim heard him yell, "Paula! He's leaving for home tomorrow!"

"Tell him I'm coming!" his mother shouted.

"Here she comes wrapped in a towel. She's on the stairs now," his father said, using his hockey-commentator voice, "dripping water as she comes. She's closing in now and soon—"

Jim pictured his mother grabbing the phone.

"Jim! At last! I am *so* relieved. Are you really coming home?"

"Yes."

"Thank God." There was a pause before she asked if he was bringing the girl.

"No."

"Because your father and I talked it over and decided it would be okay if she stayed with us."

With us. "So Dad's living with us from now on?" He had to know if it was real.

"Yes. We're trying a reconciliation," Paula said carefully. So Ron was out of the picture. After a long pause, she asked Jim if the split had been why he'd left home.

Jim told her he didn't know—he didn't think so, but it might have been one of the reasons. He said he didn't understand why she and Zack had split. It wasn't as if they didn't like each other. And they weren't divorced, only separated. It was confusing. "Did you split because of Carla and me?"

"It had *nothing* to do with you and Carla. It *only* had to do with Zack and me."

Jim waited.

"The truth is, I don't know why we separated. I know I wasn't paying attention to our marriage. I was too busy with other things. Also, I was eighteen when we married, which is way too young."

Still Jim waited. He knew that it was because he was so far away that his mother found it easier to tell him the truth.

"I was restless," she confessed. "I didn't have much life experience. Whatever you do, Jim, don't get married too young. You need life experience."

Well, he was certainly getting that.

Jim heard his father's voice in the background but he couldn't make out what he was saying. "Zack wants to have a word."

"I've been thinking," Zack said, "that Paula and I can

drive out and meet your bus and we can drive the rest of the way home together. How about that?"

"Sounds good. Any chance Carla can come with you? "It surprised Jim that more than anyone, it was his sister he wanted to tell what had happened on Majestic Farm.

"I doubt it. She says she's got a ton of work and is up all hours writing papers. But I'll ask." Zack told him where they would meet. Like Silas, his father knew the country like the back of his hand and had already chosen a place.

Paula came on the phone again.

"Do you want me to call the principal and tell her you'll be returning to school? It won't take long to catch up."

Catch up on what, Jim thought. He knew he'd learned way more in the last few weeks than he would have ever learned if he'd been in school. "I'll call the principal when I get home. There's nothing in school I can't make up."

"Right," Paula said. "We'll see you soon."

Reluctantly Jim hung up the phone.

Using the telephone directory, he dialled the number for PATSY'S POTS. After five rings, a grumpy voice asked, "Who's this?"

"Jim. I'm calling from town to say I'm going home tomorrow."

"You mean to tell me you're still around?"

Jim asked if Miriam and Thomas were okay.

"They're exhausted but okay. Right now they're sleeping." Patsy didn't say she'd been sleeping too, but Jim was sure he'd wakened her.

He told her that the pastor knew he'd helped Miriam and Thomas escape, that he was waiting inside the house after Jim returned the car and went back to Bliss.

"You went back to Bliss? After I told you not to!" Jim could hear the fury in Patsy's voice.

"I had no choice," Jim said. "Hosea and probably others from Majestic Farm were searching the town for Miriam and Thomas and I had to get out of there fast, so I got a ride with a neighbour. The pastor tried to get me to say where I'd taken them, but I didn't, and they don't know they're with you."

"Good work. You gave me a scare there, Jim."

He continued talking, telling Patsy that Ben Godshawk had fired a rifle at him to keep him inside the house, and that after he escaped, Ben and Hosea had followed him to the Chumniks'. "I called 911 and the police rescued me," he said. "Ben is in jail and Hosea has been ordered to stay on the farm. But that doesn't mean others won't be out looking for Miriam and Thomas."

Patsy said, "But they won't know where to look because no one saw you coming here and we'll be extra careful. I've made it very clear to Miriam and Thomas that they have to stay inside."

Concerned about Thomas's being separated from Blackie, Jim asked if Patsy had seen Thomas's crow.

"Thomas's crow?"

"His pet crow. He follows Thomas everywhere."

"Crows aren't pets," Patsy said crossly. "They're communal birds that flock together and don't have much to do with people." She yawned.

That's what you think. "Tell Miriam I'll be in touch," he said.

"I will. Take care of yourself, Jim."

He heard another of Patsy's yawns. "You too," he said and hung up.

For a while Jim sat by the phone imagining a crow flying across the fields toward a little boy who couldn't sleep. Although he was far gone with exhaustion, Jim didn't go to bed until Marilyn came upstairs. She was in the next room and he was behind two locked doors, yet still Jim couldn't sleep.

What he wouldn't give to have his guitar right now. No matter what his problems, he could always count on his guitar to calm him down. Playing his guitar was like having a conversation with himself, a conversation that wandered this way and that, never in a straight line—a chord here and a chord there, meandering like his life, going in one direction and then another. He liked that. Jim could tell his guitar anything and everything and it never judged him, never let him down, never made him feel left out or geeky. Tomorrow he'd phone and ask Zack to bring his guitar so he could sit in the back seat and tell his guitar how he felt about the things that had happened since he left home.

28

A damp, Scottish wind was blowing off the Firth of Forth when a tall, curly-headed young man carrying a backpack and a canvas bag stepped off the bus. Inside his pocket was a computer printout of a map with the street where Hector Bliss lived marked in yellow. Striding along, Jim drank in the sights: the walled castle dominating the city, the parkland that had once been a loch where long ago witches were drowned, the museum honouring Scotland's writers. Since leaving Bliss over a year before, Jim had stuck close to home, studying during the school months and working for a landscape gardener during the summer. The day before flying to Edinburgh, he'd written his last exam of the term and, after visiting Hector, would return home to spend the holiday with his family.

Iris Bliss had been dead ten years. Hector had mentioned her death in his first letter to Jim, his stiff, arthritic writing jumping off the page, so unlike Iris's teacherly script. By emailing a Scottish realtor, Paula had managed to find Hector's address, and he had been maintaining a sporadic correspondence with Jim for the past six months.

Hector lived on the first floor of a grey stone tenement

that, except for the red-painted door, resembled the other tenements on the narrow street. There was a row of buttons beside the door and Jim pushed the one with *Bliss* written beside it. A buzzer sounded, and letting himself in, he walked down the dark hallway as Hector had instructed in his letter.

A tiny, white-haired man waited in the apartment doorway, leaning heavily on a knobbed wooden cane. Remembering how Barbara Chumnik had described Hector Bliss as a small man, Jim had expected to tower over him, but he hadn't expected to be fully twice Hector's height. The old man's spine was bent almost double, and when he lifted his head to greet his visitor, it rose only partway. But Hector's brown eyes were lively and there was a puckish grin on his lips. Reaching out, he took Jim's hand. "Jim Hobbs," he said in a clipped Scottish voice. "How I have looked forward to this day."

"Me too," Jim said. It was hard to believe he was really here.

"Come into the sitting room," Hector said. Jim followed as the old man hobbled into a high-ceilinged room where a small fire burned in a wrought-iron grate.

Jim immediately noticed that bookshelves lined the walls, except for the far wall, where a large window overlooked a rocky cliff. He went to the window and gazed outside. "Those are the Salisbury Crags," Hector said from his place at Jim's elbow. Waving his cane at a walled garden, he added, "Down there is the drying green where Mary hangs the washing." Turning, he pointed to a small table in front of the fire. "As you can see," he said, "Mary has set out our tea." Indicating the chair where Jim was to sit, Hector sat opposite, the tea table between them. Jim noticed Hector's shaky hands and asked if he could pour the tea.

"If you would be so kind."

As the tea and the buttered scones were being passed, Hector asked Jim to tell him about "that girl you helped get away."

"Miriam."

"Ah yes, Miriam. What happened to her?"

"She's going to school in a small town in the mountains."

"There was a little boy, was there not?"

"Thomas. He's taking drawing classes, and Miriam says he's begun to speak a few words."

Jim had told Hector all this in a letter, but the old man must have forgotten. Not long after leaving Bliss, with Patsy's address embedded in his brain, Jim had sent Miriam a letter. Six weeks later he had received a note printed in her childlike hand, thanking him for his help and asking him to write to her, which he did, telling her he was back in school. Three months went by before Miriam wrote him a letter from a new address. She, Rachel and Thomas had moved farther west, to a town in the mountains where her sister had an office job in a small hospital, Thomas was in kindergarten and she was in school.

"Miriam is now writing letters on a computer," Jim said.

"Email," Hector said proudly, and swallowing the last of his tea, he set down the cup with a shaky clatter. Always the teacher, he asked Jim what Miriam intended to do with herself when she finished school.

"She's hoping to become a librarian. She reads all the time and wants to work where she'll be surrounded by books."

"Clever girl," Hector said approvingly. "Then she'll be able to think for herself."

"I hope so," Jim said. Miriam had been so brainwashed by her father that he sometimes wondered if her mind would be shackled to the Righteous Path for the rest of her life.

It seemed to be as good a time as any to mention the biscuit tin. Jim had been reluctant to mention it in a letter, and as much as delivering the canvas bag, the prospect of finding out more about the biscuit tin had made him want to visit Hector. After a moment's hesitation, he got it out. "Hector," he said, "I found a biscuit tin with an inscription on the lid. It was behind the schoolhouse near the broken-down fence. An animal—a badger, I've since been told—had dug it up. Did you bury it?"

Hector sighed. "The infant grave," he said. "Yes, I buried the biscuit tin."

"I reburied it," Jim said, "and I put the wooden cross on the grave."

"I whittled that cross. After we buried the poor wee thing, Iris and I had a modest ceremony at the grave and she recited a few lines from Wordsworth. I still remember them." His voice quavered, but without hesitation, Hector recited,

I would have planted thee . . .
Amid a world how different from this!
Beside a sea that would not cease to smile;
On tranquil land, beneath a sky of bliss.

After a while, Jim said, "Did Gila attend the burial?"

"No. She was too weak to leave the house."

"Did the pastor show up?"

"He did not," Hector said, "although he must have

known that she had got away. He had confined the lass to her room and forbade her to be with her family. After months of confinement, she came to us, undernourished and deeply depressed. It was Iris's opinion that had the lass been spared such harsh treatment, the bairn might have survived."

"So the pastor never came to Bliss?"

"No. He waited until Gila had recovered and had gone on her way before he accused Iris of being a witch and began his guerilla tactics. The pastor did not participate himself but sent his minions to do the dirty work, either at night or when we had undertaken an errand. They did everything short of murder to drive us from Bliss. You see, the pastor wanted no witnesses to the cruel way he had treated his daughter." Hector sighed. "It was hardest on Iris. She never really got over it."

"Did the baby live at all?"

"No. I never saw the wee bairn. While Gila was giving birth on the parlour sofa, I was banished to the kitchen to keep the stove going. Iris told me later that the bairn never once drew breath, though she struggled to help him breathe. He was premature by one or two months." There was another sigh. "It was Iris who put the poor wee bairn into the biscuit tin so wild animals wouldn't dig it up after it was buried."

"Did you ever hear from Gila after she left?"

"We did not. She might have tried to contact us, but of course we left Bliss a fortnight or so after her." Hector sighed. "It was difficult to leave, but we had to. After the strong-armed tactics employed against us by the people on Majestic Farm, we could not stay."

The old man looked down, as if he was studying his spotted crippled hands while he assembled his thoughts.

After a while he continued speaking, his voice careful and cautious. "When you have lived as long as I have, Jim, you see that the way you live your life comes down to ends and means."

"I don't understand."

"It's all very well for people to pursue their religious beliefs, whatever they might be, but if they use the wrong methods to achieve what they want, where's the good in it?" He turned to Jim. "Do you see what I mean?" He was almost pleading.

"I do see," Jim said quietly.

There was nothing more to say, and impulsively, Jim held up the canvas bag and asked Hector if it was his.

The old man's eyes lit up. "It is!" he cried. "It's the bag I used in Bliss! For years I missed not having it close at hand. The fact is that Iris and I left Bliss in such haste we forgot a number of things."

Reaching into the bag, Jim took out a parcel wrapped in tissue paper. "Something else you left behind," he said, and with a flourish he placed the parcel in Hector's lap.

With trembling hands, Hector unwrapped the tissue and looked at the silver-framed picture. When Jim had first stuffed the frame into the canvas bag, he'd had no idea that beneath the black was a silver frame. Later, when he was home, he'd spent hours polishing the silver until it gleamed. A beatific smile lit up Hector's face. "Our wedding day photograph," he said wonderingly. "To think you brought it to me." The corners of his eyes glistened. "Thank you, Jim."

Jim said, "If I had mailed you the photo you would have had it sooner, but I wanted to bring it to you myself so I could thank you in person." Jim cleared his throat before going on. "The thing is, Hector, you and Iris helped me to take learning seriously. Before I stumbled onto Bliss, I wasn't interested in school. I didn't see that it had much use. But hearing about how you and Iris taught"—Jim had already written Hector about meeting the Chumniks—"I began looking at school differently, and when I left Bliss and went home, I was eager to get back to it."

"Well, now, that's good to hear." Hector chuckled. "And what useful life do you intend to pursue after graduation?"

"I'm going to trade school in the West."

"Ah!" Hector said as if he had come upon a precious secret. "So you plan on seeing the lass again."

Annoyed that his reddening cheeks still gave him away, Jim attempted to make light of his feelings for Miriam. "She's not the only reason I want to live out west. Once I have my carpenter's papers and get a job, I plan to build myself a straw-bale house on the Prairies. It will have solar heat and a wind turbine for generating electricity. I want to live where there's lots of space. There again, you and Iris inspired me, Hector."

"Thank you, Jim," Hector said humbly. "I will be sure to tell Iris."

She's dead but he still talks to her. Strangely the thought didn't give him the creeps.

Jim saw the old man wipe the corners of his eyes, but Hector didn't allow himself to cry. Instead his voice became became resolute and strong.

"I miss Iris every moment I am awake," he said, "but I am grateful she has been spared the anger and hatred unleashed in the world today, the wickedness of war, the fanatics killing innocent people." He paused before going on. "Iris always believed that there is much goodness in humankind. And so do I," Hector finished stoutly.

"Sir?" Jim turned and saw Mary, a pretty dark-haired young woman, in the sitting-room doorway. He'd been aware of her presence, having heard footsteps elsewhere in the flat. "Are you finished your tea, sir?" she asked Hector.

"Yes," he replied. "We are finished, Mary. You may remove the tray."

"Don't forget your nap, sir," Mary said, and after she left with the tea tray, Jim stood up and said he must be going.

"Of course, of course. You are young. You have miles to go before you sleep."

Jim stood awkwardly by his chair, uncertain about whether he should stay a while longer or slip quietly away. The old man already seemed half asleep in the chair. But Hector wasn't quite ready to let his visitor go. Rousing himself, he said, "Not so fast there, Jim. You can't leave until I give you something." Reaching for his cane, Hector struggled to his feet and, making his way to the shelves, hooked the cane on the spine of a book and handed it to Jim. *Treasure Island,* Jim read, *Robert Louis Stevenson.* The letters were written in gold on a worn leather cover. Jim had written Hector about the pastor throwing the book into the fire.

"Iris and I want you have it," Hector said. "We think of this gift as a phoenix." Noting Jim's perplexity, he added, "Which is to say the legendary bird reborn through fire."

"Thank you" did not seem adequate, but Jim said it anyway, bowing his head, the book firm and solid between his hands. Between Hector's knowledge and the roomful of books, Jim was acutely aware of how much he didn't know. But he was young, wasn't he, so there was plenty of time to learn.

Hector said, "Robert Louis Stevenson was born in this city. His father wanted him to build lighthouses, but Robert chose to write books instead. He made the right decision, wouldn't you say?"

They went into the hallway, where Hector paused to show Jim a picture he'd painted. The picture was a large watercolour, the kind an amateur artist would make. From a cluster of trees Jim picked out the faint outlines of what he took to be a small house, a stone well, a garage and a schoolhouse. The shapes were blurred and indistinct. Above them was an immense prairie sky, below which Bliss was a small island shimmering on the horizon like a mirage. Bliss was there and not there, depending on how you looked at it.

"I remember just before we left Bliss," the old man said, "after we were packed and I had backed out of the driveway, Iris made me stop the car. There was something she wanted to do, she said. She got out of the car and went to the house. When she returned a minute or so later, I asked why she'd gone back. 'To unlock the door,' she said. 'Before our troubles with the people on Majestic Farm, Bliss was a peaceful, happy place, and I feel better leaving an open door for someone else. That way the house won't be lonely.'

Jim didn't tell Hector that finding the unlocked door had creeped him out. Instead he said, "I know what she meant."

"I will tell her that, too."

Leaving the old man to his nap, Jim walked toward the castle ramparts, thinking not about kings and queens and knights in armour but about Bliss. He realized that his sharpest memory of Bliss wasn't the small house and the smaller buildings shown in Hector's painting, but the snowy night when he stood on the road waiting for Miriam and Thomas. Jim remembered that just as they appeared, the clouds opened up and he saw a universe pulsing with planets and stars, and that a short while later, when they were on the way to their destination, he caught sight of Mars hanging in the vast prairie sky, a circle of red reflecting starlight born trillions of years ago and now on a journey toward the present.

Toward Planet Earth, Jim thought, and quickened his step.

Acknowledgments

I would like to thank the Canadian Children's Book Centre for sending me on a book tour in northern Saskatchewan, where, during a long and blissful bus ride, the genesis of this story took place. Without that experience this novel might never have been written.

I would also like to thank those who helped me in various and important ways: Norah Flynn, Merna Summers, Sara Clark, Gwen Hoover, Edna Alford, Don Dabbs, Gail Crawford and the guitarist Anthony Clark.

I am particularly grateful to my indispensable agent and friend, Dean Cooke, and for the enthusiasm, support and suggestions of my editor, Amy Black.

—JOAN CLARK